Praise for
TONY HILLERMAN
and
SKINWALKERS

> > > > « « « «

"*Skinwalkers* is a very absorbing tale."

—John D. MacDonald

"Agile . . . reflective . . . absorbing . . ."

—*The New Yorker*

"*Skinwalkers* is suspense fiction of the highest caliber."

—Jonathan Kellerman

"Hillerman transcends the mystery genre."

—*Washington Post Book World*

TONY HILLERMAN

SKINWALKERS

■ HarperPaperbacks
A Division of HarperCollinsPublishers

This is a work of fiction. The characters, incidents, and dialogues are products of the author's imagination and are not to be construed as real. Any resemblance to actual events or persons, living or dead, is entirely coincidental.

HarperPaperbacks   *A Division of* HarperCollins*Publishers*
10 East 53rd Street, New York, N.Y. 10022

A hardcover edition of this book was published in 1986 by Harper & Row, Publishers, Inc.

Cover illustration by Peter Thorpe

First HarperPaperbacks printing: April 1990

Printed in the United States of America

HarperPaperbacks and colophon are trademarks of HarperCollins*Publishers*

12 13 14 15 16 17 18 19 20

This book is dedicated to Katy Goodwin, Ursula Wilson, Faye Bia Knoki, Bill Gloyd, Annie Kahn, Robert Bergman, and George Bock, and all the Medicine People, Navajo and *belagana*, who care for The People—and about them. My thanks to Dr. Albert Rizzoli for his kindness and his help, and a tip of my hat to the good work of the too often unappreciated Indian Health Service.

AUTHOR'S NOTE

Those who read these Navajo mysteries with a map of the Big Reservation beside them should be warned that Badwater Wash, its clinic, and its trading post are as fictional as the people who inhabit them. The same is true of Short Mountain. I also use an unorthodox form of the Navajo noun for shaman/medicine man/singer, which is commonly spelled "hataalii." Finally my good friend Ernie Bulow correctly reminds me that more traditional shamans would disapprove of both the way Jim Chee was invited to do the Blessing Way mentioned in this book (such arrangements should be made face-to-face and not by letter) and of Chee practicing a sandpainting on the ground under the sky. Such sacred and powerful ritual should be done only in the hogan.

We Navajo understand Coyote is always waiting out there, just out of sight. And Coyote is always hungry.

—ALEX ETCITTY, born to the *Water Is Close* People

SKINWALKERS

≫ 1 ≪

WHEN THE CAT CAME THROUGH the little trap-
door at the bottom of the screen it made a *clack-
clack* sound. Slight, but enough to awaken Jim
Chee. Chee had been moving in and out of the
very edge of sleep, turning uneasily on the narrow bed, pressing himself uncomfortably against
the metal tubes that braced the aluminum skin
of his trailer. The sound brought him enough
awake to be aware that his sheet was tangled uncomfortably around his chest.

He sorted out the bedclothing, still half immersed in an uneasy dream of being tangled in
a rope that he needed to keep his mother's sheep
from running over the edge of something vague
and dangerous. Perhaps the uneasy dream provoked an uneasiness about the cat. What had
chased it in? Something scary to a cat—or to this
particular cat. Was it something threatening to
Chee? But in a moment he was fully awake, and
the uneasiness was replaced by happiness. Mary

Landon would be coming. Blue-eyed, slender, fascinating Mary Landon would be coming back from Wisconsin. Just a couple of weeks more to wait.

Jim Chee's conditioning—traditional Navajo—caused him to put that thought aside. All things in moderation. He would think more about that later. Now he thought about tomorrow. Today, actually, since it must be well after midnight. Today he and Jay Kennedy would go out and arrest Roosevelt Bistie so that Bistie could be charged with some degree of homicide—probably with murder. Not a complicated job, but unpleasant enough to cause Chee to change the subject of his thinking again. He thought about the cat. What had driven it in? The coyote, maybe. Or what? Obviously something the cat considered a threat.

The cat had appeared last winter, finding itself a sort of den under a juniper east of Chee's trailer—a place where a lower limb, a boulder, and a rusted barrel formed a closed cul-de-sac. It had become a familiar, if suspicious, neighbor. During the spring, Chee had formed a habit of leaving out table scraps to feed it after heavy snows. Then when the snow melt ended and the spring drought arrived, he began leaving out water in a coffee can. But easy water attracted other animals, and birds, and sometimes they turned it over. And so, one afternoon when there was absolutely nothing else to do, Chee had removed the door, hacksawed out a cat-sized rectangle through its bottom frame, and then attached a plywood flap, using leather hinges and Miracle Glue. He had done it on a whim, partly to see if the ultracautious cat could be taught to use it. If the cat did, it would gain access to a colony of field mice that seemed to have moved into Chee's trailer. And the watering problem would be solved. Chee felt slightly uneasy about the water. If he hadn't started this meddling, nature would have taken its normal course. The cat would have moved down the slope and found itself a den closer to the San Juan—which was never dry. But Chee had interfered. And now Chee was stuck with a dependent.

Chee's interest, originally, had been simple curiosity. Once, obviously, the cat had been owned by someone. It was skinny now, with a long scar over its ribs and a patch of fur missing from its right leg, but it still wore a collar, and, despite its condition, it had a purebred look. He'd described it to the woman in the pet store at Farmington—tan fur, heavy hind legs, round head, pointed ears; reminded you of a bobcat, and like a bobcat it had a mere stub of a tail. The woman had said it must be a Manx.

"Somebody's pet. People are always bringing their pets along on vacations," she'd said, disapproving, "and then they don't take care of them and they get out of the car and that's the end of them." She'd asked Chee if he could catch it and bring it in, "so somebody can take care of it."

Chee doubted if he could get his hands on the

cat, and hadn't tried. He was too much the traditional Navajo to interfere with an animal without a reason. But he was curious. Could such an animal, an animal bred and raised by the white man, call up enough of its hunting instincts to survive in the Navajo world? The curiosity gradually turned to a casual admiration. By early summer, the animal had accumulated wisdom with its scar tissue. It stopped trying to hunt prairie dogs and concentrated on small rodents and birds. It learned how to hide, how to escape. It learned how to endure.

It also learned to follow the water can into Chee's trailer rather than make the long climb down to the river. Within a week the cat was using the flap when Chee was away. By midsummer it began coming in when he was at home. At first it had waited tensely at the step until he was away from the door, kept a nervous eye on him while it drank, and bolted through the flap at his first motion. But now, in August, the cat virtually ignored him. It had come inside at night only once before—driven in by a pack of dogs that had flushed it out of its den under the juniper.

Chee looked around the trailer. Far too dark to see where the cat had gone. He pushed the sheet aside, swung his feet to the floor. Through the screened window beside his bed he noticed the moon was down. Except far to the northwest, where the remains of a thunderhead lingered, the sky was bright with stars. Chee yawned, stretched, went to the sink, and drank a palmful of water warm from the tap. The air smelled of dust, as it had for weeks. The thunderstorm had risen over the Chuskas in the late afternoon, but it had drifted northward over the Utah border and into Colorado and nothing around Shiprock had gotten any help. Chee ran a little more water, splashed it on his face. The cat, he guessed, would be standing behind the trash canister right beside his feet. He yawned again. What had driven it in? He'd seen the coyote's tracks along the river a few days ago, but it would have to be terribly hungry to hunt this close to his trailer. No dogs tonight, at least he hadn't heard any. And dogs, unlike coyotes, were easy enough to hear. But probably it was dogs, or the coyote. Probably a coyote. What else?

Chee stood beside the sink, leaning on it, yawning again. Back to bed. Tomorrow would be unpleasant. Kennedy said he would be at Chee's trailer at 8 A.M. and the FBI agent was never late. Then the long drive into the Lukachukais to find the man named Roosevelt Bistie and ask him why he had killed an old man named Dugai Endocheeney with a butcher knife. Chee had been a Navajo Tribal Policeman for seven years now— ever since he'd graduated from the University of New Mexico—and he knew now he'd never learn to like this part of the job, this dealing with sick minds in a way that would never bring them back to harmony. The federal way of curing Bistie would be to haul him before a federal magistrate, charge him with homicide on a federal reservation, and lock him away.

Ah, well, Chee thought, most of the job he liked. Tomorrow he would endure. He thought of the happy times stationed at Crownpoint. Mary Landon teaching in the elementary school. Mary Landon always there. Mary Landon always willing to listen. Chee felt relaxed. In a moment he would go back to bed. Through the screen he could see only a dazzle of stars above a black landscape. What was out there? A coyote? Shy Girl Beno? That turned his thoughts to Shy Girl's opposite. Welfare Woman. Welfare Woman and the Wrong Begay Incident. That memory produced a delighted, reminiscent grin. Irma Onesalt was Welfare Woman's name, a worker in the tribal Social Services office, tough as saddle leather, mean as a snake. The look on her face when they learned they had hauled the wrong Begay out of the Badwater Clinic and delivered him halfway across the reservation was an image he would treasure. She was dead now, but that had happened far south of the Shiprock district, out of Chee's jurisdiction. And for Chee, the shooting of Irma Onesalt didn't do as much as it might have to diminish the delight of the Wrong Begay Incident. It was said they'd never figure out who shot Welfare Woman because everybody who ever had to work with her would be a logical suspect with a sound motive. Chee couldn't remember meeting a more obnoxious woman.

He stretched. Back to bed. Abruptly he thought of an alternative to the coyote-scared-the-cat theory. The Shy Girl at Theresa Beno's camp. She had wanted to talk to him, had hung on the fringes while he talked to Beno, and Beno's husband, and Beno's elder daughter. The shy one had the long-faced, small-boned beauty that seemed to go with Beno women. He had noticed her getting into a gray Chevy pickup when he was leaving the Beno camp, and when he had stopped for a Pepsi at the Roundtop Trading Post, the Chevy had driven up. Shy Girl had parked well away from the gasoline pumps. He'd noticed her watching him, and waited. But she had driven away.

Chee moved from the sink and stood by the screen door, looking out into the darkness, smelling the August drought. She knew something about the sheep, he thought, and she wanted to tell me. But she wanted to tell me where no one could see her talking to me. Her sister's husband is stealing the sheep. She knows it. She wants him caught. She followed me. She waited. Now she will come up to the door and tell me as soon as she overcomes her shyness. She is out there, and she frightened the cat.

It was all, of course, a silly idea, product of being half asleep. Chee could see nothing through the screen. Only the dark shape of the junipers, and a mile up the river the lights that someone had left on at the Navajo Nation Shiprock Agency highway maintenance yards, and beyond that the faint glow that attempted to civilize the night at the town of Shiprock. He could smell dust and the peculiar aroma of wilted, dying leaves—an odor familiar to Chee and to all Navajos, and one that evoked unpleasant boyhood memories. Of thin horses, dying sheep, worried adults. Of not quite enough to eat. Of being very careful to take into the gourd dipper no more of the tepid water than you would drink. How long had it been since it had rained? A shower at Shiprock at the end of April. Nothing since then. Theresa Beno's shy daughter wouldn't be out there. Maybe a coyote. Whatever it was, he was going back to bed. He ran a little more water into his palm, sipped it, noticing the taste. The reservoir on his trailer would be low. He should flush it out and refill it. He thought of Kennedy again. Chee shared the prejudices of most working policemen against the FBI, but Kennedy seemed a better sort than most. And smarter. Which was good, because he would probably be stationed at Farmington a long time and Chee would be working . . .

Just then he became aware of the form in the darkness. Some slight motion, perhaps, had given it away. Or perhaps Chee's eyes had finally made the total adjustment to night vision. It was not ten feet from the window under which Chee slept, an indistinct black-against-black. But the shape was upright. Human. Small? Probably the woman at Theresa Beno's sheep camp. Why did she stand there so silently if she had come all this way to talk to him?

Light and sound struck simultaneously—a white-yellow flash which burned itself onto the retina behind the lens of Chee's eyes and a boom which slammed into his eardrums and repeated itself. Again. And again. Without thought, Chee had dropped to the floor, aware of the cat clawing its way frantically over his back toward the door flap.

Then it was silent. Chee scrambled to a sitting position. Where was his pistol? Hanging on his belt in the trailer closet. He scrambled for it on hands and knees, still seeing only the white-yellow flash, hearing only the ringing in his ears. He pulled open the closet door, reached up blindly and fumbled until his fingers found the holster, extracted the pistol, cocked it. He sat with his back pressed against the closet wall, not daring to breathe, trying to make his eyes work again. They did, gradually. The shape of the open door became a rectangle of black-gray in a black-black field. The light of the dark night came through the window above his bed. And below that small square, he seemed to be seeing an irregular row of roundish places—places a little lighter than the blackness.

Chee became aware of his sheet on the floor around him, of his foam-rubber mattress against his knee. He hadn't knocked it off the bunk. The cat? It couldn't. Through the diminishing ringing in his ears he could hear a dog barking somewhere in the distance toward Shiprock. Awakened by the gunshots, Chee guessed. And they must have been gunshots. A cannon. Three of them. Or was it four?

Whoever had fired them would be waiting out there. Waiting for Chee to come out. Or trying to decide whether four shots through the aluminum skin of the trailer into Chee's bed had been enough. Chee looked at the row of holes again, with his vision now clearing. They looked huge—big enough to stick your foot through. A shotgun. That would explain the blast of light and sound. Chee decided going through the door would be a mistake. He sat, back to the closet wall, gripping the pistol, waiting. A second distant dog joined the barking. Finally, the barking stopped. Air moved through the trailer, bringing in the smells of burned gunpowder, wilted leaves, and the exposed mud flats along the river. The white-yellow blot on Chee's retina faded away. Night vision returned. He could make out the shape of his mattress now, knocked off the bed by the shotgun blasts. And through the holes punched in the paper-thin aluminum walls, he could see lightning briefly illuminate the dying thunder-head on the northwest horizon. In Navajo mythology, lightning symbolized the wrath of the *yei,* the Holy People venting their malice against the earth.

≫ 2 ≪

LIEUTENANT JOE LEAPHORN HAD GONE to his office early. He'd awakened a little before dawn and lay motionless, feeling Emma's hip warm against his own, listening to the sound of her breathing, feeling a numbing sense of loss. He had decided, finally, that he would force her to see a doctor. He would take her. He would tolerate no more of her excuses and delays. He had faced the fact that he had humored Emma's reluctance to see a *belagana* doctor because of his own fear. He knew what the doctor would say. Hearing it said would end his last shred of hope. "Your wife has Alzheimer's disease," the doctor would say, and his face would be sympathetic, and he would explain to Leaphorn what Leaphorn already knew too well. It was incurable. It would be marked by an episodic loss of function of that territory of the brain which stored the human memory and which controlled other behavior. Finally, this loss would be so severe that the victim would simply forget, as it seemed to Leaphorn, to remain alive. It also seemed to Leaphorn that this disease killed its victim by degrees—that Emma was already partly dead. He had lain there, listening to her breathing beside him, and mourned for her. And then he had gotten up, and put on the coffeepot, and dressed, and sat at the kitchen table and watched the sky begin to brighten behind the upthrust wall of stone that gave the little town of Window Rock its name. Agnes had heard him, or smelled the coffee. He had heard water running in the bathroom, and Agnes joined him, face washed, hair combed, wearing a dressing gown covered with red roses.

Leaphorn liked Agnes, and had been happy and relieved when Emma had told him—as her headaches and her forgetfulness worsened—that Agnes would come and stay until health returned. But Agnes was Emma's sister, and Agnes, like Emma, like everyone Leaphorn knew in their branch of the Yazzie family, was deeply traditional. Leaphorn knew they were modern enough not to expect him to follow the old way and take another wife in the family when Emma died. But the thought would be there. And thus Leaphorn found himself uneasy when he was alone with Agnes.

And so he'd finished his coffee and walked through the dawn to the tribal police building, moving away from fruitless worry about his wife to a problem he thought he could solve. He would spend some quiet time before the phone began to ring, deciding, once and for all, whether he was dealing with a coincidence in homicides. He had three of them. Seemingly, absolutely nothing connected them except the exquisite level of frustration with which they confronted Joe Leaphorn. Everything in Leaphorn's Navajo blood, bones, brains, and conditioning taught him to be skeptical of coincidences. Yet for days he had seemed stuck with one—a problem so intractable and baffling that in it he was able to find shelter from the thought of Emma. This morning he intended to take a preliminary step toward solving this puzzle. He would leave the phone off the hook, stare at the array of pins on his map of the Navajo Reservation, and force his thinking into some sort of equal order. Given quiet, and a little time, Leaphorn's mind was very, very good at this process of finding logical causes behind apparently illogical effects.

A memo lay in his in-basket.

FROM: *Captain Largo, Shiprock.*

TO: *Lieutenant Leaphorn, Window Rock.*

"Three shots fired into trailer of Officer Jim Chee about 2:15 A.M. this date," the memo began. Leaphorn read it quickly. No description of either the suspect or the escape vehicle. Chee unharmed. *"Chee states he had no idea of the motive,"* the memo concluded.

Leaphorn reread the final sentence. Like hell, he thought. Like hell he doesn't. Logically, no one shoots at a cop without a motive.

And logically, the cop shot at knows that motive very well indeed. Logically, too, that motive reflects so poorly upon the conduct of the policeman that he's happy not to remember it. Leaphorn put the memo aside. When the more normal working day began, he'd call Largo and see if he had anything to add. But now he wanted to think about his three homicides.

He swiveled his chair and looked at the reservation map that dominated the wall behind him. Three pins marked the unsolved homicides: one near Window Rock, one up on the Arizona-Utah border, one north and west in the empty country not far from Big Mountain. They formed a triangle of roughly equal sides—some 120 miles apart. It occurred to Leaphorn that if the man with the shotgun had killed Chee, the triangle on his map would become an oddly shaped rectangle. He would have four unsolved homicides. He rejected the thought. The Chee business wouldn't be unsolved. It would be simple. A matter of identifying the malice, uncovering the officer's malfeasance, finding the prisoner he had abused. It would not, like the three pins, represent crime without motive.

The telephone rang. It was the desk clerk downstairs. "Sorry, sir. But it's the councilwoman from Cañoncito."

"Didn't you tell her I won't get in until eight?"

"She saw you come in," the clerk said. "She's on her way up."

She was, in fact, opening Leaphorn's door.

And now the councilwoman was sitting in the heavy wooden armchair across from Leaphorn's desk. She was a burly, big-bosomed woman about Leaphorn's middle age and middle size, dressed in an old-fashioned purple reservation blouse and wearing a heavy-silver squash blossom necklace. She was, she informed Leaphorn, staying at the Window Rock Motel, down by the highway. She had driven in all the way from Cañoncito yesterday afternoon following a meeting with her people at the Cañoncito Chapter House. The people of the Cañoncito Band were not happy with Navajo Tribal Police. They didn't like the police protection they were getting, which was no protection at all. And so she had come by the Law and Order Building this morning to talk to Lieutenant Leaphorn about this, only to find the building locked and only about two people at work. She had waited in her car for almost half an hour before the front door had been unlocked.

This discourse required approximately five minutes, giving Leaphorn time to think that the councilwoman had actually driven in to attend the Tribal Council meeting, which began today, that the Cañoncito Band had not been happy with the tribal government since 1868, when the tribe returned from its years of captivity at Fort Stanton, that the councilwoman unquestionably knew it wasn't fair to expect more than a radio dispatcher and a night staffer to be on duty at dawn, that the councilwoman had gone over this complaint with him at least twice before, and that the councilwoman was making a lot of her early rising to remind Leaphorn that Navajo bureaucrats, like all good Navajos, should be up at dawn to bless the rising sun with prayer and a pinch of pollen.

Now the councilwoman was silent. Leaphorn, Navajo fashion, waited for the signal that would tell him whether she had finished with what she had to say or was merely pausing to collect her thoughts. The councilwoman sighed, and shook her head.

"Not no Navajo police at all," she summarized. "Not one on the whole Cañoncito Reservation. All we got is a Laguna policeman, now and then, part of the time." She paused again. Leaphorn waited.

"He just sits there in that little building by the road and he doesn't do nothing. Most of the time he's not even there." The councilwoman, aware that Leaphorn had heard all this before, wasn't bothering to look at him while she recited it. She was studying his map.

"You call on the telephone and nobody answers. You go by there and knock, nobody home." Her eyes drifted from map to Leaphorn. She was finished.

"Your Cañoncito policeman is an officer of the Bureau of Indian Affairs," Leaphorn said. "He's a Laguna Indian, but he's actually a BIA policeman. He doesn't work for the Lagunas. He works for you." Leaphorn explained, as he had twice before, that since the Cañoncito Band lived on a reservation way over by Albuquerque, so far from the Big Reservation, and since only twelve hundred Navajos lived there, the Judicial Committee of the Tribal Council had voted to work out a deal with the BIA instead of keeping a full shift of the NTP stationed there. Leaphorn did not mention that the councilwoman was a member of that committee, and neither did the councilwoman. She listened with patient Navajo courtesy, her eyes wandering across Leaphorn's map.

"Just two kinds of pins on the Cañoncito," she said when Leaphorn had finished.

"Those are left over from before the Tribal Council voted to give jurisdiction to the Bureau of Indian Affairs," Leaphorn said, trying to avoid the next question, which would be What do the pins mean? The pins were all in shades of red or were black, Leaphorn's way of marking alcohol-related arrests and witchcraft complaints. The two were really Cañoncito's only disruptions of the peace. Leaphorn did not believe in witches, but there were those on the Big Reservation who claimed everybody at Cañoncito must be a skinwalker.

"Because of that decision by the Tribal Council, the BIA takes care of Cañoncito," Leaphorn concluded.

"No," the councilwoman said. "The BIA don't."

The morning had gone like that. The councilwoman finally left, replaced by a small freckled white man who declared himself owner of the company that provided stock for the Navajo rodeo. He wanted assurance that his broncos, riding bulls, and roping calves would be adequately guarded at night. That pulled Leaphorn into the maze of administrative decisions, memos, and paperwork required by the rodeo—an event dreaded by all hands in the Window Rock contingent of the tribal police. Before he could finish the adjustments required to police this three-day flood of macho white cowboys, macho Indian cowboys, cowboy groupies, drunks, thieves, con men, Texans, swindlers, photographers, and just plain tourists, the telephone rang again.

It was the principal of Kinlichee Boarding School, reporting that Emerson Tso had reopened his bootlegging operation. Not only was Tso selling to any Kinlichee student willing to make the short walk over to his place;

he was bringing bottles to the dorm at night. The principal wanted Tso locked up forever. Leaphorn, who detested whiskey as ardently as he hated witchcraft, promised to have Tso brought in that day. His voice was so grim when he said it that the principal simply said thank you and hung up.

And so finally, just before lunch, there was time for thinking about three unsolved homicides and the question of coincidence. But first Leaphorn took the telephone off the hook. He walked to the window and looked out across the narrow asphalt of Navajo Route 27 at the scattered red-stone buildings that housed the government bureaucracy of his tribe, at the sandstone cliffs behind the village, and at the thunderclouds beginning to form in the August sky, clouds that in this summer of drought would probably not climb quite high enough up the sky to release any moisture. He cleared his mind of Tribal Council members, rodeos, and bootleggers. Sitting again, he swiveled his chair to face the map.

Leaphorn's map was known throughout the tribal police—a symbol of his eccentricity. It was mounted on corkboard on the wall behind his desk—a common "Indian Country" map published by the Auto Club of Southern California and popular for its large scale and its accurate details. What drew attention to Leaphorn's map was the way he used it.

It was decorated in a hundred places with colored pins, each color representing its own sort of crime. It was inscribed in a hundred places with notes written in Leaphorn's cryptic shorthand. The notes reminded Leaphorn of information he'd accumulated in a lifetime of living on the reservation and half a lifetime of working it as a cop. The tiny q west of Three Turkey Ruins meant quicksand in Tse Des Zygee Wash. The r beside the road to Ojleto on the Utah border (and beside dozens of other such roads) recalled spots where rainstorms made passage doubtful. The c's linked with family initials marked the sites of summer sheep camps along the mountain slopes. Myriad such reminders freckled the map. W's marked places where witchcraft incidents had been reported. B's marked the homes of bootleggers.

The notes were permanent, but the pins came and went with the ebb and flow of misbehavior. Blue ones marked places where cattle had been stolen. They disappeared when the cattle thief was caught driving a truckload of heifers down a back road. Gaudy rashes of scarlet, red, and pink ones (the colors Leaphorn attached to alcohol-related crimes) spread and subsided inside the reservation with the fate of bootleggers. They made a permanent rosy blotch around reservation border towns and lined the entrance highways. Markers for rapes, violent assaults, family mayhem, and other, less damaging, violent losses of control tended to follow and mingle with the red. A few pins, mostly on the reservation's margins, marked such white-man crimes as burglary, vandalism, and robbery. At the moment, Leaphorn was interested only in three brown pins with white centers. They marked his homicides.

Homicides were unusual on the reservation. Violent death was usually accidental: a drunk stumbling in front of a passing car, drunken fights outside a bar, an alcohol-primed explosion of family tensions—the sort of unpremeditated violence that lends itself to instant solutions. When brown-and-white pins appeared, they rarely remained more than a day or two.

Now there were three. And they'd been stuck in Leaphorn's corkboard, and in his consciousness, for weeks. In fact, the oldest had been there almost two months.

Irma Onesalt was her name—pin number one. Leaphorn had stuck it beside the road between Upper Greasewood and Lukachukai fifty-four days ago. The bullet that killed her was a 30-06, the second most popular caliber in the world and the one that hung on the rifle rack across the rear window of every third pickup truck on the reservation, and around it. Everybody seemed to own one, if they didn't own a 30-30. And sometimes even if they did. Irma Onesalt, born to the Bitter Water Clan, born for the Towering House People, daughter of Alice and Homer Onesalt, thirty-one years old, unmarried, agent of the Navajo Office of Social Services, found in the front seat of her overturned Datsun two-door, hit in the jaw and throat by a bullet that smashed through the driver's-side window and, after destroying her, lodged in the opposite door. They had found a witness, more or less and maybe. A student from the Toadlena Boarding School had been en route home to visit her parents. She had noticed a man—an old man, she'd said—sitting in a pickup truck parked about where the shot would have been fired from. That theory presumed that Irma Onesalt had lost control of the Datsun the moment she'd been hit. Leaphorn had seen the body. It seemed a safe presumption.

Pin two, two weeks later, represented Dugai Endocheeney, born to the Mud People, born for the Streams Come Together Clan. Maybe seventy-five, maybe seventy-seven, depending on whom you believed. Stabbed (the butcher knife left in his body) at the sheep pen behind his hogan on the Nokaito Bench, not far from where Chinle Creek runs into the San Juan River. Dilly Streib, the agent in charge, had said there was an obvious connection between pin one and pin two. "Onesalt didn't have any

friends, and Endocheeney didn't have any enemies," Dilly had said. "Somebody is working
from both ends. Going to keep knocking off
good ones and bad ones until there's nothing
left but the middle."

"Just us average ones," Leaphorn said.

Streib had laughed. "I think he'll get to you
pretty quick, on the obnoxious end."

Delbert L. Streib wasn't your usual FBI
agent. It had always seemed to Leaphorn, who
had spent a tour at the FBI Academy and half
his life running errands for the Agency, that
Streib was smarter than most. He had a quick,
innovative intelligence, which had made him
a terrible misfit in the J. Edgar Hoover years
and got him exiled to Indian country. But
Streib, whose case it was since it was a homicide committed on a federal reservation, had
drawn a blank on Onesalt. And on Endocheeney. And so had Leaphorn.

When he had seen Leaphorn's map, Streib
had argued that pin two should be pin three.
And maybe he was right. Leaphorn had assigned the third pin to Wilson Sam, born to the
One Walks Around Clan, and born for the
Turning Mountain People. The late Mr. Sam
was fifty-seven, a herder of sheep who sometimes worked on Arizona Highway Department grader crews. He had been hit on the
back of the neck with the blade of a shovel, so
very, very hard that there was no question he

had died instantly. But there was a question of when he had been hit. Sam's nephew had found the victim's sheepdog, voiceless from howling and half dead from thirst, sitting on the rim of Chilchinbito Canyon. Wilson Sam's body was on the canyon floor below—apparently dragged to the edge and tumbled over. The autopsy suggested a time of death about the same as Endocheeney's. So who died first? Anyone's guess. Again, no witnesses, no clues, no apparent motive, not much of anything except the negative fact that if the coroner was right, it would have been very difficult for the same man to have killed them both.

"Unless he was a skinwalker," Dilly Streib had said, looking somber, "and you guys are right about skinwalkers being able to fly, and outrun turbocharged pickup trucks, and so forth."

Leaphorn didn't mind Streib kidding him, but he didn't like anyone kidding him about witches. He hadn't laughed.

Remembering it now, he still didn't laugh. He sighed, scratched his ear, shifted in the chair. Staring at the map today took him exactly where it had taken him the last time he tried it. One pin was a Window Rock pin, relatively speaking. The first one. The next two were out-in-the-boondocks pins.

The first victim was a bureaucrat, younger, female, more sophisticated. Shot. The last two were men who had followed their flocks, traditional people, probably spoke little English, killed at close quarters. Did he have two separate cases? So it would seem. In the Window Rock case, premeditation—rarity of rarities on the reservation—was obvious. In the boondocks cases, it was possible but didn't look probable. A shovel hardly seemed a likely weapon of choice. And if you were determined to kill someone, most Navajos Leaphorn knew could take along an easier weapon than a butcher knife.

Leaphorn thought about his cases separately. He got nowhere. He thought about them as a trio. Same results. He isolated the Onesalt killing, considered everything they had learned about the woman. Mean as a snake, it seemed. People hesitated to bad-mouth the dead, but they had trouble finding good to say about Irma. No, Irma was a busybody. Irma was a militant. Irma was an angry young woman. Irma made trouble. As far as he could learn, she had no jilted lovers. In fact, the only one who seemed to mourn her aside from her immediate family was a longtime and apparently devoted live-in boyfriend—a schoolteacher at Lukachukai. Leaphorn always suspected devoted boyfriends in homicide cases. But this one had been standing in front of twenty-eight students talking about math when Onesalt was killed.

The mail arrived. Without breaking his concentration on the problem, idly, he sorted through it, mind still on Onesalt. Two telexes from the FBI were on top of the stack. The first one contained the details of the Jim Chee affair. He read the telex quickly. Nothing much new. Chee had not given chase. Chee said he had no idea who might have fired the shots. Tracks left by size seven rubber-soled running shoes had been found adjoining the trailer. They led about four hundred yards to a point where a vehicle had been parked. Tracks indicated worn tires. Drippage where vehicle had parked indicated either a lengthy stay or a serious oil leak.

Leaphorn set the message aside, expression glum. Again, no motive. But there was a motive, of course. When someone tries to ambush a cop there is a strong motive, and the motive tends to be unpleasant. Well, Chee was Captain Largo's boy, and finding out what Officer Chee was doing to provoke such a reaction would be Largo's problem.

The second telex reported that Agent Jay Kennedy of the Farmington office would this date locate and interrogate subject Roosevelt Bistie in connection with the Dugai Endocheeney homicide. Two witnesses had been located who placed a vehicle owned by Bistie at the Endocheeney hogan at the time of the killing. Another witness indicated that the driver of the vehicle had said he intended to kill Endocheeney. Any officer with any information about subject Roosevelt Bistie was asked to contact Agent Kennedy.

Leaphorn turned the paper over and looked at the back. Blank, of course. He glanced at the map, mentally removing the Endocheeney pin. The triangle of unsolved crimes became a line—two dots and no real reason to link them. It looked suddenly as if his rash of homicides were, in fact, coincidences. Two unsolved was a hell of a lot better than three. And perhaps Bistie would also prove to be the Wilson Sam killer. That seemed logical. The lives of the two men might be linked in many ways. Leaphorn felt much better. Order was returning to his world.

The telephone buzzed.

"This is your day for politicians, Lieutenant," the desk clerk said. "Dr. Yellowhorse wants to talk to you."

Leaphorn tried to think of some workable reason to justify not seeing Dr. Yellowhorse, who was a tribal councilman representing the Badwater Chapter and a member of the Tribal Council Judiciary Committee, as well as a doctor. And who, as a doctor, was founder and chief of medical staff of the Badwater Clinic.

No reason occurred to Leaphorn. "Tell him to come up," he said.

"I think he's already up," the clerk said.

Leaphorn's office door opened.

Dr. Bahe Yellowhorse was a barrel of a man. He wore a black felt reservation hat with a silver-and-turquoise band and a turkey feather. A closely braided rope of hair hung, Sioux fashion, behind each ear, the end of each tied with a red string. The belt that held his jeans over his broad, flat belly was two inches wide, studded with turquoise and buckled with a sand-cast silver replica of Rainbow Man curved around the symbol of Father Sun.

"Ya-tah," said Yellowhorse, grinning. But the grin looked mechanical.

"Ya-tah-hey," Leaphorn said. "Have a ch—"

"Going to have a meeting of Judicial Committee this afternoon," Yellowhorse said, easing himself into the chair across from Leaphorn's desk. "My people want me to talk to the committee about doing something to catch that fellow that killed Hosteen Endocheeney."

Yellowhorse dug in the pocket of his denim shirt and dug out a package of cigarets, giving Leaphorn an opportunity to comment. Leaphorn didn't. Old Man Endocheeney had been a resident of that great sprawl of Utah-Arizona borderlands included in the Badwater Chapter. Leaphorn didn't want to discuss the case with Tribal Councilman Bahe Yellowhorse.

"We're working on it," he said.

"That means you're not getting nowhere,"

said Yellowhorse. "You having any luck at all?"

"The FBI has jurisdiction," Leaphorn said, thinking that this was his day for telling people what they already knew. "Felony committed on federal trust land comes under—"

Yellowhorse held up a huge brown hand. "Save it," he said. "I know how it works. The feds don't know anything unless you guys tell 'em. You finding out who killed Endocheeney? I need to know something to tell my people back at the chapter house."

He leaned back in the wooden chair, extracted a cigaret from the package, and tapped its filtered end uselessly against his thumbnail, eyes on Leaphorn.

Leaphorn considered his police academy conditioning against ever telling anybody anything about anything, weighed it against common sense. Yellowhorse was sometimes an unusually severe pain in the ass, but he did have a legitimate interest. Beyond that, Leaphorn admired the man and respected what he was trying to do. Bahe Yellowhorse, born to the Dolii Dinee, the Blue Bird People of his mother. But he had no paternal clan. His father was an Oglala Sioux. Yellowhorse had founded the Bad Water Clinic mostly with his own money. True, there was a big Kellogg Foundation grant in it, and some other foundation money, and some federal funds. But from what Leaphorn knew, most of the money, and all of the energy, had come from Yellowhorse himself.

"You can tell them we have a suspect in the Endocheeney homicide," Leaphorn said. "Witnesses put him at the hogan at the right time. Expect to pick him up today and talk to him."

"You got the right fellow?" Yellowhorse asked. "He have a motive?"

"We haven't talked to him," Leaphorn said. "We're told he said he wanted to kill Endocheeney, so you can presume a motive."

Yellowhorse shrugged. "How about the other killing? Whatever his name was?"

"We don't know," Leaphorn said. "Maybe they're connected."

"Your suspect," Yellowhorse said. He paused, put the cigaret between his lips, lit it with a silver lighter, and exhaled smoke. "He another one of my constituents?"

"Seems to live up in the Lukachukais. Long way from your country."

Yellowhorse stared at Leaphorn, waiting for further explanation. None came. He inhaled smoke again, held it in his lungs, let it trickle from his nostrils. He extracted the cigaret and came just close enough to pointing it at Leaphorn to imply the insult without delivering it. Navajos do not point at one another.

"You guys s'posed to be out of the religion

business, aren't you? Since the court cracked down on you for hassling the peyote people?"

Leaphorn's dark face turned a shade darker. "We haven't been arresting anyone for possession of peyote for years," Leaphorn said. He had been very young when the Tribal Council had passed its ill-fated law banning the use of hallucinogens, a law openly aimed at suppressing the Native American Church, which used peyote as a sacrament. He hadn't liked the law, had been glad when the federal court ruled it violated the First Amendment, and he didn't like to be reminded of it. He especially didn't like to be reminded of it in this insulting way by Yellowhorse.

"How about the Navajo religion?" Yellowhorse asked. "The tribal police got any policies against that these days?"

"No," Leaphorn said.

"I didn't think you did," Yellowhorse said. "But you got a cop working out of Shiprock who seems to think you have."

Yellowhorse inhaled tobacco smoke. Leaphorn waited. Yellowhorse waited. Leaphorn waited longer.

"I'm a crystal gazer," Yellowhorse said. "Always had a gift for it, since I was a boy. But only been practicing for the last few years. People come to me at the clinic. I tell 'em what's wrong with 'em. What kind of cure they need."

Leaphorn said nothing. Yellowhorse smoked, exhaled. Smoked again.

"If they have been fooling with wood that's been struck by lightning, or been around a grave too much, or have ghost sickness, then I tell them whether they need a Mountaintop sign, or an Enemy Way, or whatever cure they need. If they need a gallstone removed, or their tonsils out, or a course of antibiotics to knock a strep infection, then I check them into the clinic for that. Now, the American Medical Association hasn't approved it, but it's free. No charge. And a lot of the people out there are getting to know about me doing it, and it brings 'em in where we can get a look at 'em. The sick ones come in. Wouldn't have come in otherwise. They'd have gone to some other medicine man instead of me. And that way we catch a lot of early diabetic cases, and glaucoma, and skin cancer, blood poisoning, and God knows what."

"I've heard about it," Leaphorn said. He was remembering what else he'd heard. He'd heard that Yellowhorse liked to tell how his mother had died out there in that empty country of a little cut on her foot. It had led to an infection, and gangrene, because she never got any medical help. That, so the story went, was how Yellowhorse was orphaned, and got stuck in a Mormon orphanage, and got adopted into a large amount of Midwestern farm machinery money, and inherited a way to build himself a clinic—sort of a perfect circle.

"Sounds like a good idea to me," Leaphorn said. "We damn sure wouldn't have any policy against it."

"One of your cops does," Yellowhorse said. "He's telling people I'm a fake and to stay away from me. I hear the little bastard is trying to be a *yataalii* himself. Maybe he thinks I'm unfair competition. Anyway, I want you to tell me how what he's doing squares with the law. If it doesn't square, I want it stopped."

"I'll check into it," Leaphorn said. He reached for his notepad. "What's his name?"

"His name's Jim Chee," Yellowhorse said.

≫ 3 ≪

ROOSEVELT BISTIE WASN'T AT HOME, his daughter informed them. He had gone into Farmington to get some medicine yesterday, and was going to spend the night with his other daughter, at Shiprock, and then drive back this morning.

"When do you expect him?" Jay Kennedy asked. The relentless high desert sun of the reservation had burned the yellow out of Kennedy's short blond hair and left it almost white, and his skin was peeling. He looked at Chee, waiting for the translation. Bistie's Daughter probably understood English as well as Kennedy, and spoke it as well as Chee, but the way she had chosen to play the game today, she knew only Navajo. Chee guessed she was a little uneasy—that she hadn't seen many sunburned blond white men up close before.

"That's the kind of questions *belagana* ask," Chee told her in Navajo. "I'm going to tell him you expect your father when you see him. How sick is he?"

"Bad, I think," Bistie's Daughter said. "He went to a crystal gazer down there at Two Story and the crystal gazer told him he needed a Mountaintop sing. I think he's got something wrong with his liver." She paused. "What do you policemen want him for?"

"She says she expects him when he gets here," Chee told Kennedy. "We could start back and maybe meet him on the road. Or we could just wait here. I'll ask her if she knows where the old man went—what was it—two weeks ago?"

"Just a minute." Kennedy motioned Chee over toward the Agency's carryall. "I think she can understand some English," he said in just above a whisper. "We have to be careful of what we say."

"I wouldn't be surprised," Chee said. He turned back to Bistie's Daughter.

"Two weeks ago?" she asked. "Let's see. He went to see the crystal gazer the second Monday in July. That's when I go in and get all my laundry done down at Red Rock Trading Post. He took me down there. And then it was . . ." She thought, a sturdy young woman in an "I Love Hawaii" T-shirt, jeans, and squaw boots. Pigeontoed, Chee noticed. He remembered his sociology professor at the University of New Mexico saying that modern dentistry had made crooked teeth an identifying mark of those who were born into the bottommost fringe of the American socioeconomic classes. Unstraightened teeth for the white trash, uncorrected birth defects for the Navajo. Or, to be fair, for those Navajos who lived out of reach of the Indian Health Service. Bistie's Daughter shifted her weight on those bent ankles. "Well," she said, "it would have been about a week later. About two weeks ago. He took the truck. I didn't want him to go because he had been feeling worse. Throwing up his food. But he said he had to go find a man somewhere way over there around Mexican Hat or Montezuma Creek." She jerked her chin in the general direction of north. "Over by Utah."

"Did he say why?"

"What you want to see him about?" Bistie's Daughter asked.

"She says Bistie went to see a man over by the Utah border two weeks ago," Chee told Kennedy.

"Ah," Kennedy said. "Right time. Right place."

"I don't think I will talk to you anymore," Bistie's Daughter said. "Not unless you tell me what you want to talk to my father. What's wrong with that *belagana*'s face?"

"That's what sunshine does to white people's skin," Chee said. "Somebody got killed over there around Mexican Hat two weeks ago. Maybe your father saw something. Maybe he could tell us something."

Bistie's Daughter looked shocked. "Killed?"

"Yes," Chee said.

"I'm not going to talk to you anymore," Bistie's Daughter said. "I'm going into the house now." And she did.

Chee and Kennedy talked it over. Chee recommended waiting awhile. Kennedy decided they would wait one hour. They sat in the carryall, feet hanging out opposite doors, and sipped the cans of Pepsi-Cola that Bistie's Daughter had given them when they arrived. "Warm Pepsi-Cola," Kennedy said, his voice full of wonder. This remark caught Chee thinking of the way the buckshot had torn through the foam rubber of his mattress, fraying it, ripping away chunks just about over the place where his kidneys would have been. Thinking of who wanted to kill him. Of why. He had thought about the same subjects all day, interrupting his gloomy ruminations only with an occasional yearning thought of Mary Landon's impending return to Crownpoint. Neither produced any positive results. Better to think of warm Pepsi-Cola. For him, it was a familiar taste, full of nostalgia. Why did the white culture either cool things or heat them before consumption? The first time he had experienced a cold bottle of pop had been at the Teec Nos Pos Trading Post. He'd been about twelve. The school bus driver had bought a bottle for everyone on the baseball team. Chee remembered drinking it, standing in the shade of the porch. The remembered pleasure faded into the thought that anyone with a shotgun in any passing car could have mowed him down. Someone now, on the ridgeline behind Bistie's hogan, could be looking over a rifle sight at the center of his back.

Chee moved his shoulders uneasily. Took a sip

of the Pepsi. Turned his thoughts back to why whites always iced it. Less heat. Less energy. Less motion in the molecules. He poked at that for a cultural conclusion, found himself drawn back to the sound of the shotgun, the flash of light. What had he, Jim Chee, done to warrant that violent reaction?

Suddenly, he badly wanted to talk to someone about it. "Kennedy," he said. "What do you think about last night? About . . ."

"You getting shot at?" Kennedy said. They had covered that question two or three times while driving out from Shiprock, and Kennedy had already said what he thought. Now he said it again, in slightly different words. "Hell, I don't know. Was me, I'd been examining my conscience. Whose lady I'd been chasing. Anybody's feelings I'd hurt. Any enemies I'd made. Anybody I'd arrested who just recently got out of jail. That sort of thing."

"The kind of people I arrest are mostly too drunk to remember who arrested 'em. Or care," Chee said. "If they have enough money to buy shotgun shells they buy a bottle instead. They're the kind of people who have eaten a lot of shaky soup." As for whose lady he had been chasing, there hadn't been any lady lately.

"Shaky soup?" Kennedy asked.

"Local joke," Chee said. "Lady down at Gallup runs her own soup line for drunks when the cops let 'em out of the tank. They're shaking, so everybody calls it shaky soup." He decided not to try to explain another reason it was called shaky soup: the combination of Navajo gutturals used to express it was almost identical to the sounds that said penis—thereby producing the material for one of those earthy puns Navajos treasure. He had tried once to explain to Kennedy how the similarity of Navajo words for rodeo and chicken could be used to produce jokes. Kennedy hadn't seen the humor.

"Well," Kennedy said. "I'd examine my conscience, then. Somebody shoots at a cop . . ." Kennedy shrugged, let the sentence trail off without finishing the implication.

Captain Largo had not bothered to be so polite this morning in Largo's office. "It's been my experience," the captain had rumbled, "that when a policeman has got himself in a situation where somebody is coming after him to kill him, then that policeman has been up to something." Captain Largo had been sitting behind his desk, examining Chee pensively over his tented fingers, when he said it, and it hadn't angered Chee until later, when he was back in his patrol car remembering the interview. Now the reaction was quicker. He felt a flush of hot blood in his face.

"Look," Chee said. "I don't like—"

Just then they heard a vehicle clanking and groaning up the track.

Kennedy removed the pistol from the holster under his jacket on the seat, put on the jacket, dropped the pistol into the jacket pocket. Chee watched the track. An elderly GMC pickup, rusty green, emerged from the junipers. A 30-30 lever-action carbine was in the rack across the back window. The pickup eased to a slow, almost dust-less stop. The man driving it was old and thin, with a black felt reservation hat pushed back on his head. He looked at them curiously while the engine wheezed to a stop, sat for a moment con-sidering them, and then climbed out.

"Ya-tah-hey," Chee said, still standing beside the carryall.

Bistie responded gravely with the Navajo greeting, looking at Chee and then at Kennedy.

"I am born for Red Forehead People, the son of Tessie Chee, but now I work for all of the Dinee. For the Navajo Tribal Police. This man"—Chee indicated Kennedy Navajo fashion, by shifting his lips in Kennedy's direction—"is an FBI officer. We have come here to talk to you."

Roosevelt Bistie continued his inspection. He dropped his ignition key in his jeans pocket. He was a tall man, stooped a little now by age and illness, his face the odd copper color peculiar to advanced jaundice. But he smiled slightly. "Po-lice?" he said. "Then I guess I hit the son-of-a-bitch."

It took Chee a moment to digest this—the ad-mission, then the nature of the admission.

"What did he—" Kennedy began. Chee held up his hand.

"Hit him?" Chee asked. "How?"

Bistie looked surprised. "Shot the son-of-a-bitch," he said. "With that rifle there in the truck. Is he dead?"

Kennedy was frowning. "What's he saying?"

"Shot who?" Chee asked. "Where?"

"Over there past Mexican Hat," Bistie said. "Over there almost to the San Juan River. He was a Mud Clan man. I forget what they call him." Bistie grinned at Chee. "Is he dead? I thought maybe I missed him."

"Oh, he's dead," Chee said. He turned to Kennedy. "We have a funny one here. He says he shot Old Man Endocheeney. With his rifle."

"Shot?" Kennedy said. "What about the butcher knife? He wasn't—"

Chee stopped him. "He probably speaks some English. Let's talk. I think we should take him back over there. Have him show us what happened."

Kennedy's face flushed under the peeling epidermis. "We haven't read him his rights," he said. "He's not supposed—"

"He hasn't told us anything in English yet," Chee said. "Just in Navajo. He's still got a right to remain silent in English until he talks to a lawyer."

Bistie told them just about everything on the long, dusty drive that took them out of the Lukachukais, and back through Shiprock, and westward into Arizona, and northward into Utah.

"Navajo or not," Kennedy had said, "we better

read him his rights." And he did, with Chee translating it into Navajo.

"Better late than never, I guess," Kennedy said. "But who would guess a suspect would walk right up and tell you he shot the guy?"

"When he didn't," Chee said.

"When he stuck him with a butcher knife," Kennedy said.

"Why is the white man talking all this bullshit about a knife?" Bistie asked.

"I'll explain that," Chee said. "You haven't told us why you shot him."

And he didn't. Bistie continued his account. Of making sure the 30-30 was loaded. Of making sure the sights were right, because he hadn't fired it since shooting a deer last winter. Of the long drive to Mexican Hat. Of asking people there how to find the Mud Clan man. Of driving up to the hogan of the Mud Clan man, just about this time of day, with a thunderstorm building up, and taking the rifle down off the rack, and cocking it, and finding nobody at the hogan, but a pickup truck parked there, and guessing that the Mud Clan man would be around somewhere. And hearing the sound of someone hammering, and seeing the Mud Clan man working on a shed back in an arroyo behind the hogan—nailing on loose boards. And then Bistie described standing there looking over the sights at the Mud Clan man, and seeing the man looking back at him just as he pulled the trigger. And he told them how, when the smoke had cleared, the man was no longer on the roof. He told them absolutely everything about the chronology and the mechanics of it all. But he told them absolutely nothing about why he had done it. When Chee asked again, Bistie simply sat, grimly silent. And Chee didn't ask why he was claiming to have shot a man who had been knifed to death.

While Roosevelt Bistie talked, describing this insanity in a calm, matter-of-fact, old man's voice, Chee found other questions forming in his mind.

"You were in Shiprock last night? At your daughter's house? Tell me her name. Where she lives."

Chee wrote the name and place in his notebook. It would have taken Old Man Bistie ten minutes to drive from that Shiprock address to Chee's trailer.

"What are you writing?" Kennedy asked.

Chee grunted.

"Do you have a shotgun?" he asked Bistie.

There is no Navajo word for shotgun and Kennedy caught the noun.

"Hey," he said. "What are you getting into?"

"Just the rifle," Bistie said.

"I'm getting into who tried to shoot Jim Chee," Jim Chee said.

> **4** <

Awakening was abrupt. An oblong of semi-blackness against the total darkness. The door of the summer hogan left open. Through it, against the eastern horizon, the faint glow of false dawn. Had the boy cried out? There was nothing but silence now. No air moved. No night insect stirred. Anxiety alone seemed to have overcome sleep. There was the smell of dust, of the endless, sheep-killing drought. And the smell, very faint, of something chemical. Oil, maybe. More and more, the truck engine leaked oil. Where it stood in the yard beside the brush arbor, the earth was hard and black with the drippings. A quart, at least, every time they drove it. More than a dollar a quart. And not enough money, not now, to get it fixed. All the money had gone with the birth of the boy, with the time they had had to spend at the hospital while the doctors looked at him. Anencephaly, the doctor had called it. The woman had written the word on a piece of paper for them, standing beside the bed in a room that seemed too cold, too full of the smell of white-man medicines. "Unusual," the woman had said. "But I know of two other cases on the reservation in the past twenty years. It happens to everybody. So it happens to Navajos too."

What did anencephaly mean? It meant Boy Child, the son, would live only a little while. "See," the woman had said, and she had brushed back the thin hair on the top of Boy Child's head. But it had already been apparent. The top of the head was almost flat. "The brain has not formed," the woman had said, "and the child cannot live long without that. Just a few weeks. We don't know what causes it. And we don't know anything to do about it."

Well, there were things that the *belagana* doctors didn't know. There was a cause, for this and for everything. And because there was a cause, something could be done about it. The cure lay in undoing that cause, restoring the harmony inside the small, fragile skull of Boy Child. The skinwalker had caused it, for some reason lost in the dark heart of malicious evil. Thus the skinwalker must die. His brain must shrivel so the brain of Boy Child could grow. And quickly. Quickly. Quickly. Kill the witch. The anxiety rose into something close to panic. Stomach knotted. Despite the predawn chill, the blanket roll against the cheek was damp with sweat.

The shotgun had seemed a good idea—fired through the thin skin of the trailer into the bed where the witch was sleeping. But skinwalkers were hard to kill. Somehow the skinwalker had known. It had flown from the bed and the bone had missed.

Boy Child stirred now. Sleep for him was always momentary, a fading out of consciousness that rarely lasted an hour. And then the whimpering would start again. A calling out to those who loved him, were bone of his bone and flesh of his flesh. The whimpering began, the only sound in the darkness. Just a sound, like that the newborn young of animals make. It seemed to say: Help me. Help me. Help me.

There would be no more sleep now. Not for a while. No time to sleep. Boy Child seemed weaker every day. He had already lived longer than the *belagana* woman at the hospital had said he would. No time for anything except finding the way to kill the witch. There had to be a way. The witch was a policeman, and hard to kill, and being a skinwalker, he had the powers skinwalkers gain—to fly through the air, to run as fast as the wind can blow, to change themselves into dogs and wolves and maybe other animals. But there must be a way to kill him.

The rectangle of the door frame grew lighter. Possibilities appeared and were considered, and modified, and rejected. Some were rejected because they might not work. Most were rejected because they were suicidal: The witch would die, but there would be no one left to keep Boy Child

from starving. There must be a way to escape un-
detected. Nothing else was a useful solution.

In the cardboard box where he was kept, Boy
Child whimpered endlessly—a pattern of sound
as regular and mindless as an insect might make.
A faint breeze moved the air, stirring the cloth
that hung beside the hogan doorway—Dawn Girl
awakening to prepare the day. About then the
thought came: how it could be done. It was simple. It would work. And the witch they called Jim
Chee would surely die.

> 5 <

LIEUTENANT JOE LEAPHORN nosed his patrol car into the shade of the Russian olive tree at the edge of the parking lot. He turned off the ignition. He eased himself into a more comfortable position and considered again how he would deal with Officer Chee. Chee's vehicle was parked in a row of five patrol cars lined along the sidewalk outside the entrance of the Navajo Tribal Police Station, Shiprock subagency. Unit 4. Leaphorn knew Chee was driving Unit 4 because he knew everything officially knowable about Chee. He had called the records clerk at 9:10 this morning and had Chee's personnel file sent upstairs. He'd read every word in it. Just a short time earlier, he had received a call from Dilly Streib. Streib had bad news.

"Weird one," Streib had said. "Kennedy picked up Roosevelt Bistie, and Roosevelt Bistie said he shot Endocheeney."

It took only a millisecond for the incongruity to register. "Shot," Leaphorn said. "Not stabbed?"

"Shot," Streib said. "Said he'd gone over to Endocheeney's hogan, and Endocheeney was fixing the roof of a shed, and Bistie shot him, and Endocheeney disappeared—fell off, I guess—and Bistie drove on home."

"What do you think?" Leaphorn asked.

"Kennedy didn't seem to have any doubt Bistie was telling the truth. Said they were waiting at Bistie's house, and he drove up and saw they were cops, and right away said something about shooting Endocheeney."

"Bistie speak English?"

"Navajo," Streib said.

"Who'd we have along? Who interpreted?" What Streib was telling him seemed crazy. Maybe there had been some sort of misunderstanding.

"Just a second." Leaphorn heard papers rustling. "Officer Jim Chee," Streib said. "Know him?"

"I know him," said Leaphorn, wishing he knew him better.

"Anyhow, I'll send you the paperwork on it. Thought you'd want to know it turned funny."

"Yeah. Thanks," Leaphorn said. "Why did Bistie want to kill Endocheeney?"

"Wouldn't say. Flatass refused to talk about it at all. Kennedy said he seemed to think he might have missed the man, and then he was glad when he found out the guy was dead. Wouldn't say a word about what he had against him."

"Chee did the questioning?"

"Sure. I guess so. Kennedy doesn't speak Navajo."

"One more thing. Was it Chee on this from the beginning? Working with Kennedy, I mean, back when the investigation opened?"

"Just a sec," Streib said. Papers rustled. "Here it is. Yeah. Chee."

"Well, thanks," Leaphorn said. "I'll look for the report."

He clicked the receiver cradle down with a finger, got the file room, and ordered Chee's folder.

While he waited for it, he pulled open the desk drawer, extracted a brown pin with a white center, and carefully stuck it back in the hole where the Endocheeney pin had been. He looked at the map a minute. Then he reached into the drawer again, took out another brown-and-white pin, and stuck it at the *p* in "Shiprock." Four pins now. One north of Window Rock, one on the Utah borderlands, one on Chilchinbito Canyon, one over in New Mexico. And now there was a connection. Faint, problematical, but something. Jim Chee had investigated the Endocheeney killing before someone had tried to kill Chee. Had Chee learned something that made him a threat to Endocheeney's killer?

Leaphorn had been smiling, but as he thought, the smile thinned and disappeared. He could see no possible way this helped. Getting old, Leaphorn thought. He had reached the ridge and now the slope was downward. The thought didn't depress him, but it gave him an odd sense of pressure, of time moving past him, of things that needed to be done before time ran out. Leaphorn considered this, and laughed. Most un-Navajo thinking. He had been around white men far too long.

He picked up the phone and called Captain Largo at Shiprock. He told Largo he wanted to talk to Jim Chee.

"What's he done now?" Largo said. And he sounded relieved, Leaphorn thought, when Leaphorn explained.

The short route from Window Rock to Shiprock, through Crystal and Sheep Springs, is a 120-mile drive over the hump of the Chuska Mountains. Leaphorn, who rarely broke the speed limit, drove it far too fast. It was mostly a matter of nerves.

And sitting here in the parking lot at Shiprock, he was still tense. Cumulus clouds climbing the sky over the Chuskas were tall enough to form the anvil tops that promised rain. But here the August sun glared off the asphalt beyond the small shade of Leaphorn's olive. He'd told Largo he'd be here by one, almost forty-five minutes away. Largo had said he'd have Chee on hand at one. Now Largo would be out to lunch. Leaphorn considered lunch for himself. A quick hamburger at the Burgerchef out on the highway. But he wasn't hungry. He found himself thinking of

Emma, of the appointment he'd made with the neurologist at the Indian Health Service hospital in Gallup.

("Joe," Emma had said. "Please. You know how I feel about it. What can they do? It's headaches. I am out of *hozro*. I will have a sing and be well again. What can the *belagana* do? Saw open my head?" She'd laughed then, as she always laughed when he wanted to talk about her health. "They would cut open my head and let all the wind out," she'd said, smiling at him. He had insisted, and she had refused. "What do you think is wrong with me?" she asked, and he could see that she was, for once, half serious. He had tried to say "Alzheimer's disease," but the words wouldn't form, and he had simply said, "I don't know, but I worry," and she had said, "Well, I'm not going to have any doctor poking around in my head." But he had made the appointment anyway. He inhaled, exhaled. Maybe Emma was right. She could go to a listener, or a hand trembler, or a crystal gazer like Yellowhorse pretended to be, and have a curing ceremonial prescribed. Then call in the singer to perform the cure, and all the kinfolks to join in the blessing. Would that make her any worse than she'd be when the doctors at Gallup told her that something they didn't understand was killing her and there was nothing they could do about it? What would Yellowhorse tell her if she went to him? Did he know the man well enough to guess? What did he know about him? He knew Yellowhorse was pouring his inherited money and his life into Badwater Clinic, feeding an obsession. He knew he was hiring foreign-trained refugee doctors and nurses—a Vietnamese, a Cambodian, a Salvadoran, a Pakistani—because he could no longer afford the domestic brand. So maybe the money was smaller than the obsession. He knew Yellowhorse was an adept politician. But he didn't know him well enough to guess what his prescription would be for Emma. Would he leave her to the singers or to the neurologists?)

The door of the station opened and three men in the khaki summer uniforms of Navajo Policemen emerged. One was George Benaly, who long ago had worked with Leaphorn out of Many Farms. One was a jolly-looking, plump young man with a thin mustache whom Leaphorn didn't recognize. The other was Jim Chee. The round brim of Chee's hat was tilted, shading his face, but Leaphorn could see enough of it to match the photo in Chee's personnel file. A longish, narrow face fitting a longish, narrow body—all shoulders and no hips. The "Tuba City Navajo," as some anthropologist had labeled the type. Pure Athapaskan genetics. Tall, long torso, narrow pelvis, destined to be a skinny old man. Leaphorn himself fell into the "Checkerboard type." He represented—according to this authority—a blood/gene mix with the Pueblo peoples. Leaphorn didn't particularly like the theory, but it was useful ammunition when Emma pressed him to get his weight and belt size down a bit.

The three officers, still talking, strolled toward their patrol cars. Leaphorn watched. The plump officer had not noticed Leaphorn's car parked under the olive tree. Benaly had seen it without registering any interest. Only Chee was conscious of it, instantly, aware that it was occupied, that the occupant was watching. Perhaps that alertness was the product of being shot at two nights earlier. Leaphorn suspected it was permanent—a natural part of the man's character.

Benaly and Plump Cop climbed into their cars and drove out of the lot. Chee extracted something from the back seat of his vehicle and strolled back toward the station, conscious of Leaphorn's watching presence. Why wait? Leaphorn thought. He would check in with Largo later.

At Leaphorn's suggestion, they took Chee's police car to Chee's trailer. Chee drove, erect and nervous. The trailer, battered, dented, and looking old and tired, sat under a cluster of cottonwoods not a dozen yards from the crumbling north bank of the San Juan River. Cool, Leaphorn thought. Great spot for someone who wasn't bothered, as Leaphorn was, by mosquitoes. He inspected the three patches of duct tape Chee had used to heal the shotgun wounds in the aluminum skin of his home. About evenly spaced, he noticed. About two feet apart. Each a little more than hip high. Nicely placed to kill somebody in bed if you knew exactly where the bed was located in such a trailer.

"Doesn't look random," Leaphorn said, half to himself.

"No," Chee said. "I think some thought went into it."

"Trailer like this . . . Any trouble for anyone to find out where the bed would be located? How far off the floor?"

"How high to shoot?" Chee said. "No. It's a common kind. When I bought it in Flagstaff there were three just about like it on the used lot. See 'em all the time. Anyway, I think they're all pretty much alike. Where they put the beds."

"I think we'll ask around, anyway. See if somebody who sells them at Farmington, or Gallup, or Flag, can remember anything." He glanced at Chee. "Maybe a customer came in and asked to see this particular model, and pulled out a tape measure and said he had to measure the bed off to see where to hold the shotgun to get himself a Navajo Policeman."

Chee's expressionless face eased into what might have been a smile. "I'm not usually that lucky."

Leaphorn's fingers were on the tape that covered the hole nearest the front of the trailer. He glanced at Chee again.

"Pull it off," Chee said. "I've got more tape."

Leaphorn peeled off the patch, inspected the ragged hole punched through the aluminum, then stooped to peer inside. He could see only blue-and-white cloth. Flowers. Chee's pillow slip. It looked new. Hole torn in the old one, Leaphorn guessed. He was impressed that a bachelor would put a pillowcase on his pillow. Pretty tidy.

"You were lucky when this happened," said Leaphorn, who was always skeptical about luck, who was always skeptical about anything that violated the orderly rules of probability. "The report said your cat woke you up. You keep a cat?"

"Not exactly," Chee said. "It's a neighbor. Lives out there." Chee pointed upstream to a sun-baked slope of junipers. But Leaphorn was still looking thoughtfully at the shotgun hole—measuring its width with his fingers. "Lives out there under that juniper," Chee added. "Sometimes when something scares it, it comes in."

"How?"

Chee showed him the flap he'd cut in the trailer door. Leaphorn examined it. It didn't look new enough to have been put there after the shooting. He noticed that Chee was aware of his examination, and of the suspicion it suggested.

"Who tried to kill you?" Leaphorn asked.

"I don't know," Chee said.

"A new woman?" Leaphorn suggested. "That can cause trouble." Chee's expression became totally blank.

"No," Chee said. "Nothing like that."

"It could be something mild. Maybe just talking too often to a woman with a boyfriend who's paranoid."

"I've got a woman," Chee said slowly.

"You've thought all this out?" Leaphorn asked.

He motioned toward the holes in the side of the trailer. "It's your ass somebody's after."

"I've thought about it," Chee said. He threw his hands apart, an angry gesture aimed at himself. "Absolutely damned nothing."

Leaphorn studied him, and found himself half persuaded. It was the gesture as much as the words. "Where did you sleep last night?"

"Out there," Chee said, gesturing toward the hillside. "I have a sleeping bag."

"You and the cat," Leaphorn said. He paused, dug out his pack of cigarets, offered one to Chee, took one himself. "What do you think about Roosevelt Bistie? And Endocheeney?"

"Funny," Chee said. "That whole thing's odd. Bistie's . . ." He paused, hesitated. "Why not come on in," Chee said. "Have a cup of coffee."

"Why not," Leaphorn said.

It was left-over-from-breakfast coffee. Leaphorn, made an authority on bad coffee by more than two decades of police work, rated it slightly worse than most. But it was warm, and it was coffee, and he sipped it appreciatively while Chee, sitting on the bunk where he had so nearly died, told him about meeting Roosevelt Bistie.

"I don't believe he was faking anything," Chee concluded. "He didn't act surprised to see us. Seemed pleased when he heard Endocheeney was dead, and then the whole business about shooting at Endocheeney on the roof, thinking he'd killed him, not really wondering about it until he got home, not going back to make sure because he figured if he hadn't killed him, En-docheeney wouldn't have stuck around to give him a second chance at it." Chee shrugged, shook his head. "Genuine satisfaction when he heard Endocheeney was dead. I just don't think he could have been faking any of that. No reason to. Why not just deny everything?"

"All right," Leaphorn said. "Now, tell me again exactly what he said when you asked him why he wanted to kill Endocheeney."

"Just like I said," Chee said.

"Tell me again."

"He wouldn't say anything. Just shut his mouth and looked grim and wouldn't say a word."

"What do you think?"

Chee shrugged. The light through the window over the trailer sink dimmed slightly. The shadow of the thunderhead over the Chuskas had moved across the Shiprock landscape. With the shadow, the cloud's advance guard of breeze sighed through the window screen. But it wouldn't rain. Leaphorn had studied the cloud. Now he was considering Chee's face, which wore a look of uneasy distaste. Leaphorn felt his own face beginning a smile, a wry one. Here we go again, he thought.

"Witchcraft?" Leaphorn asked. "A skin-walker?"

Chee said nothing. Leaphorn sipped the stale coffee. Chee shrugged. "Well," he said. "That could explain why Bistie wouldn't talk about it."

"That's right," Leaphorn said. He waited.

"Of course," Chee added, "so could other things. Protecting somebody in the family."

"Right," Leaphorn said. "If he tells us his motive, it's also the motive for the guy with the butcher knife. Brother. Cousin. Son. Uncle. What relatives does he have?"

"He's born to the Streams Come Together Dinee," Chee said, "and born for the Standing Rock People. Three maternal aunts, four uncles. Two paternal aunts, five uncles. Then he's got three sisters and a brother, wife's dead, and two daughters and a son. So not even counting his clan brothers and sisters, he's related to just about everybody north of Kayenta."

"Anything else you can think of? For why he won't talk?"

"Something he's ashamed of," Chee said. "Incest. Doing something wrong to some relative. Witchery."

Leaphorn could tell Chee didn't like the third alternative any better than he did.

"If it's witchcraft, which one is the skinwalker?"

"Endocheeney," Chee said.

"Not Bistie," Leaphorn said, thoughtfully. "So if you're right, Bistie killed himself a witch, or intended to." Leaphorn had considered this witch theory before. Nothing much wrong with the idea, except proving it. "You pick up anything about Endocheeney to support it? Or try it on Bistie?"

"Tried it on Bistie. He just looked stubborn.

Talked to people up there on the Utah border who knew Endocheeney. Got nothing." Chee was looking at Leaphorn, judging the response.

He's heard about me and witches, Leaphorn thought. "In other words, everybody just shut up," he said. "How about Wilson Sam. Anything there?"

Chee hesitated. "You mean any connection?"

Leaphorn nodded. It was exactly what he was driving at. They were right. Chee was smart.

"That's out of our jurisdiction here," Chee said. "Where he was killed, that's in Chinle's territory. The subagency at Chinle has that case."

"I know that," Leaphorn said. "Did you go out there and look around? Ask around?" It was exactly what Leaphorn would have done under the circumstances—with two killings almost the same hour.

Chee looked surprised, and a little abashed. "On my day off," he said. "Kennedy and I hadn't gotten anything helpful on the Endocheeney thing yet, and I thought—"

Leaphorn held up his palm. "Why not?" he said. "You seeing anything that links them?"

Chee shook his head. "No family connections. Or clan connections. Endocheeney ran sheep, used to work when he was younger with that outfit that lays rails for the Santa Fe railroad. He got food stamps, and now and then sold firewood. Wilson Sam was also a sheepherder, had a job as a flagman on a highway construction job down near Winslow. He was fifty-something years old. Endocheeney was in his middle seventies."

"Did you try Sam's name on people who knew Endocheeney? To see if . . ." Leaphorn made a sort of inclusive gesture.

"No luck," Chee said. "Didn't seem to know the same people. Endocheeney's people didn't know Sam. Sam's people never heard of Endocheeney."

"Did you know either one of them? Ever? In any way? Even something casual?"

"No connection with me, either," Chee said. "They're not the kind of people policemen deal with. Not drunks. Not thieves. Nothing like that."

"No mutual friends?"

Chee laughed. "And no mutual enemies, as far as I can learn."

The laugh, Leaphorn thought, seemed genuine.

"Okay," he said. "How about the shooting-at-you business."

Chee described it again. While he talked, the cat came through the flap in the screen.

It was a large cat, with short tan hair, a stub of a tail, and pointed ears. It stopped just inside the screen, frozen in the crouch, staring at Leaphorn with intense blue eyes. Quite a cat, Leaphorn thought. Heavy haunches like a bobcat. The hair was matted on the left side of its head, and what looked like a scar distorted the smoothness of its flank. Some *belagana* tourist's pet, he guessed. Probably taken along on a vacation and lost. Leaphorn listened to Chee with half of his mind, alert only for some variation in an account he had already read twice in the official report, and heard from Largo over the phone. The other half of his consciousness focused on the cat. It still crouched by the door—judging whether this strange human was a threat. The flap probably had made enough noise when the cat came in to waken a man sleeping lightly, Leaphorn decided. The cat was thin, bony; its muscles had the ropy look of wild predators. If it had, in fact, been a pampered pet, it had adapted well. It had got itself in harmony with its new life. Like a Navajo, it had survived.

Chee had finished his account, without saying anything new. Or anything different. The metal seat of the folding chair was hard against Leaphorn's tailbone. He felt more tired than he should have felt after nothing much more than the drive from Window Rock. Chee was said to be smart. He seemed smart. Largo insisted he was. A smart man should have some idea who was trying to kill him. And why. If he wasn't a fool, was he a liar?

"When it got light, you looked outside," Leaphorn prompted. "What did you find?"

"Three empty shotgun shells," Chee said. His eyes said he knew Leaphorn already knew all this. "Twelve gauge. Center fire. Rubber sole tracks of a small shoe. Size seven. Fairly new. Led off up the slope to the road up there. Top of the slope, a vehicle had been parked. Tires were worn and it leaked a lot of oil."

"Did he come in the same way?"

"No," Chee said. The question had interested him. "Tracks down along the bank of the river."

"Past where this cat has its den."

"Right," Chee said.

Leaphorn waited. After a long silence, Chee said, "It seemed to me that something might have happened there. To spook the cat out of his hiding place. So I looked around." He made a deprecatory gesture. "Ground was scuffed. I think somebody had knelt there behind the juniper. It's not far from where people dump their trash and there's always a lot of stuff blowing around. But I found this." He got out his billfold, extracted a bit of yellow paper, and handed it to Leaphorn. "It's new," he said. "It hadn't been out there in the dirt very long."

It was the wrapper off a stick of Juicy Fruit gum. "Not much," Chee said, looking embarrassed.

It *wasn't* much. Leaphorn couldn't imagine how it would be useful. In fact, it seemed to symbolize just how little they had to work on in any of these cases. "But it's something," he said. His imagination made the figure squatting behind the juniper, watching the Chee trailer, a small figure holding a pump shotgun in his right hand, reaching into his shirt pocket with his left hand, fishing out a package of gum. No furious emotion here. Calm. A man doing a job, being careful, taking his time. And, as an accidental by-product, giving the cat crouched under the juniper a case of nerves, eroding its instinct to stay hidden until this human left, sending it into a panicky dash for a safer place. Leaphorn smiled slightly, enjoying the irony.

"We know he chews gum. Or she does," Chee said. "And what kind he sometimes chews. And that he's . . ." Chee searched for the right word. "Cool."

And I know, Leaphorn thought, that Jim Chee is smart enough to think about what might have spooked the cat. He glanced at the animal, which was still crouched by the flap, its blue eyes fixed on him. The glance was enough to tilt the decision. Two humans in a closed place were too many. The cat flicked through the flap, *clack-clack*, and was gone. Loud enough to wake a light sleeper, especially if he was nervous. Did Chee have something to be nervous about? Leaphorn shifted in the chair, trying for a more comfortable position. "You read the report on Wilson Sam," Leaphorn said. "And you went out there. When? Let's go over that again."

They went over it. Chee had visited the site four days after the killing and he'd found nothing to add significant data to the original report. And that told little enough. A ground-water pond where Wilson Sam's sheep drank was going dry. Sam had been out looking for a way to solve that problem—checking on his flock. He hadn't returned with nightfall. The next morning some of the Yazzie outfit into which Sam was married had gone out to look for him. A son of his sister-in-law had remembered hearing a dog howling. They found the dog watching the body in an arroyo that runs into Tyende Creek south of the Greasewood Flats. The investigating officers from Chinle had arrived a little before noon. The back of Sam's head had been crushed, just above where head and neck join. The subsequent autopsy confirmed that he'd been struck with a shovel that was found at the scene. Relatives agreed that it wasn't Sam's shovel. The body apparently had fallen, or had rolled, down the bank and the assailant had climbed down after it. The nephew had driven directly out to the Dennehotso Trading Post, called the police, and then followed instructions to keep everybody away from the body until they arrived.

"There were still some pretty good tracks when I got there," Chee said. "Been a little shower there the day before the killing and a little runoff down the arroyo bottom. Cowboy boots, both heels worn, size ten, pointed toes. Heavy man, probably two hundred pounds or over, or he was carrying something heavy. He walked around the body, squatted beside it." Chee paused, face thoughtful. "He got down on both knees beside the body. Spent a little time, judging from the scuff marks and so forth. I thought maybe they were made by our people when they picked up the body. But I asked Gorman, and he said no. They were there when he'd checked originally."

"Gorman?"

"He's back with us now," Chee said. "But he was loaned out to Chinle back in June. Vacation relief. He was that guy who was walking out in the parking lot with me at noon. Gorman and Benaly. Gorman is the sort of fat one."

"Was the killer a Navajo?" Leaphorn asked.

Chee hesitated, surprised. "Yes," he said. "Navajo."

"You sound sure," Leaphorn said. "Why Navajo?"

"Funny. I knew he was Navajo. But I didn't think about why," Chee said. He counted it off on his fingers. "He didn't step over the body, which could have just happened that way. But when he walked down the arroyo, he took care not to walk where the water had run. And on the way back to the road, a snake had been across there, and when he crossed its path he shuffled his feet." Chee paused. "Or do white men do that too?"

"I doubt it," Leaphorn said. The don't-step-over-people business grew out of families living in one-room hogans, sleeping on the floor. A matter of respect. And the desert herders' respect for rain must have produced the taboo against stepping in water's footprints. Snakes? Leaphorn tried to remember. His grandmother had told him that if you walk across a snake's trail without erasing it by shuffling your feet, the snake would follow you home. But then his grandmother had also told him it was taboo for a child to keep secrets from grandmothers, and that watching a dog urinate would cause insanity. "How about the killer at Endocheeney's place? Another Navajo? Could it have been the same person?"

"Not many tracks there," Chee said. "Body was about a hundred yards from the hogan, with the whole family milling around after he was found. And we hadn't had the rain there. Everything dry."

"But what do you think? Another Navajo?"

Chee thought. "I don't know," he said. "Couldn't be absolutely sure. But when we eliminated what everybody who lived there was wearing, I think it was a boot with a flat rubber heel. And probably a smallish hole worn in the right sole."

"Different suspect, then," Leaphorn said. "Or different shoes." In fact, three different suspects. In fact, maybe four different suspects, counting Onesalt. He shook his head, thinking of the implausible, irrational insanity of it. Then he thought of Chee. An impressive young man. But why didn't he have at least an inkling of who had tried to kill him? Or why? Could he possibly not know? Leaphorn's back hurt. Sitting too long always did it these days. Easing himself out of the chair, he walked to the window over the sink and looked out. He felt something gritty under his boot sole, leaned down, and found it. The round lead pellet from a shotgun shell.

He showed it to Chee. "This one of them?"

"I guess so," Chee said. "I swept up, but when

they went through the bedclothes, they bounced around. Got into everything."

Into everything except Jim Chee, Leaphorn thought. Too bad he had so much trouble learning to believe in luck. "Did you see anything at all that would connect the Endocheeney and Sam things? Anything at all? Anything to connect either one of them to this?" Leaphorn gestured at the three patched shotgun holes.

"I've thought about that," Chee said. "Nothing."

"Did the name Irma Onesalt turn up either place?"

"Onesalt? The woman somebody shot down near Window Rock? No."

"I'm going to ask Largo to take you off of everything else and have you rework everything about Endocheeney and Sam," Leaphorn said. "You willing? I mean talk to everybody about everything. Who people talked to. Who people saw. Try to get a fix on whatever the killers were driving. Just try to find out every damn thing. Work on it day after day after day until we get some feeling for what the hell went on. All right?"

"Sure," Chee said. "Fine."

"Anything else about this shooting of your own here that didn't seem to fit on the FBI report?"

Chee thought about it. His lips twitched in a gesture of doubt or deprecation.

"I don't know," he said. "Just this morning, I found this. Might not have anything to do with anything. Probably doesn't." He pulled out his wallet again and extracted from it something small and roundish and ivory-colored. He handed it to Leaphorn. It was a bead formed, apparently, from bone.

"Where was it?"

"On the floor under the bunk. Maybe it fell out when I changed the bedding."

"What do you think?" Leaphorn asked.

"I think I never had anything that had beads like that on it, or knew anybody who did. And I wonder how it got here."

"Or why?" Leaphorn asked.

"Yes. Or why."

If you believed in witches, Leaphorn thought, as Chee probably did, you would have to think of a bone bead as a way witches killed—the bone being human, and the fatal illness being "corpse sickness." And if you loaded your own shotgun shells, or even if you didn't, you would know how simple it would be to remove the little plug from the end, and the wadding, and add a bone bead to the lead pellets.

» 6 «

THE WIND BLEW OUT OF THE SOUTHWEST, hot and
dry, whipping sand across the rutted track in
front of Jim Chee's patrol car. Chee had backed
the car a hundred yards up the gravel road that
led to Badwater Wash Trading Post. He'd parked
it under the gnarled limbs of a one-seed juniper—a place that gave him a little shade and a
long view back down the road he had traveled.
Now he simply sat, waiting and watching. If anyone was following, Chee intended to know it.

"I'm going to go along with the lieutenant,"
Captain Largo had told him. "Leaphorn wants
me to rearrange things and let you work on our
killings." As usual when he talked, Captain
Largo's hands were living their separate life,
sorting through papers on the captain's desk, re-
arranging whatever the captain kept in the top
drawer, trying to reshape a crease in the captain's hat. "I think he's wrong," Largo said. "I
think we ought to leave those cases to the FBI.

The FBI's not going to break them, and neither are we, but the FBI's getting paid for it, and nobody's going to do any good on them until we have some luck—and taking you off your regular work isn't going to make us lucky. Is it?"

"No, sir," Chee had said. He wasn't sure Largo expected an answer, or wanted one, but being agreeable seemed a good policy. He didn't want the captain to change his mind.

"I think that Leaphorn thinks you getting shot is connected with one or the other of those killings, or maybe both of them. He didn't say so, but that's what I think he thinks. I can't see any connection. How about it?"

Chee shrugged. "I don't see how there could be."

"No," Largo agreed. His expression, as he looked at Chee, was skeptical. "Unless you're not telling me something." The tone of the statement included a question mark.

"I'm not not telling you anything," Chee said.

"Sometimes you haven't," Largo said. But he didn't pursue it. "Real reason I'm going along with this is I want you to stay alive. Just getting shot at is bad enough." Largo pointed to the folder on his desk. "Look at that, and it's not finished yet. If somebody kills you, think how it would be." Largo threw out his arms in a gesture encompassing mountains of forms. "When we had that man killed over in the Crownpoint subagency back in the sixties, they were doing reports on that for two years."

"Okay," Chee said. "That's okay with me."

"What I mean is, poke around on Endocheeney and Wilson Sam and see what you can hear, but mostly I want you out where it would be hard for anybody to get a shot at you. In case they're still trying. Let 'em cool off. Be careful."

"Good," Chee had said, meaning it.

And while he was out there, Largo had added, he might as well get some useful work done. For instance, the people at the refinery over at Montezuma Creek were sore because somebody was stealing drip gasoline out of the collector pipeline. And somebody seemed to be hanging out around the tourist parking places at the Goosenecks, and other such places, and stealing stuff out of the cars. And so forth. The litany had been fairly long, indicating that the decline of human nature on the Utah part of the reservation was about the same as it was in Chee's usual New Mexico jurisdiction. "I'll get you the paperwork," Largo said, shuffling papers out of various files into a single folder. "Xerox copies. I wish we could put a stop to this getting into people's cars," he added. "People raise hell about it, and it gets to the chairman's office and then he raises hell. Be careful. And get some work done."

And now, parked here out of sight watching his back trail, Chee was being careful, exactly as instructed. If the man (or the woman) with the shotgun was following, it would have to be down this road. The only other way to get to the trading post at Badwater Wash was to float down the San

Juan River, and then take one of the tracks that connected it to the hogans scattered where terrain allowed along the river. Badwater wasn't a place one passed through by accident en route to anywhere else.

And now the only dust on the Badwater road was wind dust. The afternoon clouds had formed over Black Mesa, far to the south, producing lightning and air turbulence. As far as Chee could estimate from thirty miles away, no rain was falling. He studied the cloud, enjoying the range of blues and grays, its shapes and its movement. But he was thinking of more somber things. The hours of thinking he had done about who would want to kill him had depressing effects. His imagination had produced an image in his mind—himself standing at the face of a great cliff of smooth stone, as blank as a mirror, feeling hopelessly for fingerholds that didn't exist. There was a second unpleasant effect. This persistent hunt for malice, for ill will, for hatred— examining relationships with friends and associates with cynical skepticism—had left him gloomy. And then there was Lieutenant Leaphorn. He'd gotten what he wanted from the man—more than he'd expected. But the lieutenant hadn't trusted him when they'd met, and he hadn't trusted him when they'd parted. Leaphorn hadn't liked the bone bead. When Chee had handed it to him, the lieutenant's face had changed, expressing distaste and what might have been contempt. In the small universe of the

Navajo Police, total membership perhaps less than 120 sworn officers, Lieutenant Leaphorn was a Fairly Important Person, and somewhat of a legend. Everybody knew he hated bootleggers. Chee shared that sentiment. Everybody also knew Leaphorn had no tolerance for witchcraft or anything about it—for those who believed in witches, or for stories about skinwalkers, corpse sickness, the cures for same, and everything connected with the Navajo Wolves. There were two stories about how Leaphorn had acquired this obsession. It was said that when he was new on the force in the older days he had guessed wrong about some skinwalker rumors on the Checkerboard. He hadn't acted on what he'd heard, and a fellow had killed three witches and got a life term for murder and then committed suicide. That was supposed to be why the lieutenant didn't like witchcraft, which was a good enough reason. The other story was that he was a descendant of the great Chee Dodge and had inherited Dodge's determination that belief in skinwalkers had no part in the Navajo culture, that the tribe had been infected with the notion while it was held captive down at Fort Sumner. Chee suspected both stories were true.

Still, Leaphorn had kept the bone bead.

"I'll see about it," he'd said. "Send it to the lab. Find out if it is bone, and what kind of bone." He'd torn a page from his notebook, wrapped the bead in it, and placed it in the coin compartment of his billfold. Then he'd looked at Chee for a moment in silence. "Any idea how it got in here?"

"Sounds strange," Chee had said. "But you know you could pry out the end of a shotgun shell and pull out the wadding and stick a bead like this in with the pellets."

Leaphorn's expression became almost a smile. Was it contempt? "Like a witch shooting in the bone?" he asked. "They're supposed to do that through a little tube." He made a puffing shape with his lips.

Chee had nodded, flushing just a little.

Now, remembering it, he was angry again. Well, to hell with Leaphorn. Let him believe whatever he wanted to believe. The origin story of the Navajos explained witchcraft clearly enough, and it was a logical part of the philosophy on which the Dinee had founded their culture. If there was good, and harmony, and beauty on the east side of reality, then there must be evil, chaos, and ugliness to the west. Like a nonfundamentalist Christian, Chee believed in the poetic metaphor of the Navajo story of human genesis. Without believing in the specific Adam's rib, or the size of the reed through which the Holy People emerged to the Earth Surface World, he believed in the lessons such imagery was intended to teach. To hell with Leaphorn and what he didn't believe. Chee started the engine and jolted back down the slope to the road. He wanted to get to Badwater Wash before noon.

But he couldn't quite get Leaphorn out of his

mind. Leaphorn posed a problem. "One more thing," the lieutenant had said. "We've got a complaint about you." And he'd told Chee what the doctor at the Badwater Clinic had said about him. "Yellowhorse claims you've been interfering with his practice of his religion," Leaphorn said. And while the lieutenant's expression said he didn't take the complaint as anything critically important, the very fact that he'd mentioned it implied that Chee should desist.

"I have been telling people that Yellowhorse is a fake," Chee said stiffly. "I have told people every chance I get that the doctor pretends to be a crystal gazer just to get them into his clinic."

"I hope you're not doing that on company time," Leaphorn said. "Not while you're on duty."

"I probably have," Chee said. "Why not?"

"Because it violates regulations," Leaphorn said, his expression no longer even mildly amused.

"How?"

"I think you can see how," Leaphorn had said. "We don't have any way to license our shamans, no more than the federal government can license preachers. If Yellowhorse says he's a medicine man, or a hand trembler, or a road chief of the Native American Church, or the Pope, it is no business of the Navajo Tribal Police. No rule against it. No law."

"I'm a Navajo," Chee said. "I see somebody cynically using our religion . . . somebody who doesn't believe in our religion using it in that cynical way . . ."

"What harm is he doing?" Leaphorn asked. "The way I understand it, he recommends they go to a *yataalii* if they need a ceremonial sing. And he points them at the white man's hospital only if they have a white man's problem. Diabetes, for example."

Chee had made no response to that. If Leaphorn couldn't see the problem, the sacrilege involved, then Leaphorn was blind. But that wasn't the trouble. Leaphorn was as cynical as Yellowhorse.

"You, yourself, have declared yourself to be a *yataalii*, I hear," Leaphorn said. "I heard you performed a Blessing Way."

Chee had nodded. He said nothing.

Leaphorn had looked at him a moment, and sighed. "I'll talk to Largo about it," he said.

And that meant that one of these days Chee would have an argument with the captain about it and if he wasn't lucky, Largo would give him a flat, unequivocal order to say nothing more about Yellowhorse as shaman. When that happened, he would cope as best he could. Now the road to Badwater had changed from bad to worse. Chee concentrated on driving.

It was the policy of the Navajo Tribal Police, as a matter of convenience, to consider Badwater to be in the Arizona portion of the Big Reservation. Local wisdom held that the store itself was actually in Utah, about thirty feet north of the imaginary line that marked the boundary. One of the local jokes was that Old Man Isaac Ginsberg, who built the place, used to move out of his room behind the trading post and into a stone hogan across the road one hundred yards to the south because he couldn't stand the cold Utah winters. Nobody seemed to know exactly where the place was, mapwise. Its location, in a narrow slot surrounded by the fantastic, thousand-foot, red-black-blue-tan cliffs, made pinpointing it on surveys mostly guesswork. And nobody cared enough to do more than guess.

Historically, it had been a watering place for herdsmen. In the immense dry badlands of Casa del Eco Mesa, it was a rare place where a reliable spring produced pools of drinkable water. Good water is a magnet anywhere in desert country. In a landscape like Caso del Eco, where gypsum and an arsenal of other soluble minerals tainted rainwater almost as fast as it fell, the stuff that seeped under the sandy arroyo bottoms was such a compound of chemicals that it would kill even tumbleweeds and salt cedar. Thus, the springs in Badwater Wash were a magnet for all living things. They attracted those tough little mammals and reptiles which endure in such hostile places. Eventually it attracted goats that strayed from the herds the Navajos had stolen from the Pueblo Indians. Then came the goatherders. Next came sheepherders. Finally, geologists discovered the shallow but persistent Aneth oil deposit, which brought a brief, dusty boom to the

plateau. The drilling boom left behind a little refinery at Montezuma Creek, a scattering of robot
pumps, and a worn-out spiderweb of truck trails
connecting them with the world. Sometime in
this period between boom and dust, it had attracted Isaac Ginsberg, who built the trading
post of slabs of red sandstone, earned the Navajo
name Afraid of His Wife, and died. The wife to
whom Ginsberg owed his title was a Mud Clan
Navajo called Lizzie Tonale, who had married
Ginsberg in Flagstaff, had converted to Judaism,
and, it was locally believed, had persuaded Ginsberg to establish his business in such an incredi-
bly isolated locale because it was the hardest
possible place for her relatives to reach. It would
have been a sensible motive. Otherwise, the trading post would have been bankrupt in a month,
since Lizzie Tonale could refuse no kin who
needed canned goods, gasoline, or a loan, and
maintain her status as a respectable woman.
Whatever her motives, the widow Tonale-
Ginsberg had run the post for twenty years before her own death, steadfastly closing on the
Sabbath. She had left it to their daughter, the
only product of their union. Chee had met this
daughter only twice. That was enough to understand how she had earned her local name, which
was Iron Woman.

Now, as he rolled his patrol car down the final
slope and into the rutted yard of Badwater Wash
Trading Post, he saw the bulky form of Iron
Woman standing on the porch. Chee parked as

much of the car as he could in the scanty shade of a tamarisk and waited. It was a courtesy learned from boyhood in a society where modesty is prized, privacy is treasured, and visitors, even at a trading post, are all too rare. "You don't just go run up to somebody's hogan," his mother had taught him. "You might see something you don't want to see."

So Chee sat, without giving it a thought, to allow the residents of Badwater Wash to get in harmony with the idea of a visit from a tribal policeman, to button up and tidy up, or to do whatever was required by Navajo good manners. While he sat, perspiring freely, he looked in his rearview mirror at the people on the porch. Iron Woman had been joined by another woman, as thin and bent as Iron Woman was stout and ramrod rigid. Then two young men appeared in the front door, seeming, in the dusty rearview glass, to be dressed exactly alike. Each wore a red sweatband around the forehead, a faded red plaid shirt, jeans, and cowboy boots. Iron Woman was saying something to the bent woman, who nodded and looked amused. The two young men, standing side by side, stared with implacable rudeness at Chee's car. An old Ford sedan was parked at the corner of the building, a cinder block supporting the right rear axle. Beside it, perched high on its backcountry suspension, was a new GMC four-by-four. It was black with yellow pinstripes. Chee had priced a similar model in Farmington and couldn't come close to affording it. He admired it now. A vehicle that would go anywhere. But richer than anything you expected to see parked at Badwater Wash.

Through his windshield, beyond the thin screen of Russian olive leaves, the red mass of the cliff rose to the sky, reflecting the sun. The patrol car was filled with dry heat. Chee felt uneasiness stirring. He was getting used to it, finding the anxiety familiar but not learning to like it. He got out of the car and walked toward the porch, keeping his eyes on the men, who kept their eyes on him.

"*Ya-tah-hey,*" he said to Iron Woman.

"*Ya-tah,*" she said. "I remember you. You're the new policeman from Shiprock."

Chee nodded.

"Out here the other day with the government officer seeing about the Endocheeney business."

"Right," Chee said.

"This man is born to the Slow Talking People and born for the Salts," Iron Woman told the bent woman. She named Chee's mother, and his maternal aunt, and his maternal grandmother, and then recited his father's side of the family.

Bent Woman looked pleased. She faced Chee with her head back and her eyes almost closed, looking at him under her lids, a technique the descending blindness of glaucoma and cataracts taught its victims. "He is my nephew," Bent Woman said. "I am born to the Bitter Water People, born for the Deer Spring Clan. My mother was Gray Woman Nez."

Chee smiled, acknowledging the relationship. It was vague—the Bitter Waters being linked to the Salt Clan and thereby to his father's family. The system meant that Chee, and all other Navajos, had wholesale numbers of relatives.

"On business?" Iron Woman asked.

"Just out poking around," Chee said. "Seeing what I can see."

Iron Woman looked skeptical. "You don't get out here much," she said. "Nobody gets out here except on purpose."

Chee was aware of the two men watching him. Barely men. Late teens, he guessed. Obviously brothers, but not twins. The one nearest him had a thinner face, and a half-moon of white scar tissue beside his left eye socket. Under the old rules of Navajo courtesy, they would have identified themselves first, since he was the stranger in their territory. They didn't seem to care about the old rules.

"My clan is Slow Talking People," Chee said to them. "Born for the Salt Dinee."

"Leaf People," the thinner one said. "Born for Mud." His face was sullen.

Chee's efficient nose picked up a whiff of alcohol. Beer. The Leaf Clan man let his eyes drift from Chee to study the police car. He gestured vaguely toward the other man. "My brother," he said.

"What's happening over your way?" Iron

Woman asked. "I heard on the radio they had a knifing at a wedding over at Teec Nos Pos. One of the Gorman outfit got cut. Anything to that?"

Chee knew very little about that one—just what he'd overheard before the morning patrol meeting. Normally he worked east and south out of Shiprock—not this mostly empty northwestern area. He put the beer (possession illegal on the reservation) out of his mind and tried to remember what he had heard.

"Didn't amount to much," Chee said. "Fella was fooling with a girl and she had a knife. Stuck him in the arm. I think she was a Standing Rock girl. Not much to it."

Iron Woman looked disappointed. "It got on the radio, though," she said. "Lot of people around here related to the Gorman outfit."

Chee had gone to the battered red pop cooler just inside the front door, inserted two quarters, and tried to open the lid.

"Takes three," Iron Woman said. "Costs too much to get that stuff hauled way out here. And icing it down. Now everybody wants it cold."

"No more change," Chee said. He fished out a dollar and handed it to Iron Woman. It was dark inside the store and much cooler. At the cash register, Iron Woman handed him four quarters.

"Last time you were with that FBI man—asking about the one that got killed," she said, respecting the Navajo taboo of not speaking the name of the dead. "You find out who killed that man?"

Chee shook his head.

"That fellow that came through here looking for him the day he was killed. Sounded to me like he did it."

"That's a crazy thing," Chee said. "We found that man at his hogan over in the Chuskas. A man they call Roosevelt Bistie. Bistie told us he came over here to kill that man who got killed. And the man Bistie was after was up on his roof fixing something, and Bistie shot at him and he fell off. But whoever killed the man did it with a butcher knife."

"That's right," Iron Woman said. "Sure as hell, it was a knife. I remember his daughter telling me that." She shook her head, peered at Chee again. "Why would that fellow tell you he shot him?"

"We can't figure that out, either," Chee said. "Bistie said he wanted to kill the man, but he won't say why."

Iron Woman frowned. "Roosevelt Bistie," she said. "Never heard of him. I remember when he stopped in here asking directions, I never had seen him before. The man's kinfolks, do they know this Bistie?"

"None of them we've talked to," Chee said. He was thinking of how disapproving Kennedy would be if he could hear Chee discussing this case with a layman. Captain Largo too, for that matter, Largo having been a cop long enough to start acting secretive. But Kennedy was FBI to the bone, and the first law of the Agency was, Say nothing to nobody. If Kennedy were here, listening to this Navajo talk, he'd be waiting impatiently for a translation—knowing that Chee must be telling this woman more than she needed to know. However, Kennedy wasn't here, and Chee had his own operating theory. The more you tell people, the more people tell you. Nobody, certainly no Navajo, wants to be second in the business of telling things.

Chee dropped in quarters and selected a Nehi Orange. Cold and wonderful. Iron Woman talked. Chee sipped. Outside, noonday heat radiated from the packed earth of the yard, causing the light to shimmer. Chee finished his soda pop. The four-by-four drove away with a roar, dust spurting from its wheels. Beer in the four-by-four, Chee guessed. Unless the boys had bought it here. But if Iron Woman was a bootlegger, he hadn't heard it, and he hadn't remembered seeing this place on the map Largo kept of liquor sources in his subagency territory. Beer in the morning, and an expensive rig to drive. Iron Woman had said the two were part of the Kayonnie outfit, which ran goats down along the San Juan to the north and sometimes worked in the oil fields. But Iron Woman obviously did not want to discuss the Kayonnie boys, her neighbors, with a stranger. The local murder victim was another matter. She couldn't understand who would do it. He was a harmless old man. He stayed at home. Since his wife had died, he rarely came even as far as the trading post. Maybe two or three times a year, sometimes riding in on a horse, sometimes coming with a relative when a relative came to see him. No Endocheeney daughters to bring home their husbands, so the old man had lived alone. Only thing important she could remember happening involving him was a Red Ant Way sing done for him six or seven years ago to cure him of something or other after his woman died. In all the years she'd been at Badwater, which was all her life, she couldn't remember him getting into any kind of trouble, or being involved in bad problems. "Like getting your wood on somebody else's wood-gathering place, or getting into some other family's water, or running his sheep where they shouldn't be, or not helping out somebody that needed it. Never heard anything bad about him. Never been in any trouble. Always helping out at sheep dippings, always tried to take care of his kinfolks, always there when somebody was having a sing."

"I don't know if I ever told you that I have studied to be a *yataalii* myself," Chee said. "I do the Blessing Way and some others." He got out his billfold, extracted a card, and handed it to Iron Woman. The card said:

THE BLESSING WAY
and other ceremonials sung
by a singer who studied with
Frank Sam Nakai
Contact Jim Chee

The next lines provided his address and telephone number at the Shiprock Police Station. He had mentioned this to the dispatcher, thinking he would square it with Captain Largo if the captain ever learned about it. So far, the risk seemed small. There had been no calls, and no letters.

Iron Woman seemed to share the general lack of enthusiasm. She glanced at the card and laid it on the counter.

"Everybody liked him," Iron Woman said, getting back on the subject. "But now he's dead, some people are saying he was a skinwalker." Her face reflected distaste. "Sons-a-bitches," she added, clarifying that the distaste was not for skinwalkers but for the gossips. "When you live by yourself, people say things like that."

Or when you get stabbed to death, Chee thought. Violent death always seemed to provoke witch talk.

"If everybody around here liked him," Chee said, "then whoever killed him must have come from someplace else. Like Bistie. Did he know anybody anywhere else?"

"I don't think so," Iron Woman said. "Long as I been here, he only got one letter."

Chee felt a stir of excitement. Something at last. "You remember anything about it? Who it was from?" Of course she would remember. The arrival of any mail on this isolated outpost would be something to talk about, especially a letter to a man who never received letters and who couldn't read them if he did. It would lie in the little shoebox marked MAIL on the shelf above Iron Woman's cash register, the subject of conjecture and speculation until Endocheeney came in, or a relative showed up who might be trusted to deliver it to him.

"Wasn't from anybody," Iron Woman said. "It was from the tribe. There in Window Rock."

The excitement evaporated. "One of the tribal offices?"

"Social Services, I think it was. One of those that are always messing around with people."

"How about his pawn?" Chee asked. "Anything unusual in that?"

Iron Woman led him behind the counter, fished a key out of the folds of her voluminous reservation skirt, and unlocked the glass-topped cabinet where she kept the pawn.

The Endocheeney possessions held hostage for credit included one belt of heavy, crudely hammered conchas, old-fashioned and heavily tarnished; a small sack containing nine old Mexican twenty-peso coins, their silver as tarnished as the belt; two sand-cast rings; and a belt buckle of sand-cast silver. The buckle was beautiful, a simple geometric pattern that Chee favored, with a single perfect turquoise gem set in its center. He turned it in his hand, admiring it.

"And this," Iron Woman said. She thumped a small deerskin pouch on the countertop and poured out a cluster of unset turquoise nuggets and fragments. "The old man made some jewelry now and then. Or he used to. Guess he got too old for it after the old woman died."

There was nothing remarkable about the turquoise. It was worth maybe two hundred dollars. Add another two hundred for the belt and maybe one hundred for the buckle and probably fifteen or twenty dollars each for the old pesos. They were once standard raw material for belt conchas on the reservation, and cheap enough, but Mexico had long since stopped making them, and the price of silver had soared. Nothing remarkable about any of this, except the beauty of the buckle. He wondered if Endocheeney had cast it himself. And he wondered why some of his kin had not claimed these belongings. Once, tradition would have demanded that such personal stuff be disposed of with the body. But that tradition was now often ignored. Or perhaps Endocheeney's relatives didn't know about this pawn. Or perhaps they didn't have the cash to redeem it.

"How much do you have on the old man's bill?" Chee asked.

Iron Woman didn't have to look it up. "One hundred eighteen dollars," she said. "And some cents."

Not much, Chee thought. Far less than the stuff was worth. Someone without any cash could raise that much by selling a few goats.

"And then there's them," Iron Woman said. She tilted her head toward a corner behind the counter. There stood a posthole digger, two axes, a pair of crutches, a hand-turned ice cream freezer, and what seemed to be an old car axle converted into a wrecking bar.

Chee looked puzzled.

"The crutches," Iron Woman said impatiently. "He wanted to pawn them too, but hell, who wants crutches? They loan 'em to you free, up there at the Badwater Clinic, so I didn't want to get stuck with 'em as pawn. Anyway, he just left 'em there. Said give him half if I could sell 'em."

"Was he hurt?" Chee asked, thinking as he did that he could have found a smarter way to ask the question.

Iron Woman seemed to think so too. "Broke his leg. Fell off of something and they had to put a cast on it over at the clinic and he came back with the crutches."

"And then he climbed right back on the roof," Chee said. "Sounds like he was a slow learner."

"No, no," Iron Woman said. "Broke his leg way last autumn doing something else. Think he fell off of a rail fence. Leg caught." Iron Woman broke an imaginary stick with her fingers. "Snap," she said.

Chee was thinking of relatives who didn't come in and collect pawn. "Who buried the old man?" he asked.

"They got a man that works on those old well pumps out there." Iron Woman made a sweeping gesture with both hands to take in the entire plateau. "White man. He does that sometimes for people. Doesn't mind about corpses."

"This witch talk. You hear that a long time or just now?"

Iron Woman looked uneasy. From what Chee had heard about her, she had gone to school over at Ganado, at the College of Ganado, a good school. And she was a Jew, more or less, raised in that religion. But she was also a Navajo, a member of the Halgai Dinee, the People of the Valley Clan. She didn't like talking about witches in any specific way with a stranger.

"I heard about it just now," she said. "Since the killing."

"Was it just the usual stuff? What you'd expect when somebody gets killed?"

Iron Woman licked her lips, caught the lower lip between her teeth, looked at Chee carefully. She shifted her weight and in the silence the creak of the floorboard plank under her shoe was a loud groaning sound. But her voice was so faint when she finally spoke that, even in the silence, he had to strain to hear.

"They say that when they found him, they found a bone in the wound—where the knife had gone in."

"A bone?" Chee asked, not sure that he'd heard it.

Iron Woman held her thumb and forefinger

up—an eighth of an inch apart. "Little corpse bone," she said.

She didn't need to explain it more than that. Chee was remembering the bone bead he'd found in his trailer.

» 7 «

DR. RANDALL JENKS HELD a sheet of paper in his fist. Presumably it was the laboratory report on the bead, since Jenks's office had called Leaphorn to tell him the report was ready. But Jenks gave no sign he was ready to hand it over.

"Have a seat," Dr. Jenks said, and sat down himself beside the long table in the meeting room. He wore a headband of red fabric into which the Navajo symbol of Corn Beetle had been woven. His blond hair was shoulder length and under his blue laboratory jacket Leaphorn could see the uniform—a frayed denim jacket. Leaphorn, who resented those who stereotyped Navajos, struggled not to stereotype others. But Dr. Jenks fell into Leaphorn's category of Indian Lover. That meant he irritated Leaphorn even when he was doing him favors. Now Leaphorn was in a hurry. But he sat down.

Jenks looked at him over his glasses. "The bead

is made out of bone," he said, checking for reaction.

Leaphorn was not in the mood to pretend surprise. "I thought it might be," he said.

"Bovine," Jenks said. "Modern but not new, if you know what I mean. Dead long enough to be totally dehydrated. Maybe twenty years, maybe a hundred—more or less."

"Thanks for the trouble. Appreciate it," Leaphorn said. He got up, put on his hat.

"Did you expect it to be human?" Jenks asked. "Human bone?"

Leaphorn hesitated. He had work to do back at Window Rock—a rodeo that would probably be causing problems by now and a meeting of the Tribal Council that certainly would. Getting that many politicians together always caused some sort of problem. He wanted to confirm Emma's appointment before he left the hospital, and talk to the neurologist about her if he could. And then there were his three homicides. Three and a half if you counted Officer Chee. Besides, he wanted to think about what he had just learned—that the bone wasn't human. And what he had expected was none of Jenks's business. Jenks's business was public health, more specifically public health of the Navajos, Zunis, Acomas, Lagunas, and Hopis served by the U.S. Indian Service hospital at Gallup. Jenks's business, specifically, was pathology—a science that Lieutenant Leaphorn often wished he knew more about so he wouldn't be asking favors of Jenks.

"I thought it might be human," Leaphorn said. "Any connection with Irma Onesalt?"

The question startled Leaphorn. "No," he said. "Did you know her?"

Jenks laughed. "Not exactly. Not socially. She was in here a time or two. Wanting information."

"About pathology?" Why would the Onesalt woman want information from a pathologist?

"About when a bunch of people died," Jenks said. "She had a list of names."

"Who?"

"I just glanced at it," Jenks said. "Looked like Navajo names, but I didn't really study it."

Leaphorn took off his hat and sat down.

"Tell me about it," he said. "When she came in, everything you can remember. And tell me why this bone bead business made you think of Onesalt."

Dr. Jenks told him, looking pleased.

Irma Onesalt had come in one morning about two months earlier. Maybe a little longer. If it was important, maybe he could pin down the date. He had known her a little bit before. She had come to see him way back when the semiconductor plant was still operating at Shiprock—wanting to know if that kind of work was bad for the health. And he had looked stuff up for her a couple of times since.

Jenks paused, getting his thoughts in order.

"What kind of stuff?" Leaphorn asked.

Jenks's long, pale face looked slightly embarrassed. "Well, one time she wanted some details about a couple of diseases, how they are treated, if hospitalization is needed, how long, so forth. And one time she wanted to know if an alcohol death we had in here might have been beaten."

Jenks didn't say beaten by whom. He didn't need to say. Irma Onesalt would have been interested, Leaphorn suspected, only if police, and preferably Navajo Tribal Police, had been the guilty party. Irma Onesalt did not like police, particularly Navajo Police. She called them Cossacks. She called them oppressors of The People.

"This time she had a sheet of paper with her—just names typed on it. She wanted to know if I could go back through my records and come up with the date each one had died."

"Could you?" Leaphorn asked.

"A few of them, maybe. Only if they had died in this hospital, or if we did the postmortem workup for some reason. But you know how that works. Most Navajo families won't allow an autopsy and usually they can stop it on religious grounds. I'd have a record of it only if they died here, and then only if there was some good reason—like suspicious causes, or the FBI was interested, or something like that."

"She wanted to know cause of death?"

"I don't think so. All she seemed to want was dates. I told her the only place I could think of she could get them all was the vital statistics offices in the state health departments. In Santa Fe and Phoenix and Salt Lake City."

"Dates," Leaphorn said. "Dates of their death." He frowned. That seemed odd. "She say why?"

Jenks shook his head, causing the long blond hair to sway. "I asked her. She said she was just curious about something." Jenks laughed. "She didn't say what, but that little bone bead of yours made me think of her because she was talking about witchcraft. She said something about the problem with singers and the health situation. People getting scared by the singers into thinking a skinwalker has witched them, and then getting the wrong medical treatment, or treatment they don't need because they're not really sick. So when I saw your little bead I made the connection." He studied Leaphorn to see if Leaphorn understood. "You know. Witches blowing a little piece of bone into somebody to give 'em the corpse sickness. But she never said that had anything to do with her list of names and what she was curious about. She said it was too early. She shouldn't talk about it yet—not then, she meant—and she said if anything came of it she would let me know."

"But she didn't come back?"

"She came back," Jenks said. He looked thoughtful, running the tip of his thumb under the headband, adjusting it. "Must have been a couple of weeks before she got killed. This time she wanted to know what sort of treatment would be indicated for two or three diseases, and how long you'd be hospitalized. Things like that."

"What diseases?" Leaphorn asked, although

when he asked it he couldn't imagine what the answer would mean to him.

"One was TB," Jenks said. "I remember that. And I think one was some sort of liver pathology." He shrugged. "Nothing unusual. Sort of routine ailments we deal with around here, I remember that."

"And did she tell you then? I mean tell you why she wanted the dates those people died?" He was thinking of Roosevelt Bistie—the man who tried to kill Endocheeney—the man they had locked up at Shiprock, with not much reason to keep him, according to Kennedy's report. Roosevelt Bistie had something wrong with his liver. But so did a lot of people. And what the hell could that mean, anyway?

"I was in a hurry," Jenks said. "Two of our staff were on vacation and I was covering for one of them and I was trying to get my own operation caught up so I could go on vacation myself. So I didn't ask any questions. Just told her what she wanted to know and got rid of her."

"Did she ever explain it to you? In any way at all?"

"When I got back from vacation—couple of weeks after that—somebody told me somebody had shot her."

"Yeah," Leaphorn said. Shot her and left Leaphorn to guess why, since nobody else seemed to care a lot. And here might be the motive—this further example of Irma Onesalt in the role of busybody, to use the *belagana* term for it. His mother would have called her, in Navajo, a "one who tells sheep which weed to eat." Onesalt's job in the Navajo Office of Social Services, obviously, had no more to do with death statistics than it did with the occupational hazards of the semiconductor plant or, to get closer to Leaphorn's own emotional scar tissue, with punishing bad judgment in the Navajo Tribal Police.

"Do you think what she was working on had anything to do with why . . ." Jenks didn't complete the sentence.

"Who knows," Leaphorn said. "FBI handles homicides on Indian reservations." He heard himself saying it, his voice curt and unfriendly, and felt a twinge of self-disgust. Why this animus against Jenks? It wasn't just that he felt Jenks's attitude was patronizing. It was part of a resentment against all doctors. They seemed to know so much, but when he gave them Emma, the only thing that mattered, they would know absolutely nothing. That was the principal source of this resentment. And it wasn't fair to Jenks, or to any of them. Jenks had come to the Big Reservation, as many of the Indian Health Service doctors did, because the federal loans that had financed his education required two years in the military or the Indian Health Service. But Jenks had stayed beyond the two-year obligation, as some other IHS doctors did—delaying the Mercedes, the country club membership, the three-day work week, and the winters in the Bahamas—to help Navajos fight the battle of diabetes, dysen-

tery, bubonic plague, and all those ailments that
follow poor diets, bad water, and isolation. He
shouldn't resent Jenks. Not only wasn't it fair;
showing it would hurt his chances of learning
everything Jenks could tell him.

"However," Leaphorn added, "we know something about it. And from what we know, the FBI
hasn't a clue about motive." Nor do I, Leaphorn
thought. Not about motive. Not about anything
else. Certainly not about how to connect three
and a half murders whose only connection
seems to be an aimless lack of motive. "Maybe
this list Irma had would help. All Navajo names,
you said. Right? Could you think of any of them?"

Jenks's expression suggested he was probing
his brain for names. All the homicide victims
were still alive when Jenks had seen the list,
Leaphorn thought, but wouldn't it be wonderful
and remarkable if . . .

"One was Ethelmary Largewhiskers," Jenks
said, faintly amused. "One was Woody's Mother."

Leaphorn rarely allowed his face to show irri-
tation, and he didn't now. These were exactly the
sort of names he'd expect Jenks to remember:
names that were quaint, or cute, that would provoke a smile at a cocktail party somewhere when
Dr. Jenks had become bored with Navajos—
when too few of them drove wagons, and hauled
drinking water forty miles, and slept in the desert with their sheep, and too many drove station
wagons and got their teeth straightened by the
orthodontist.

"Any others?" Leaphorn asked. "It might be important."

Jenks put on the expression of a man trying hard for a recall. And failing. He shook his head.

"Would you remember any, if you heard?"

Jenks shrugged. "Maybe."

"How about Wilson Sam?"

Jenks wrinkled his face. Shook his head. "Isn't he that guy who got killed early this summer?"

"Right," Leaphorn said. "Was his name on the list?"

"I don't remember," Jenks said. "But he was still alive then. He didn't get killed until after Onesalt. If I remember it right, and I think I do because they did the autopsy at Farmington and the pathologist there called me about it."

"You're right. I'm just fishing around. How about Dugai Endocheeney?"

Jenks produced the expression that signifies deep thought. "No," he said. "I mean no, I can't remember. Been a long time." He shook his head. Stopped the gesture. Frowned. "I've heard the name," he said. "Not on the list, I think, but . . ." He paused, adjusted the headband. "Wasn't he a homicide victim too? The other one that was killed about then?"

"Yes," Leaphorn said.

"Joe Harris did the autopsy too, at Farmington," Jenks said. "He told me he got a dime out of one of the wounds. That's why I remembered it, I guess."

"Harris found a dime in the wound?" Harris

was the San Juan County coroner working out of the Farmington hospital. Pathologists, like police, seemed to know one another and swap yarns.

"He said Endocheeney got stabbed a bunch of times through the pocket of his jacket. In knifings we're always finding threads and stuff like that in the wound. Whatever the knife happens to hit on the way in through the clothing. Buttons. Paper. Whatever. This time it hit a dime."

Leaphorn, whose memory was excellent, recalled reading the autopsy report in the FBI file. No mention of a dime. But there had been mention of "foreign objects," which would cover a dime as well as the more usual buttons, thread, gravel, and broken glass. Could a knife punch a dime into a wound? Easily enough. It seemed odd, but not unreasonable.

"But Endocheeney wasn't on the list."

"I don't think so," Jenks said.

Leaphorn hesitated. "How about Jim Chee?" he asked.

Dr. Jenks thought hard again. But he couldn't remember whether or not Jim Chee's name was on the death date list.

> 8 <

It was almost dark when Chee pulled into the
police parking lot in Shiprock. He parked where
a globe willow would shade the car from the
early sun the next morning and walked, stiff and
weary, toward his pickup truck. He had left it
that morning where another of the police department willows would shade it from the afternoon
sun. Now the same tree hid it from the dim red
twilight in a pool of blackness. The uneasiness
Chee had shaken off at Badwater Wash and on
the long drive home was suddenly back in possession. He stopped, stared at the truck. He could
see only its shape in the shadows. He turned
abruptly and hurried into the Police Building.

Nelson McDonald was working the night shift,
lounging behind the switchboard with the two
top buttons of his uniform shirt open, reading
the sports section of the Farmington *Times*. Officer McDonald glanced up at Chee, nodded.

"You still alive?" he asked, with no hint of a smile.

"So far," Chee said. But he didn't think it was funny. He would later, perhaps. Ten years later. Crises past, in police work, tended to transmute themselves from fear into the stuff of jokes. But now there was still the fear, a palpable something affecting the way Chee's stomach felt. "I guess nobody noticed anyone tinkering around with my truck?"

Officer McDonald sat up a little straighter, noticing Chee's face and regretting the joke. "Nobody mentioned it," he said. "And it's parked right out there where everybody could see it. I don't think . . ." He decided not to finish the sentence.

"No messages?" Chee asked.

McDonald sorted through the notes impaled on a spindle on the clerk's desk. "One," he said, and handed it to Chee.

"Call Lt. Leaphorn as soon as you get in," it said, and listed two telephone numbers.

Leaphorn answered at the second one, his home.

"I want to ask you if you learned anything new about Endocheeney," Leaphorn said. "But there's a couple of other loose ends. Didn't you say you met Irma Onesalt just recently? Can you tell me exactly when?"

"I could check my logs," Chee said. "Probably in April. Late April."

"Did she say anything to you about a list of

names she had? About trying to find out what date the people on that list died?"

"No, sir," Chee said. "I'm sure I'd remember something like that."

"You said you went to the Badwater Clinic and picked up a patient there and took him to a chapter meeting for her and they gave you the wrong man. And she was sore about it. That right?"

"Right. Old man named Begay. You know how it is with Begays." How it was with Begays on the reservation is how it is with Smiths and Joneses in Kansas City or Chavezes in Santa Fe. It was the most common name on the reservation.

"She said nothing about names? Nothing about a list of names? Nothing about how to go about finding out dates of deaths? Nothing that might lead into that?"

"No, sir," Chee said. "She just said a word or two when I got to the chapter house. She was waiting. Wanted to know why I was late. Then she took the old man in to the meeting. I waited because I was supposed to take him back after he had his say. After a while, she came out and raised hell with me for bringing her the wrong Begay, and then he came out and got in and I took him back to the clinic. Not much of a chance for chatting."

"No," Leaphorn said. "I had some dealing with the woman myself." Chee heard the sound of a chuckle. "I imagine you learned a few new dirty words?"

"Yes, sir," Chee said. "I did."

A long silence. "Well," Leaphorn said. "Just remember that a little while before she was shot she showed up at the pathologist's office at the Gallup hospital with a list of names. She wanted to know how to find out when each of them died. If you hear anything that helps explain that, I want to know about it right away."

"Right," Chee said.

"Now. What did you learn out around Badwater?"

"Not much," Chee said. "He had several hundred dollars' worth of pawn left at the post there—a lot more than he owed for—and his kinfolks haven't picked it up. And he broke a leg last summer falling off a fence. Nothing much."

Silence again. Then Leaphorn said, in a very mild voice: "I've got a funny way of working. Instead of telling me 'Not much,' I like people to tell me all the details and then I'll say, 'Well, that's not much,' or maybe I'll say, 'Hey, that part about the pawn explains something else I heard.' Or so forth. What I'm saying is, give me all the details and let me sort it out."

And so Chee, feeling slightly resentful, told Leaphorn of the bent woman, and the Kayonnie brothers with morning beer on their breath, and the letter from Window Rock, and the crutches which Iron Woman wouldn't accept as pawn and couldn't sell, and all the other details. He finished, and listened to a silence so long that he wondered if Leaphorn had put down the telephone. He cleared his throat.

"That letter," Leaphorn said. "From Window Rock. But what agency? And when?"

"Navajo Social Services," Chee said. "That's what Iron Woman remembered. It came back in June."

"That's who Irma Onesalt worked for," Leaphorn said.

"Oh," Chee said.

"Where'd he get the crutches?"

"Badwater Clinic," Chee said. "They set his leg. Guess they loan out their crutches."

"And don't get them back," Leaphorn said. "You learn anything else you're not telling me?"

"No, sir," Chee said.

Leaphorn noticed the tone. "You can see why I need the details. You haven't been working on the Onesalt case, so you had no way of knowing—or giving a damn—who she worked for. Now we have a link. Victim Onesalt wrote a letter to victim Endocheeney. Or somebody in her office did."

"That help?"

Leaphorn laughed. "I don't see how. But nothing else helps, either. You figured out yet why you got shot at?"

"No, sir."

Another pause. "Something I want you to think about." Silence. "I'm going to bet you that when we find out who did it and why, it's going to be based on something you know. You're going to say, 'Hell, I should have thought of that.'"

"Maybe," Chee said. But he thought about it as

he put down the telephone. And he doubted it. Leaphorn was a hotshot. But Leaphorn was wrong about this.

He glanced at McDonald, immersed again in the *Times*. Chee had come in mostly to get the station's portable spotlight out of the storeroom and shine it on his truck. But now, in this well-lit room with his friend waiting behind the newspaper, curious and embarrassed, doing that seemed ridiculous. Instead he went to his typewriter and pounded out a note to Largo.

TO: *Commanding Officer*
FROM: *Chee*
SUBJECT: *Investigation thefts from vehicles at tourist parking sites and theft of drip gasoline in Aneth field.*
    At Badwater Wash Trading Post ran into two young men, Kayonnie family, driving a new GMC 4 × 4 and drinking in the morning. Am told they are unemployed. Will check more out there again.

He initialed the memo and handed it to Officer McDonald.

"Going home," he said, and left.

He stood a moment in the darkness beyond the entrance until his eyes adjusted enough to make his pickup visible. By then the fear had reestablished itself, and the thought of walking up to that truck in the darkness, and then of driving into the darkness surrounding his trailer, was more than he wanted to handle. He'd walk.

It was less than two miles from the station down along the river to his homesite under the cottonwoods. An easy walk, even at night. It would work out the stiffness of a day spent mostly in his patrol car. He trotted across the asphalt of U.S. 666 and found the path that led toward the river.

Chee was a fast walker and normally this trip took less than thirty minutes. Tonight, moving soundlessly, he took almost forty and used another ten carefully scouting, pistol in hand, the places around his trailer where someone with a shotgun might wait. He found nothing. That left the trailer itself.

He paused behind a juniper and studied it. Light from a half-moon made the setting a pattern of cottonwood shadows. The only sound on the breezeless air was a truck changing gears on the highway far behind him, growling up the long slope out of the valley en route to Colorado. As to whether someone with a shotgun was waiting in the trailer, Chee could think of no safe way to answer that question. He'd left the door locked, but the lock would be easy to pick. He slipped the pistol out of its holster again, thinking that this was a hell of a way to live, thinking that he might give up on the trailer, walk back to the station, get his patrol car, and spend the night in a motel, thinking that he might just say to hell with it and walk up to the door, pistol cocked, and unlock it, and go in. Then he remembered the cat.

The cat was probably out hunting the nocturnal rodents it had lived on until Chee began supplementing its diet with his table scraps. But maybe not. Maybe it was still a little early for rodents and the predators that hunt them. More than once when he had risen early he'd seen Cat returning to its den about dawn. So perhaps it slept early and hunted late. The juniper under which Cat made its home was along the slope to Chee's left. He picked up a handful of dirt and gravel and threw it into the bush.

Later, he thought that the cat must have been crouched, alert, under the juniper listening to his prowling. It shot from the bush, moving almost too fast to be seen in the poor light for its refuge in the trailer. He heard the *clack-clack* of the cat door. He relaxed. No one would be waiting for him inside.

But now he knew he couldn't sleep in the trailer. He got out his sleeping bag, packed his toothbrush and a change of clothing, and walked back to the police station. He was tired now, and the incident of the cat had broken the tension. The fear that had lived in his truck was gone now. It was simply a friendly, familiar vehicle. He unlocked the door, climbed in, and started the engine. He drove across the San Juan and then west on 504, with the dark shape of the Chuskas looming in the moonlight to the south. Just past Behclahbeto, he pulled onto the shoulder, turned off his lights, and waited. The car lights he'd noticed miles behind him turned out to belong to a U-Haul truck, which roared past him and disappeared over the hill. He restarted his engine and turned onto a dirt road that jolted through the dusty sagebrush and dipped into an arroyo. Up the arroyo, he parked and rolled out his sleeping bag. He lay on his back, looking up at the stars, thinking about the nature of fear and how it affected him, and about what Iron Woman had told him of the bone being found in Dugai Endocheeney. It could be false, one of those witch rumors that spring up like tumbleweeds after rain when bad things happen. Or it could be true. Perhaps someone thought he had been witched by Endocheeney, and had killed him and returned the bone of corpse poison to reverse the witching. Or it could be that a witch had killed Dugai Endocheeney and left the bone as its marker. In either case, how would the people at Badwater Wash have learned of it? Chee considered that and found an answer. The bone would have shown up in the autopsy. The surgeon would have seen it only as a piece of foreign matter lodged in the wound. But it was odd, and he would have mentioned it. The word would have spread. A Navajo would have heard it—a nurse, an orderly. To a Navajo, any Navajo, the significance would have been apparent. The word of the bone would have reached Badwater Wash with the speed of light.

So why hadn't he mentioned the bone gossip to the lieutenant who insisted on knowing every detail? Chee examined his motives. It was too vague to mention, he thought, but the real reason was his expectation of Leaphorn's reaction to anything associated with witchery. Ah, well, perhaps he would mention it to Leaphorn the next time he saw him.

Chee rolled onto his side, seeking comfort and sleep. Tomorrow he would go to the Farmington jail, where Roosevelt Bistie was being held until the federals could decide what to do with him. He would try to get Bistie to talk about witchcraft.

> 9 <

"**I** THINK YOU'RE TOO LATE," the officer on the jail information desk telephone said. "I think his lawyer's coming to get him."

"Lawyer?" Chee asked. "Who?"

"Somebody from DNA," the deputy said. "Some woman. She's driving over from Shiprock."

"So am I," Chee said, checking his memory for the name to go with the deputy's voice, and finding it. "Listen, Fritz, if she gets there first, maybe you could stall around a little. Take some time getting him checked out."

"Maybe so, Jim," Fritz said. "Sometimes people say we're slow. Can you be here by nine?"

Chee glanced at his watch. "Sure," he said.

From the police station in Shiprock to the jail in Farmington is about thirty miles. While he drove it, Chee considered how he would deal with the lawyer, or try to deal with her. DNA was the popular acronym for Dinebeiina Nahiilna be

Agaditahe, which translates roughly into "People Who Talk Fast and Help the People Out," and which was the Navajo Nation's version of Legal Aid Society/public defender organization. Earlier in its career it had attracted mostly young militant social activists whose relationship with the Navajo Tribal Police had ranged from icy to hostile. Things had improved gradually. Now, generally, the iciness had modified to coolness, and the hostility to suspicion. Chee expected no trouble.

However . . .

The young woman in the white silk shirt sitting against the wall in the D Center reception room was looking at him with something stronger than suspicion. She was small, skinny, a Navajo, with short black hair and large angry black eyes. Her expression, if not hostile, showed active distaste.

"You're Chee," she said, "the arresting officer?"

"Jim Chee," Chee said, checking his reflex offer of a handshake in midmotion. "Not the arresting officer, technically. The federal—"

"I know that," said Silk Shirt, getting to her feet with a graceful motion. "Did Agent Kennedy explain to you . . . did Agent Kennedy explain to Mr. Bistie . . . that a citizen, even a Navajo citizen, has a right to consult with an attorney before he undergoes a cross-examination?"

"We read him—"

"And do you know," Silk Shirt asked, forming each word with icy precision, "that you have absolutely no legal right to hold Mr. Bistie here in this jail with no charge against him whatsoever, and knowing that he didn't commit the homicide you arrested him for, just because you 'want to talk to him'?"

"He's being held for investigation," Chee said, aware that his face was flushed, aware that Officer Fritz Langer of the Farmington Police Department was standing there behind the reception desk, watching all this. Chee shifted his position. From the corner of his eye he could see Langer was not only listening, he was grinning. "He admitted taking a shot—"

"Without advice of counsel," Silk Shirt said. "And now, just at your request and without any legal grounds at all, Mr. Bistie is being held here by the police while you take your time driving over from Shiprock so you can talk to him. Just a favor from one good old boy to another."

The grin disappeared from Langer's face. "The paperwork," he said. "It takes time when the federals are involved."

"Paperwork, my butt," Silk Shirt snapped. "It's the good old boy network at work." She pointed a thumb in Chee's direction, something one polite Navajo did not do to another. "Your buddy here calls you and says keep him locked up until I can get around to talking to him. Stall around all day if you have to."

"Naw," Langer said. "Nothing like that. You know how the Federal Bureau of Investigation is about crossing all the *t*'s and dotting the *i*'s."

"Well, Mr. Chee is here now. Can you get the *i* dotted and release Mr. Bistie?"

Langer made a wry face at Chee, lifted the telephone, and talked to someone. "He'll be out in a minute," he said. He reached under the counter, extracted a brown paper grocery bag, and put it on the countertop. It bore the legend R. BISTIE, WEST WING in red Magic Marker. Chee felt a yearning to explore that paper sack. He should have thought of it earlier. Much earlier. Before Silk Shirt arrived. He smiled at Silk Shirt.

"All I need is just a few minutes. Just some information."

"About what?"

"Well," Chee said, "if we knew why Bistie wanted to kill Endocheeney—and he says he wanted to kill him," he inserted hastily, "then maybe we'd know more about why someone else did kill Endocheeney. Stabbed Endocheeney. Later."

"Make an appointment," Silk Shirt said. "Maybe he'll want to talk to you." She paused, looking at Chee. "And maybe he won't."

"I guess we could pick him up again," Chee said. "As a material witness. Something like that."

"I guess you could," she said. "But it better be legal this time. Now he'll be represented by someone who understands that even a Navajo has some constitutional rights."

Roosevelt Bistie came through the door, trailed by an elderly jailer. The jailer patted him on the shoulder. "Come see us," he said, and disappeared back through the doorway.

"Mr. Bistie," Silk Shirt said. "I am Janet Pete. We were told you needed legal counsel and the DNA sent me over to represent you. To be your lawyer."

Bistie nodded to her. *"Ya-tah-hey,"* he said. He looked at Chee. Nodded. Smiled. "I don't need no lawyer," he said. "They told me somebody else killed the son-of-a-bitch. I missed him." Bistie chuckled when he said it, but to Chee he still looked sick.

"You need a lawyer to tell you to be careful what you say," Janet Pete said, glancing at Chee. And then, to Langer: "And we need a place where my client and I can talk. In private."

"Sure," Langer said. He handed Bistie the sack and pointed. "Down the hall. First door to the left."

"Miss Pete," Chee said. "When you're talking to your client, would you ask him if I can talk to him for a minute or two? Otherwise . . ."

"Otherwise what?"

"Otherwise I'll have to drive all the way up into the Lukachukais to his place and talk to him there," Chee said meekly. "And just to ask three or four questions I forgot to ask him earlier."

"I'll see," Janet Pete said, and disappeared down the hall after Bistie.

Chee looked out the window. The lawn needed water. What was it about white men that caused them to plant grass in places where grass couldn't possibly grow without them fiddling with it all the time? Chee had thought about that a lot, and talked to Mary Landon about it. He'd told Mary he thought it represented a subconscious need to remind themselves that they could defy nature. Mary said no, it wasn't need for remembered beauty. Chee looked at the lawn, and at the desert country visible across the San Juan beyond it. He preferred the desert. Today even the fringe of tumbleweeds along the sidewalk looked wilted. Dry heat everywhere and the sky almost cloudless.

"I didn't tell her you'd asked me to stall," Langer said, apologetically. "She figured that out for herself."

"Oh, well," Chee said. "I don't think she likes cops, anyway." A thought materialized abruptly. "You remember what was in Bistie's sack?"

Langer looked surprised at the question. He shrugged. "Usual stuff. Billfold. Keys to his truck. Pocket knife. One of those little deerskin sacks some of you guys carry. Handkerchief. Nothing unusual."

"Did you look in the billfold?"

"We have to inventory the money," Langer said. He sorted through papers on a clipboard. "Had a ten and three ones and seventy-three cents in change. Driver's license. So forth."

"Anything else you remember?"

"I didn't check him in," Langer said. "Al did. On the evening shift. Says here: 'Nothing else of value.'"

Chee nodded.

"What you looking for?"

"Just fishing," Chee said.

"Speaking of which," Langer said, "can you get a permit for fishing up there at Wheatfields Lake? Free, I mean."

"Well," Chee said. "I guess you know—"

Janet Pete appeared at the hall door. "He says he'll talk to you."

"I thank you," Chee said.

The room held a bare wooden table and two chairs. Roosevelt Bistie sat in one of them, eyes half closed, face sagging. But he returned Chee's salutation. Chee put his hand on the back of the other chair, glanced at Janet Pete. She was leaning against the wall behind Bistie, watching Chee. The paper sack was under Bistie's chair.

"Could we talk in private?" Chee asked her.

"I'm Mr. Bistie's legal counsel," she said. "I'll stay."

Chee sat down, feeling defeated. It had never been likely that Bistie would talk. He hadn't, after all, in the past. It was even less likely that he would talk about the subject Chee intended to raise, which was witchcraft. There was a simple enough reason for that. Witches hated to be talked about—to even have their evil business discussed. Therefore the prudent Navajo discussed witchcraft, if at all, only with those known and trusted. Not with a stranger. Certainly not with two strangers. However, there was no harm in trying.

"I have heard something which I think you would like to know," Chee said. "I will tell you what I heard. And then I will ask you a question. I hope you will give me an answer. But if you won't, you won't."

Bistie looked interested. So did Janet Pete.

"First," Chee said, speaking slowly, intent on Bistie's expression, "I will tell you what the people over at the Badwater Wash Trading Post hear. They hear that a little piece of bone was found in the body of that man you took a shot at."

There was a lag of a second or two. Then Bistie smiled a very slight smile. He nodded at Chee.

Chee glanced at Janet Pete. She looked puzzled. "Understand that I do not know if this is true," Chee said. "I will go to the hospital where the body of that man was taken and I will try to find out if it was true. Should I tell you what I find out?"

No smile now. Bistie was studying Chee's face. But he nodded.

"Now I have a question for you to answer. Do you have a little piece of bone?"

Bistie stared at Chee, face blank.

"Don't answer that," Janet Pete said. "Not until I find out what's going on here." She frowned at Chee. "What's this all about? It sounds like an attempt to get Mr. Bistie to incriminate himself. What are you driving at?"

"We know Mr. Bistie didn't kill Endocheeney," Chee said. "Somebody else killed him. We don't know who. We aren't likely to find out who until we know why. Mr. Bistie here seems to have had a good reason to kill Endocheeney, because he tried to do it. Maybe it was the same reason. Maybe it was because Endocheeney was a skinwalker. Maybe he witched Mr. Bistie. Put the witch bone into him. Maybe Endocheeney witched somebody else. If what I heard at Badwater Wash isn't just gossip, maybe Mr. Endocheeney had a bone put in him because that other person, the one who knifed Endocheeney, put it in him when he stabbed Endocheeney to turn the witching around." Chee was talking directly to Janet Pete, but he was watching Bistie from the corner of his eye. If Bistie's face revealed any emotion, it was satisfaction.

"It sounds like nonsense to me," Janet Pete said.

"Would you recommend to your client that he answer my question, then?" Chee asked. "Did he believe Mr. Endocheeney was a witch?"

"I'll talk to him about this," she said. "There are no charges against him. None. He's not accused of anything. You're just holding him to satisfy your curiosity."

"About a murder," Chee said. "And there may be a charge filed by now. Attempted homicide."

"Based on what?" Janet Pete asked. "On what he told you and Kennedy before consulting with his attorney? That's absolutely all you have."

"That, and some other stuff," Chee said. "Witnesses who put him where it happened. His li-

cense number. The ejected shell from his rifle."
Which, as far as Chee knew, hadn't been found
and wasn't being looked for. Why look for a shell
casing from a shot that missed when they had a
butcher knife, which didn't miss? But Janet Pete
wouldn't know they hadn't found it.

"I don't think there's any basis for charges,"
Janet Pete said.

Chee shrugged. "It's not up to me. I think Kennedy—"

"I think I will call Kennedy," Janet Pete said.
"Because I don't believe you." She walked to the
door, stopped with her hand on the knob, smiled
at Chee. "Are you coming?"

"I'll just wait," Chee said.

"Then my client is coming," she said. She motioned to Bistie. He got up, steadied himself with
a hand on the tabletop.

"This interview is over," Janet Pete said, and
she closed the door behind them.

Chee waited. Then he went to the door and
glanced down the hall. Janet Pete was using the
telephone in the pay booth. Chee closed the door
again, picked up Bistie's sack, sorted quickly
through it. Nothing interesting. He extracted Bistie's billfold.

In it, in the corner of the currency pocket that
held a ten and three ones, Chee found a bead. He
turned it over between thumb and first finger, examining it. Then he put it back where he had
found it, put the wallet back in the sack, and the

sack back on the floor under Bistie's chair. The bead seemed to be made of bone. In fact, it looked exactly like the one he'd found on the floor of his trailer.

≫ 10 ≪

THE TURBULENCE CAUSED BY THE THUNDERHEAD was sweeping across the valley floor toward them. It kicked up an opaque gray-white wall of dust which obscured the distant shape of Black Mesa and spawned dust devils in the caliche flats south of them. They were standing, Officer Al Gorman and Joe Leaphorn, beside Gorman's patrol car on the track that led across the sagebrush flats below Sege Butte toward Chilchinbito Canyon.

"Right here," Gorman said. "Here's where he parked his car, or pickup, or whatever."

Leaphorn nodded. Gorman was sweating. A trickle of it ran down his neck and under his shirt collar. It was partly the heat, and partly that Gorman should lose a few pounds, and partly, Leaphorn knew, because he made Gorman nervous.

"Tracks lead right back here." Gorman pointed. "From over there near the rim of Chilchinbito Canyon, where he killed Sam, and down that slope there, where the shale outcrops are, and then across the sagebrush right up to here."

Leaphorn grunted. He was watching the dust storm moving down the valley with its outrider of whirlwinds. One of them had crossed a gypsum sink, and its winds had sucked up that heavier mineral. The cone changed from the yellow-gray of the dusty earth to almost pure white. It was the sort of thing Emma would have noticed, and found beauty in, and related in some way or other to the mythology of The People. Emma would have said something about the Blue Flint Boys playing their games. They were the *yei* personalities credited with stirring up whirlwinds. He would describe it to her tonight. He would if she was awake and aware—and not in that vague world she now so often retreated into.

Beside him, Gorman was describing the sign he had followed from killing scene to car, and the sign the car had left, and his conclusion that the killer had raced away. "Spun his wheels in the grass," Gorman was saying. "Tore it up. Threw dirt. And then, right down there, he backed around and drove on back toward the road."

"Where was the killing?"

"See that little bunch of juniper? Look across the shale slope, and then to the right. That man . . ." Gorman stopped, glanced at Leaphorn for a reading of whether the lieutenant would allow him to avoid "wearing out the name" of a dead man. He made his decision and restated the sentence. "That's where Wilson Sam was, by the juniper. Looked like it was a regular stopping place for him when he was out with the sheep. And the killer got him about twenty-five, thirty yards to the right of those junipers."

"Looks like he took sort of a roundabout way to get back here, then," Leaphorn said. "If he circled all the way around and came down that shale."

"Looks that way," Gorman said. "But it's not. It fools you. You can't see it from here because of the way the land folds, but if you try to go straight across, then over that ridge there—the ridge that shale is in—over that there's an arroyo. Cut deep. To get across it you got to skirt way up, or way down, where there's sheep crossing. So the short way—"

Leaphorn interrupted him. "Did he go the same way he came back?"

Gorman looked puzzled.

Leaphorn rephrased the question, partly to clarify his own thinking. "When he drove along here, we'll say he was looking for Sam. Hunting him. He sees Sam, or maybe just the flock of sheep Sam was watching, over there across the flats by the junipers. This is as close as he can get the vehicle. So he parks here. Gets out. Heads for Sam. You say the fastest way to get there is angling way to the right, and then up that shale slope over there, and across the ridge, and then across an arroyo at a sheep crossing, and then swing left again. Long way around, but quickest. And that's the way he came back. But is that the way he went?"

"Sure," Gorman said. "I guess so. I didn't notice. I wasn't looking for that. Just tracking him to see where he went."

"Let's see if we can find out," Leaphorn said. It wouldn't be easy, but for the first time since he'd awakened that morning, with the homicides instantly on his mind, he felt a stirring of hope. This might be a way to learn whether or not the person who'd killed Wilson Sam was a stranger to Sam's territory. Small though that would be, it would satisfy Leaphorn's quota for this unpromising day.

Leaphorn had given himself the quota as he'd eaten his breakfast: Before the day was done, he would add one single hard fact to what he knew about his unsolved homicides. He'd eaten a bowl of cornmeal mush, a piece of Emma's fried bread, and some salami from the refrigerator. Emma, who for all the almost thirty years of their marriage had risen with the dawn, was still asleep. He'd dressed quietly, careful not to disturb her.

She'd lost weight, he thought. Not eating. Before Agnes had come to help, she would simply forget to eat when he wasn't home. He would make her a lunch before he left for the office and find it untouched when he came home at the end of the day. Now she would sometimes forget to eat even when the food was on her plate in front of her. "Emma," he would say. "Eat." And she would look at him with that embarrassed, confused, disoriented smile and say, "It's good, but I forget." He had looked down at her as he buttoned his shirt, seeing an unaccustomed hollowness below the cheekbones, under the eyes. When he was away from her, her face would always have the same smooth roundness he'd noticed that day he first saw her—walking with two other Navajo girls across the campus at Arizona State.

Arizona State. His mother had buried his umbilical cord at the roots of a piñon beside their hogan—the traditional Navajo ritual for binding a child to his family and his people. But for Leaphorn, Emma was the tie. A simple physical law. Emma could not be happy away from the Sacred Mountains. He could not be happy away from Emma. He had frowned down at her, studying her, seeing the flatness of her cheek, the lines under her eyes and at the corners of her mouth. ("I'm feeling fine," she would say. "I never felt better. You must not have any work to do down at the police to be worrying about me all the time.") But now she would admit the headaches. And there was no way she could hide the forgetfulness, nor those odd blank moments when she seemed to be awakening, confused, from some bad dream. Day after tomorrow was the appointment. At 2 P.M. They would leave early, and drive to Gallup, and check her in at the Indian Health Service hospital. And then they would find out.

Now there was no reason to think about it, about what it might be. No reason to let his mind reexamine again and again and again all he had heard and read of the horrors of Alzheimer's disease. Maybe it wasn't that. But he knew it was. He'd called the toll-free number of the Alzheimer's Disease and Related Disorders Association, and they had sent him a package of information.

> *. . . initially a patient with AD*
> *exhibits the following symptoms:*
> *1. Forgetfulness.*
> *2. Impairment of judgment.*
> *3. Inability to handle routine tasks.*
> *4. Lack of spontaneity.*
> *5. Lessening of initiative.*
> *6. Disorientation of time and place.*
> *7. Depression and terror.*
> *8. Disturbance of language.*
> *9. Episodic confusional states.*

He had read it in the office, checking them off. The suddenly faltering unfinished sentences, the business of always thinking today was his day off, the lethargy, the trouble with getting the garbage bag installed in the garbage can, the preparation for Agnes's arrival two days after Agnes had arrived. Worst of all, his awakening in the night to find Emma clutching at him, frantic with some nightmare fear. He had, as was his fashion, made notes in the margin. Emma had scored nine for nine.

Leaphorn had every reason to think of something else.

And so that morning he had thought, first, of Irma Onesalt's list of the dead, and why death dates would be important to her. As he left Emma still sleeping he heard Agnes stirring in her room. He drove to his office in the clear, sunrise light of another day of heat and drought. Dust was already rising from the rodeo grounds down at the highway intersection—the dust of stock feeding. Sometime today he would think of the rodeo and the myriad of problems it always brought. Now he wanted to think of his homicides.

At the office, he composed a letter to go to the various county health departments in Arizona, New Mexico, and Utah that would have been contacted by Onesalt if she followed the advice of Dr. Randall Jenks. It was too complicated, and too sensitive, to be handled by the half-dozen telephone calls it would require. And there was no real urgency. So he put the letter together— very carefully. He explained who he was, explained that the investigation of the murder of Irma Onesalt was involved, described the list as best he could, trying to recall for them the question she might have asked. Finally, with these needed preliminaries out of the way, he inquired if anyone in the department had received a letter or a telephone call from Ms.

Onesalt concerning these names, asking death dates. If so, could he have a copy of the letter, or the name of the person who had handled the telephone call, so he could question that person more closely.

He wrote a clean copy of the final draft and a cover memo for the clerk, listing to whom copies should be sent. That done, he considered what Jenks had told him about Chee's bone bead. It was made of cow bone. A witch, if one believed bona fide witches existed, would have used human bone, presuming the bona fide witch believed Navajo witchcraft mythology in a literal meaning. So if a real witch was involved, presuming such existed, said witch had been swindled by his bone supplier. On the other hand, if someone was merely pretending to be a witch, such things didn't matter. Those who believed witches magically blew bone particles into their victims would hardly subject said bone to the microscope. And of course, cow-bone beads would be easy to get. Or would they? It seemed likely. Every slaughterhouse would produce mountains of cattle bones. Raw material for mass producing beads for the costume jewelry market. Leaphorn found his thought process leading him into the economics of producing bone beads as opposed to molding plastic beads. Chee's bone beads would certainly be old, something from old jewelry, or perhaps clothing. Jenks had said the bead was fairly old. Perhaps the FBI, with its infinite resources, could track down the source. But he couldn't imagine how. He tried to imagine Delbert Streib phrasing the memo about corpse poison and witches to touch off such an effort. Streib would simply laugh at the idea.

Leaphorn wrote another memo, instructing Officer Jimmy Tso, who handled liaison with the Gallup police department, to check suppliers for jewelry makers, pawnshops, and wherever else he could think of, to learn how a Navajo/Zuni/Hopi jewelry maker might obtain beads, and particularly bone beads. He dropped that memo in his out-basket atop the drafted letter. Then he extracted his homicide folders from the cabinet, put them on his desk, and looked at them.

He pushed the Onesalt file aside. Onesalt had been the first to die. Something in his instinct told him she was the key, and he knew her file by heart. It baffled him. It seemed as lacking in purpose as death by lightning—as cruel and casual as the malicious mischief of the Holy People. He picked up the file labeled WILSON SAM, opened it, and read. He saw nothing that he hadn't remembered. But when he'd first read it, he hadn't noticed that the tribal policeman working with Jay Kennedy on this investigation was Officer Al Gorman. The name then had meant nothing to him. It had simply identified a new, probably young, officer whom Leaphorn did not know. Now the name carried with it a visual image.

Leaphorn put the file on the desk and looked out his window at the early morning sunlight on the scattered roofs of Window Rock village. Gorman. The plump cop walking across the Shiprock parking lot with Chee and Benaly. Chee instantly conscious of the parked car, of what car it was, of its occupant, all with hardly a glance. But the walk became a little stiffer, the shoulders a little straighter, knowing he was watched. Benaly becoming aware of Chee's awareness, noticing the car, not being interested. And Gorman, talking, noticing nothing. Oblivious. Blind to everything except the single thought that occupied him. Officer Gorman had never noticed Leaphorn sitting in the shade in his car. If he missed that, what had he missed at the scene of Wilson Sam's death? Maybe nothing, but it was worth checking. To be honest, perhaps he should say it gave him an excuse.

It was nine minutes until eight. In nine minutes his telephone would start ringing. The world of the troublesome rodeo, the Tribal Council meeting, indignant school principals, bootleggers, too few men and too many assignments, would capture him for another day. He looked past the clock at the world outside the window, the highway leading away over the ridge toward everywhere but Window Rock, the world in which his job had once allowed him to pursue his own curiosity and to hell with the paperwork. He picked up the telephone and

called the Shiprock station. He asked for Officer
Al Gorman.

Now it was early afternoon. Gorman had met
him, as requested, at the Mexican Water Trading
Post. They'd made the bone-jarring drive back
into the Chilchinbito Canyon country. Rather
quickly, Officer Gorman had proved he was the
sort of man who—as Leaphorn's grandmother
would have said—counted the grass and didn't
see the grazing.

Gorman was sitting now in Leaphorn's car,
waiting (uneasily, Leaphorn hoped) for Leaphorn to finish whatever the hell Leaphorn was
doing. What Leaphorn was doing was looking
past the grass at the grazing. They had
established by two hours of dusty work that the
route the killer had taken to reach the growth of
junipers where Wilson Sam was waiting was
very different from his return route. Broken
twigs here, dislodged rocks there, a footprint
sheltered enough to survive two months of
rainless days, showed them that he had headed
in an almost straight line through the sagebrush
toward the junipers. He had crossed the ridge,
maintaining that direction except when heavy
brush forced a detour, until he reached the
arroyo. He had walked down its bank perhaps a
hundred yards, presumably looking for a
crossing point. Then he had reversed direction
almost a quarter mile, to cross at a sheep trail—
the same trail he'd used on his return trip.

Leaphorn spent the remainder of the morning having Gorman shown him just what he had found, and where he had found it, when Gorman had worked this scene for Kennedy early in the summer. Gorman had shown him where Wilson Sam's body had been found on the bottom of the narrow wash draining into Chilchinbito. He had pointed out the remains of the little rock slides that showed Sam had been tumbled down from above. The rainless summer had left the sign pretty much undisturbed. Ants had carried away most of the congealed blood from the sand where the body had lain, but you could still find traces. In this protected bottom, the winds had only smoothed the tracks of those who had come to carry Sam away.

Above, the scouring had been more complete. Gorman had shown Leaphorn where Sam had been and where the killer had come from. "Easy enough to tell 'em apart," Gorman said. "The ground was softer then. Sam had boots on. Flat heels. Easy to match them with his tracks. And the other fellow had on cowboy boots." He glanced at Leaphorn. "Bigger. Maybe size eleven."

All that had been in Kennedy's report. So had the answer to the question Leaphorn had decided to ask. But he wanted to hear it for himself.

"And they didn't stand and talk at all? No sign of that?"

"No, sir," Gorman said. "No sign of that. When I tracked the suspect back, it showed he started running about forty yards out there." Gorman had pointed into the sparse sagebrush to the south. "No more heel prints. He was running."

"And Sam? Where did he start running away?"

Gorman showed him. Sam had not run far. Perhaps twenty-five yards. Old men are poor runners, even when they are running for their life.

Back at the car, Leaphorn stood where the killer had parked and stared across the broken landscape toward the junipers where this person must have seen Sam, or Sam's sheep. He stood with his lower lip held between his teeth, nibbling thoughtfully, trying to recreate what the killer must have been thinking, retracing with his eyes the route the man had taken.

"Let's make sure we agree—that I'm not overlooking anything," Leaphorn said. "He's driving along here. He sees Sam, or maybe Sam's flock, over there by the junipers. He parks. He heads directly toward Sam." Leaphorn glanced at Gorman, saw no sign of disagreement. "In a hurry, I'd say, because of the way he crashed through the sagebrush. He didn't know the arroyo was there behind the ridge, and couldn't get across it there, so he had to skirt upstream to where the banks get lower."

"Not too smart," Gorman said.

"Could be that," Leaphorn said, although being smart had nothing to do with it. "And when he got close to Sam he was in such a hurry to kill him that he started running. Right?"

"I'd say so," Gorman said.

"Why did Sam start running?"

"Scared," Gorman said. "Maybe the guy was yelling at him. Or waving that shovel he killed him with."

"Yeah," Leaphorn said. "That's what I'd guess. When we catch him, who do you think it will turn out to be?"

Gorman shrugged. "No way of telling," he said. "It'd be a man. Big, man-sized feet. Probably some kinfolks or other." He looked at Leaphorn, smiling slightly. "You know how it is. It's always some sort of fight with some of his wife's folks, or some fight with some neighbor over where he's grazing his sheep. That's the way it always is."

It was, in fact, the way it always was. But this time it wasn't. "Think about him not knowing the arroyo was there. Not knowing where to find the sheep crossing," Leaphorn said. "That tell you anything?"

Gorman's pleasant round face looked puzzled. He thought. "I didn't think about that," he said. "I guess it wasn't a neighbor. Anybody lives around here, they'd know how the land lays. How it drains."

"So our man was a stranger."

"Yeah," Gorman said. "That's funny. Think it will help any?"

Leaphorn shrugged. He couldn't see how. It did form a sort of crazy harmony with the Endocheeney affair. Bistie and Endocheeney seemed to have been strangers. What did that mean? But he'd met his quota. He'd added one fact to his homicide data. Wilson Sam had been killed by a stranger.

>> 11 <<

AFTER MANY PAINSTAKING RECONSIDERATIONS,
Jim Chee finally decided he didn't know what the
hell to do about the bone bead in Roosevelt Bistie's billfold. He had walked out of the visiting
room and closed the door behind him, leaving
Bistie's paper sack of belongings on the floor beside the chair, exactly where Bistie had put it.
Then he stood by the door, looking at Bistie with
a curiosity intensified by the thought that Bistie
had tried to blast him out of bed with a shotgun.
Bistie was sitting on the hard bench against the
wall looking out of the window at something, his
face in profile to Chee. Chee memorized him. A
witch? Why had this man fired the shotgun
through the skin of his trailer? He looked no different from any other human, of course. None
of those special characteristics that the white culture sometimes gives its witches. No pointy nose,
sharp features, broomstick. Just another man
whose malice had led him to try to kill. To shoot

Dugai Endocheeney, a stranger, on the roof of his hogan. To shoot Jim Chee, another stranger, asleep in his bed. To butcher Wilson Sam amid his sheep. As Bistie sat now, slumped on the bench, Chee had no luck relating his shape to the shape he had seen, or dreamed he had seen, in the darkness outside his trailer. His only impression had been that the shape had been small. Bistie seemed a little larger than the remembered shape. Could Bistie actually be the man?

Bistie lost interest in whatever he'd been watching through the window and glanced down the hall toward Chee. Their eyes met. Chee read nothing in Bistie's expression except a mild and guarded interest. Then the door of the phone booth pushed open and Janet Pete emerged. Chee walked down the hall, away from her, and out the exit into the parking lot and to his car, away from all the impulsive actions his instinct urged. He wanted to rearrest Bistie. He wanted to take the wallet and confront Bistie—in front of witnesses—with the bone bead. He wanted to make Bistie's possession of the bone a matter of record. But keeping a bone bead in one's billfold was legal enough. And Chee had absolutely no right to know it was there. He'd found it in an illegal search. There was a law against that. But not against bone possession or—for that matter—against being a skinwalker.

Having thought of nothing he could do, he sat in his car waiting for Pete and Bistie to emerge. Maybe they would leave without Bistie's sack.

Simply forget it. If that happened, he would go to the jail, tell Langer that Bistie had left his belongings behind, get Langer to make another, more complete inventory, which would include all the billfold's contents. But when Pete and Bistie emerged, Bistie had the sack clutched in his hand. They drove out of the jail lot, turning toward Farmington. Chee turned west, toward Shiprock.

His mind worked on it as he drove. Reason told him that Bistie might not have been the shape in the darkness that had fired the shotgun into his trailer. Bistie had used the 30-30 on the rack across the back window of his pickup to shoot at Endocheeney. Or said he did. Not a shotgun. There had been no reason to search Bistie's place for a shotgun. Maybe he didn't have one. And the complex mythology of Navajo witchcraft, which Chee knew as well as any man, usually attached a motive to the malice of the skinwalkers. Bistie had no conceivable motive for wanting to kill Chee. Perhaps Bistie was not the one who had tried to kill him.

But even as he thought this, he was aware that his spirit was light again. The dread had lifted. He was not afraid of Bistie, as he had been afraid of the unknown. He felt an urge to sing.

The in-basket on his desk held two envelopes and one of the While You Were Out memos the tribal police used to record notes and telephone calls. One envelope, Chee noticed with instant delight, was the pale blue of Mary Landon's stationery. He put it in his shirt pocket and looked at the other one. It was addressed to Officer Chee, Police Station, Shiprock, in clumsy letters formed with a pencil. Chee glanced at the telephone memo, which said merely: "Call Lt. Leaphorn immediately," and tore open the envelope.

The folded letter inside had been written on the pulpy lined tablet paper schoolchildren use, in the format students are taught in grade school.

In the block where one is taught to put one's return address, the writer had printed:

> Alice Yazzie
> Sheep Springs Trading Post
> Navajo Nation 92927

Dear Nephew Jim Chee:

I hope you are well. I am well. I write you this letter because your Uncle Frazier Denetsone is sick all this summer and worst sick about this month. We took him to the Crystal Gazer over at the Badwater Clinic and the Crystal Gazer said he should let the belagana doctor there give him some medicine. He is taking that green medicine now but he is still sick. The Crystal Gazer said he should take that medicine but that he needs a sing too. That will get him better faster, having the sing. And the sing should be a Blessing Way. I heard that you did the Blessing Way sing for the Niece of Old Grandmother Nez and everybody said it was good. Everybody said you got it all right and the dry paintings were

right. They said the Niece of Old Grandmother Nez got better after that.

We want you to talk about it. We want you
to come to the place of Hildegarde Goldtooth
and we will talk to you about having the sing.
We have about $400 but maybe there could
be more.

Chee read with intense satisfaction. The Blessing Way he had conducted last spring had been
his first job as a *yataalii.* And his last. The niece
of Old Grandmother Nez was a niece by the
broad Navajo definition—the daughter of a first
cousin on the maternal side of Chee's family—
and hiring him as singer had been family courtesy. In fact, the event had been a trial balloon—
as much to inform the north central slice of the
Big Reservation that Chee had begun his practice
as to cure the girl of nothing more serious than
the malaise of being sixteen.

Now, finally, a summons had come. Alice Yazzie called him nephew, but the title here reflected
good manners and not ties of either clan or family. Frazier Denetsone was probably some sort of
uncle, as Navajos defined such things, through
linkage with his father's paternal clan. But a call
for a *yataalii* didn't come from the patient. It
came from whoever in the patient's circle of family took responsibility for such things. Chee
glanced at Alice Yazzie's signature, which included, in the custom of old-fashioned Navajos,
her clan. Streams Come Together Dinee. Chee

was born to the Slow Talking People, and for the Salt Clan. No connections with the Streams Clan. Thus her invitation was the first clue that Jim Chee was becoming accepted as a singer outside his own kinfolk.

He finished the letter. Alice Yazzie wanted him to come to Hildegarde Goldtooth's place the next Sunday evening, when she and the patient's wife and mother could be there to work out a time for the ceremony. "We want to hold it as soon as we can because he is not good. He is not going to last long, I think."

That pessimistic note diminished Chee's jubilation. It was much better for a *yataalii* to begin his career with a visible cure—with a ceremony that not only restored the patient to harmony with his universe but also returned him to health. But Chee would tolerate nothing negative today. It would be better still to effect a cure on a hopeless case. If Frazier Denetsone's illness was indeed subject to correction by the powers evoked by the Blessing Way ritual, if Jim Chee was good enough to perform it precisely right, then all things were possible. Chee believed in penicillin and insulin and heart bypass surgery. But he also believed that something far beyond the understanding of modern medicine controlled life and death. He folded Alice Yazzie's letter into his shirt pocket. With his thumbnail he opened the letter from Mary Landon.

Dearest Jim:

I think of you every day (and even more every night). Miss you terribly. Can't you get some more leave and come back here for a while? I could tell you didn't enjoy yourself on your visit in May, but now we are having our annual two weeks of what passes for summer in Wisconsin. Everything is beautiful. It hasn't rained for two or three hours. You would like it now. In fact, I think you could learn to love it—to live somewhere away from the desert—if you would give it a chance.

Dad and I drove down to Madison last week and talked to an adviser in the College of Arts and Sciences. I will be able to get my master's degree—with a little luck—in just two more semesters because of those two graduate courses I took when I was an undergraduate. Also found a cute efficiency apartment within walking distance of the university and picked up the application papers for graduate admission. I can start taking classes on nondegree status while they process the grad school admission. The adviser said there shouldn't be any problem.

Classes will start the first week of September, which means that, if I enroll, I won't have time to come back out to see you until semester break, which I think is about Thanksgiving. I'm going to hate not seeing you until then, so try to find a way to come. . . .

Chee read the rest of it without much sense of what the words meant. Some chat about something that had happened when he'd visited her in Stevens Point, a couple of sentences about her mother. Her father (who had been painfully polite and had asked Chee endless questions about the Navajo religion and had looked at him as Chee thought Chee might look at a man from another planet) was well and thinking about retirement. She was excited about the thought of returning to school. Probably she would do it. There were more personal notes too, tender and nostalgic.

He read the letter again, slowly this time. But that changed nothing. He felt a numbness—a lack of emotion that surprised him. What did surprise him, oddly, he thought, was that he wasn't surprised. At some subconscious level he seemed to have been expecting this. It had been inevitable since Mary had arranged the leave from the teaching job at Crownpoint. If he hadn't known it then, he must have learned it during that visit to her home—which had left him on the flight back to Albuquerque trying to analyze feelings that were a mixture of happiness and sorrow. He glanced at the opening salutation again. "Dearest Jim . . ." The notes she'd sent him from Crownpoint had opened with "Darling . . ."

He stuffed the letter into his pocket with the Yazzie letter and picked up the memo.

It still said: "Call Lt. Leaphorn immediately."

He called Lieutenant Leaphorn.

≫ 12 ≪

THE TELEPHONE ON Joe Leaphorn's desk buzzed.

"Who is it?"

"Jim Chee from Shiprock," the switchboard said.

"Tell him to hold it a minute," Leaphorn said. He knew what to learn from Chee, but he took a moment to reconsider exactly how he'd go about asking the questions. He held the receiver lightly in his palm, going over it.

"Okay," he said. "Put him on."

Something clicked.

"This is Leaphorn," Leaphorn said.

"Jim Chee. Returning your call."

"Do you know any of the people who live out there around Chilchinbito Canyon. Out there where Wilson Sam lived?"

"Let me think," Chee said. Silence. "No. I don't think so."

"You ever worked anything out there? Enough to be familiar with the territory?"

"Not really," Chee said. "Not my part of the reservation."

"How about the country around Badwater Wash? Around where Endocheeney lived?"

"A lot better," Chee said. "It's not what Captain Largo has me patrolling, but I spent some time out there trying to find a kid who got washed down the San Juan last year. Several days. And then I handled the Endocheeney business. Went out there twice on that."

"I'm right that Bistie wouldn't say anything about whether he knew Endocheeney?"

"Right. He wouldn't say anything. Except he was glad Endocheeney was dead. He made that plain. So you guess he knew the man."

You do, Leaphorn thought. But maybe you guess wrong.

"Did he say anything that would give you an idea whether he knew that Badwater country? Like about having trouble finding Endocheeney's place? Anything like that?"

"You mean beyond stopping at the trading post to ask directions? He did that."

"That was in Kennedy's report," Leaphorn said. "What I meant was did you hear anything from him, or from the people you talked to at Badwater, that would tell you he was totally strange to that country? Afraid of not finding the road? Getting lost? Anything like that?"

"No." The word was said slowly, indicating the thought wasn't finished. Leaphorn waited. "But I didn't press it. We just got his description, and a make on his truck. Didn't look for that sort of information."

Obviously it wouldn't have seemed to have any meaning at that stage of the game. Perhaps it didn't now. He waited for Chee to make unnecessary excuses. None materialized. Leaphorn began phrasing his next question, but Chee interrupted the thought.

"You know," he said slowly, "I think the fellow who knifed Endocheeney was a stranger too. Didn't know the country."

"Oh?" Leaphorn said. He'd heard Chee was smart. He'd heard right. Chee was saving him his question.

"He came down out of the rocks," Chee said. "Have you seen that Endocheeney place? It's set back from the San Juan maybe a hundred yards. Cliffs to the south of it. The killer came down off of those. And went back the same way to get to where he'd left his car. I spent some time looking around. There were two or three easier ways to get down to Endocheeney. Easier than the way he took."

"So," Leaphorn said, half to himself. "Two strangers show up the same day to kill the same man. What do you think of that?"

There was silence. Through his window Leaphorn watched an unruly squadron of crows flying in from the cottonwoods along Window Rock Ridge toward the village. Lunchtime for crows in the garbage cans. But he wasn't thinking of crows. He was thinking of Chee's intelligence. If he told Chee now that the man who killed Wilson Sam was also a stranger, and how he knew it, Chee would quickly detect the reason for his first question. They had established that Chee, too, was a stranger to Wilson Sam's landscape. They established Leaphorn's suspicions. But to hell with that. A cop who got himself shot at from ambush should expect to be under close scrutiny. Chee might as well. He would tell Chee what he'd learned.

"It's possible," Chee was saying, slowly, "that there weren't two strangers coming to find Endocheeney. Maybe there was just one."

"Ah," said Leaphorn, who had the very same thought.

"It could be," Chee went on, "that Bistie knew he missed Endocheeney when he shot at him on the roof. So he drove away, parked up on the mesa, climbed down, and killed Endocheeney with the knife. And then—"

"He confesses to shooting Endocheeney," Leaphorn concluded. "Pretty smart. Is that what happened?"

Chee sighed. "I don't think so," he said.

Neither did Leaphorn. It violated what he'd learned of people down the years. People who prefer guns don't use knives, and vice versa. Bistie had preferred a rifle. He still had the rifle. Why not use it on the second attempt?

"Why not?" Leaphorn asked.

"Different tracks. I don't think Bistie would have brought along a change of footwear, and what few tracks I found at Endocheeney's didn't match Bistie's boots. Anyway, why would he do that? And why not shoot him on the second attempt? Why use a knife? It gave him an alibi, sure. And fooled us. But think of the advance planning it would take to make it all work out like that. And the things that could go wrong. It doesn't match my impression of Bistie."

"Okay," Leaphorn said. "Do you know anything from talking to Bistie, or from anything, that would suggest that Bistie might have known Wilson Sam?"

"No, sir. Nothing."

"Well, we seem to have another strange situation, then." He told Chee what he'd learned at Chilchinbito Canyon.

"Doesn't make much sense," Chee said. "Does it?"

"That bone bead in your trailer," Leaphorn said. "It turned out to be bovine. Made out of old cow bone."

Chee made a noncommittal sound.

"Anything else happened with you? Anything suspicious?"

"No, sir."

"You learning anything?"

"Well . . ." Chee hesitated. "Nothing much. I heard gossip at Badwater Trading Post. They say a bone was found in Endocheeney's corpse."

Leaphorn exhaled, surprised. "Like he had been witched?"

"Yeah," Chee said. "Or like he'd witched some-body else and they put it back into him."

And this was, in Leaphorn's thinking, the very worst part of a sick tradition—this cruel business of killing a scapegoat when things went wrong. It was what Chee Dodge had railed against when he tried to stamp it out. It was what had made Joe Leaphorn, young then and new to the Navajo Tribal Police, responsible for the deaths of four people. Two men. Two women. Three witches and the man who killed them. He had heard the gossip. He had laughed at it. He had collected the bodies—three murders and a suicide. That was twenty years ago. It had converted Leaphorn's contempt for witchcraft into hatred.

"Nothing about any foreign bone fragment showed up in the autopsy," Leaphorn said. But even as he said it, he knew it wasn't necessarily true. The pathologist might not list—probably wouldn't list—such odds and ends. When the cause of death was so obvious—a butcher knife blade driven repeatedly through clothing into the victim's abdomen and side—why list the threads and buttons, lint and gum wrappers, the blade might drive through the skin?

"I thought it might be worth asking about," Chee said.

"It is," Leaphorn said. "I will."

"Also," Chee said. And then paused.

Leaphorn waited.

"Also, Bistie had a bone bead in his wallet. Just

like the one I found in my trailer. Looked like it, anyway."

Leaphorn exhaled again. "He did? What did he say about it?"

"Well, nothing," Chee said. He explained what had happened at the jail. "So I just put it back where I found it."

"I think we better go talk to Bistie again," Leaphorn said. "In fact, I think we better pick him up, and lock him up until we get this sorted out a little better." Leaphorn imagined trying to persuade Dilly to file the complaint. Dilly Streib would be hard to persuade. Dilly had been FBI too long not to care about his batting average. The Agency didn't like cases it didn't win. Still . . .

Leaphorn swiveled in his chair and looked at his map. A line of bone beads now connected two of his dots. And Roosevelt Bistie must know how they connected. And why.

"We can charge him with attempted murder, or attempted assault, or hold him as a material witness."

"Umm," Chee said. A sound full of doubt.

"I'll call the feds," Leaphorn said. He glanced at his watch. "Can you meet me in an hour at . . ." He looked at the map again, picking the most practical halfway point between Window Rock and Shiprock for their drive into the Chuskas. "At Sanostee," he concluded. "Sanostee in an hour?"

"Yes, sir," Chee said. "Sanostee in an hour."

≫ 13 ≪

SANOSTEE WAS HARDLY A HALFWAY POINT, but it was convenient for where they were going. For Chee it was fast—twenty miles south on the worn pavement of U.S. 666 to Littlewater, and then nine miles westward, into the teeth of the gusting, dusty wind, up the long slope of the Chuska range to the trading post. For Leaphorn it was triple that distance—from Window Rock to Crystal and over Washington Pass to Sheep Springs, then north to the Littlewater intersection. When Leaphorn reached Sanostee it was sundown, the copper-colored twilight of one of those days when the desert sky is translucent with hanging dust.

Chee was sitting under his steering wheel, feet out the door, drinking an orange crush. They left Leaphorn's car and took Chee's. Leaphorn asked questions. Chee drove. They were astute questions, intended to duplicate as much of Chee's memory in Leaphorn's as was possible. At first the focus was on Bistie, on everything he'd said and how he'd said it, and then on Endocheeney, and finally on Janet Pete.

"I had a little mixup with her last year," Leaphorn said. "She thought we'd roughed up a drunk—or said she did."

"Had we?"

Leaphorn glanced at him. "Somebody had. Unless the officer was lying about it, it was somebody else."

The road that wandered northward from Sanostee had been graded once, and graveled at some time in the dim past when this part of the Chuskas had elected an unusually fierce advocate to the Tribal Council. The perpetual cycle of January snows and April thaws had swallowed the gravel long ago, and the highway superintendent for that district had solved the problem by erasing the road from his map. But it was still passable in dry weather and still used by the few families who grazed their sheep in this part of the highlands. Chee drove it carefully, skirting washouts and avoiding its washboard pattern of surface erosion when he could. Sunrays from below the curve of the planet lit cloud banks on the western horizon and reflected red now, converting the yellow hue of the universe into a vague pink tint.

"I've been wondering who called her in on this," Chee said. "When we told Bistie he could call a lawyer, he wasn't interested."

"Probably his daughter," Leaphorn said.

"Probably," Chee agreed. He remembered the daughter standing in the yard of Bistie's house. Would she have thought of calling a lawyer? Driven back to Sanostee to make the call? Known whom to call? He amended the "probably." "Maybe so," he said.

That concluded the conversation. They rode in silence. Leaphorn sat back straight against the seat, his eyes memorizing what he could see of the landscape in fading yellow light, his mind drawn to the intolerable problem of Emma's illness and then flinching away from that to escape into the merely frustrating puzzle of the four pins on his map. Chee rode slumped against the door, right hand on the wheel, a taller man and slender, thinking of the bone bead in Bistie's wallet, of what questions he might ask to cause the stubborn Bistie to talk about witchcraft to hostile strangers, of whether Leaphorn would allow him any questions, of how Leaphorn, the famous Leaphorn, the Leaphorn of tribal police legends, would handle this. And thinking of Mary Landon's letter. He found he could see the words, dark blue ink against the pale blue of the paper.

"Dad and I drove down to Madison last week and talked to an adviser in the College of Arts and Sciences. I will be able to get my master's degree—with a little luck—in just two more semesters . . ."

Just two semesters. Only two semesters. Only two. Or, put another way, I will only take two long steps away from you. Or, I promised I would come back to you at the end of summer, but now I am going away. Or, rephrased again, former lover, you are now a friend. Or . . .

The patrol car slanted up into the thicket of piñon and stunted ponderosa. Chee shifted into second gear.

"Just over this ridge," he said.

Just over the ridge, the light became visible. It was below them, still at least half a mile away, a bright point in the darkening twilight. Chee remembered it from the afternoon they had arrested Bistie. A single bare bulb protected by a metal reflector atop a forty-foot ponderosa pine stem. Bistie's ghost light. Would a witch be worried about ghosts? Would a witch keep a light burning to fend off the *chindi* which wandered in the darkness?

"His place?" Leaphorn asked.

Chee nodded.

"He's got electricity out here?" Leaphorn sounded surprised.

"There's a windmill generator behind the house," Chee said. "I guess he runs that light off batteries."

Bistie's access route required a right turn off the road, bumped over a rocky hummock and past a scattering of piñons, to drop again down to his place. In the harsh yellow light it looked worse than Chee had remembered it—a rectangular plank shack, probably with two rooms, roofed with blue asphalt shingles. Behind it stood a dented metal storage shack, a brush arbor, a pole horse corral, and, up the slope by the low cliff of the mesa, a lean-to for hay storage. Beyond that, against the cliff, the yellow light reflected from a hogan made of stacked stone slabs. Beside the shack, side by side and with their vanes turned away from the gusting west wind, were Bistie's windmill and his wind generator.

Chee parked his patrol car under Bistie's yard light.

There was no sign of the truck and no light on in the house.

Leaphorn sighed. "You know enough about him to do any guessing about where he might be?" he said. "Visiting kinfolks or anything?"

"No," Chee said. "We didn't get into that."

"Lives here with his daughter. Right?" Leaphorn said.

"Right."

They waited for someone to appear at the door and acknowledge the presence of visitors, delaying the moment when they'd admit the long drive had been for nothing. Delaying what would be either a return trip to Sanostee or a fruitless hunt for neighbors who might know where Roosevelt Bistie had gone.

"Maybe he didn't come back here when the lawyer got him out," Chee said.

Leaphorn grunted. The yellow light from the bare bulb above them lit the right side of his face, giving it a waxy look.

No one appeared at the door.

Leaphorn got out of the car, slammed the door noisily behind him, and leaned against the roof, eyes on the house. The door wouldn't be locked. Should he go in, and look around for some hint of where Bistie might be?

The wind gusted against him, blowing sand against his ankles above his socks and pushing at his uniform hat. Then it died. He heard Chee's door opening. He smelled something burning— a strong, acrid odor.

"Fire," Chee said. "Somewhere."

Leaphorn trotted toward the house, rapped on the door. The smell was stronger here, seeping between door and frame. He turned the knob, pushed the door open. Smoke puffed out, and was whipped away by another gust of the dry wind. Behind him, Chee yelled: "Bistie. You in there?"

Leaphorn stepped into the smoke, fanning with his hat. Chee was just behind him. The smoke was coming from an aluminum pot on top of a butane stove against the back wall of the room. Leaphorn held his breath, turned off the burner under the pan and under a blue enamel coffeepot boiling furiously beside it. He used his hat as a potholder, grabbed the handle, carried it outside, and dropped it on the packed earth. It contained what seemed to have been some sort of stew, now badly charred. Leaphorn went back inside.

"No one's here," Chee said. He was fanning the

residual smoke with his hat. A chair lay on its side on the floor.

"You checked the back room?"

Chee nodded. "Nobody home."

"Left in a hurry," Leaphorn said. He wrinkled his nose against the acrid smell of burned meat and walked back into the front yard. With the butt of his flashlight, he poked into the still-smoking pan, inspected the residue it collected.

"Take a look at this," he said to Chee. "You're a bachelor, aren't you? How long does it take you to burn stew like this?"

Chee inspected the pot. "The way he had the fire turned up, maybe five, ten minutes. Depends on how much water he put in it."

"Or she," Leaphorn said. "His daughter. When you were here with Kennedy, they just have one truck?"

"That's all," Chee said.

"So they must be off somewhere in it," Leaphorn said. "One or both. And they drove off the other way from the way we were coming. But if it was that way, why didn't we see their headlights? They would have just left." Leaphorn straightened, put his hands on his hips, stretched his back. He stared into the deepening twilight, frowning. "Just one plate on the table. You notice that?"

"Yeah," Chee said. "And the chair turned over."

"Five or ten minutes," Leaphorn said. "If you know how long it takes to incinerate stew, then we didn't scare him off. The truck was already gone. And the stew was already burning before we got here."

"I'll go in and look around again," Chee said. "A little closer."

"Let me do it," Leaphorn said. "See if you can find anything out here."

Leaphorn stood at the doorway first, not wishing to further disturb any signs that might have been left. He suspected Chee might be good at this, but he knew he was good. The floor was covered with dark red linoleum, seamed near the middle of the room. It was fairly new, which was good, and dusty, which was almost inevitable considering the weather, and absolutely essential considering what Leaphorn hoped to do. But before he did anything, he looked. This front room was used for cooking, eating, general living, and the woman's bedroom. One corner of the bed, a single wooden frame neatly made up, was visible behind a curtain of blankets which walled off a corner. Shelves loaded with canned goods, cooking utensils, and an assortment of boxes lined the partition wall. Except for the overturned chair, nothing seemed odd or out of place. The room showed the habitual neatness imposed by limited living space.

But the floor was dusty.

Leaphorn squatted on the step and inspected the linoleum with his eyes just an inch or so above its surface. The pattern of dust newly disturbed by his footsteps, and Chee's, was easy enough to make out. He could easily separate the treads of Chee's bigger feet from his own. But the angle of light was wrong. Walking carefully, he went in and pulled the chain to turn off the light bulb. He clicked on his flashlight. Working the light carefully, squatting at first and then on his stomach with his cheek against the floor, he studied the marks left in the dust.

He ignored the fresh scuffs he and Chee had made—looking for other marks. He found them. Dimmer but fairly fresh and plain enough to an eye as experienced at this as Leaphorn's. Waffle marks left by the soles of someone who had apparently sat beside the table, someone who had pulled his feet back under the chair, leaving the drag marks of the toes. Also under the table, and near the fallen chair, another pattern, left by a rubber sole. Some sort of jogging or tennis shoes, perhaps. Smaller than the big-footed person who wore the waffle soles. Bistie and daughter? If so, Bistie's Daughter had large feet.

Leaphorn emerged from under the table, whacking his ear in the process. Behind the curtain of blankets, on a chest beside the bed, stood two pair of shoes. Worn tan squaw boots and low-heeled black slippers. They were narrow and about size six. He took a left slipper back to the table, relocated the track, and made the comparison. The slipper was far too small. Bistie had been entertaining a visitor not long before Leaphorn and Chee arrived.

But where the devil had they gone? And why

had they left the stew to burn and the coffee to boil away?

He found nothing interesting in the back room. Against the wall, a bedroll on which Bistie apparently slept was folded neatly. Bistie's clothing hung with equal neatness from a wire strung taut along the wall—two pairs of well-worn jeans, a pair of khaki trousers with frayed cuffs. A plaid wool jacket, four shirts, all with long sleeves and one with a hole in the elbow. Leaphorn clicked his tongue against his teeth, thinking, studying the room. He pushed his forefinger into the enamel washbasin on the table beside Bistie's bedroom, testing water temperature without thinking why. It was tepid. Exactly what one would expect. He picked up the crumpled washcloth beside the basin. It was wet. Leaphorn looked at it, frowning. Not what one would expect.

The cloth had been used to clean something. Leaphorn studied it in the flashlight beam. In three places the cloth was heavily smudged with dirt—as if to clean spots from the dusty floor. He held one of the spots to his nose and smelled it.

"Chee!" he shouted. "Chee!"

He examined the floor, moving the flash beam methodically back and forth, looking for a wiped place and seeing none. Perhaps it had been done in the front room. He squatted, holding the flash close to the linoleum, looking for tracks. He saw, instead, a path. It was fairly regular, possibly eighteen inches wide—a strip of the plastic surface wiped clean of dust. A pathway leading from the doorway into the front room, down the center of this back room, to the back door.

The back door opened and Chee looked in. "I think somebody, or maybe something, got dragged out of here," Chee said. "Drag marks leading up toward the rocks."

"Through here too," Leaphorn said. He drew the flashlight beam along the polished, dust-free path. "To the back door. But look at this." He handed Chee the damp cloth. "Smell it," he said.

Chee smelled.

"Blood," Chee said. "Smells like it." He glanced at Leaphorn. "Wonder what was in that stew. Fresh mutton, you think?"

"I doubt it," Leaphorn said. "I think we ought to find where those drag marks take us. I want to know what's being dragged."

"Or who's being dragged," Chee said.

Bare earth that has been lived on for years and as dry as drought can make it becomes almost as hard as concrete. From the back door, Leaphorn saw nothing until Chee's flashlight beam, held close to the earth, created shadows where something even harder had been pulled across its surface. Scratches. The scratches led past the windmill tower, past the metal storage building, and beyond. On the slope, where the earth was less pounded, the scratches became scuff marks between the scattering of wilted weeds and clumps of grass.

"Up toward the hogan," Leaphorn said. "It leads that way."

Even in the less compacted earth the drag marks were hard to follow. The twilight had faded into almost full dark now, with only a flush of dark red in the west. The wind had risen again, kicking up dust in front of Leaphorn. He walked with his flashlight focused on the ground, picking up the sign of dislodged earth and crushed weeds.

Even in retrospect, Leaphorn didn't remember hearing the shot—being aware first of pain. Something that felt like a hammer struck his right forearm and the flashlight was suddenly gone. Leaphorn was sitting on the ground, aware of Chee's voice yelling something, aware that his forearm hurt so badly that something must have broken it. The sound of Chee's pistol firing, the muzzle flash, brought him out of the shock and made him aware of what had happened. Roosevelt Bistie, that son-of-a-bitch, had shot him.

› 14 ‹

THE "OFFICER DOWN" CALL provokes a special re-action in each police jurisdiction. In the Ship-rock subagency of the Navajo Tribal Police, Cap-tain A. D. Largo commanding, it produced an im-mediate call to Largo himself, who was home watching television, and almost simultaneous radio calls to all Navajo Police units on duty in the district, to the New Mexico State Police, and the San Juan County Sheriff's Office. Then, since the Chuska Mountains sprawl across the New Mexico border into Arizona, and Sanostee is only a dozen or so miles from the state boundary, and neither the dispatcher at Shiprock nor anyone else was quite sure in which state all this was happening, the call also went out to the Arizona Highway Patrol and, more or less out of cour-tesy, to the Apache County Sheriff's Office, which might have some legitimate jurisdiction even though it was a hundred miles south, down at St. Johns.

The Farmington office of the Federal Bureau of Investigation, which had ultimate jurisdiction when such a lofty crime is committed on an Indian reservation, got the word a little later via telephone. The message was relayed to Jay Kennedy at the home of a lawyer, where he was engaged in a penny-a-point rotating-partner bridge game. Kennedy had just won two consecutive rubbers and was about to make a small slam, properly bid, when the telephone rang. He took the call, finished the slam, added up the score, which showed him to be ahead 2,350 points, collected his $23.50, and left. It was a few minutes after 10 P.M.

A few minutes after 10:30, Jim Chee got back to the Bistie place. He had met the ambulance from Farmington at Littlewater on U.S. 666. While Leaphorn was being tucked away in the back, Captain Largo had arrived—Gorman riding with him—and had taken charge. Largo asked a flurry of questions, sent the ambulance on its way, and made a series of quick radio checks to ensure roadblocks were in place. He'd hung up the microphone and sat, arms folded, looking at Chee.

"Too late for roadblocks, probably," he said.

It had been a long day for Chee. He was tired. All the adrenaline had drained away. "Who knows," he said. "Maybe he stopped to fix a flat. Maybe he didn't even have a car. If it was Bistie himself, maybe he just went back to his house. If—"

"You think it might be somebody besides Bistie?"

"I don't know," Chee said. "It's his place. He shoots at people. But then maybe somebody doesn't like him any better than he likes other people, and they came and shot him and dragged him off into the rocks."

Largo's expression, which had already been sour, suggested he didn't like Chee's tone. He stared at Chee.

"How did it happen?" he asked. "One old man, sick, and two cops with guns?"

Largo obviously didn't expect an answer and Chee didn't attempt one.

"You and Gorman go back up there and see if you can find him," Largo said. "I'll have the state police and the sheriff's people follow you. Don't let 'em get lost."

Chee nodded.

"I'm meeting Kennedy here," Largo said. "Then we'll come along and join you."

Chee headed for his car.

"One more thing," Largo shouted. "Don't let Bistie shoot you."

And now, at 10:55, Chee parked beside Bistie's now-dark light pole, got out, and waited for the entourage to finish its arrival. He felt foolish. Bistie's truck was still absent. Bistie's shack was dark. Everything seemed to be exactly as they had left it. The chance of Bistie's hanging around to await this posse simply didn't exist.

There was a general slamming of doors.

Chee explained the layout, pointed up into the darkness to the hogan from which the shots had come. They moved up the slope, weapons drawn, the state policeman carrying a riot gun, the deputy carrying a rifle. What had happened here two hours before already seemed unreal to Chee, something he had imagined.

No one was at the hogan, or in it.

"Here's some brass," the state policeman said. He was an old-timer, with red hair and a freckled, perpetually sunburned face. He stood frowning down at a copper-colored metal cylinder which reflected the beam of his flashlight. "Looks like thirty-eight caliber," he said. "Who'll be handling the evidence?"

"Just leave it there for Kennedy," Chee said. "There should be another one." He was thinking that the empty cartridge certainly wasn't from a 30-30. It was shorter. Pistol ammunition. And, since it had been ejected, probably from an automatic—not a revolver. If Bistie had fired it, he seemed to have quite an arsenal.

"Here it is," the state policeman said. His flashlight was focused on the ground about a long step from where the first cartridge lay. "Same caliber."

Chee didn't bother to look at it. He considered asking everyone to be careful of where they walked, to avoid erasing any useful tracks. But as dry and windy as it was, he couldn't imagine tracking as anything but a waste of time. Except for the drag marks. Whatever had been dragged up here should be easy to find.

It was.

"Hey," Gorman shouted. "Here's a body."

It was half hidden in a clump of chamiso, head downhill, feet uphill, legs still spraddled apart as if whoever had dragged it there had been using them to pull the body along and had simply dropped them.

The body had been Roosevelt Bistie. In the combined lights of Chee's and Gorman's flashlights, the yellow look of his face was intensified—but death had done little to change his expression. Bistie still looked grim and bitter, as if being shot was only what he'd expected—a fitting ending for a disappointing life. The dragging had pulled his shirt up over his shoulders, leaving chest and stomach bare. The waxy skin where the rib cage joined at the sternum showed two small holes, one just below the other. The lower one had bled a little. Very small holes, Chee thought. It seemed odd that such trivial holes would let out the wind of life.

Gorman was looking at him, a question in his face.

"This is Bistie," Chee said. "Looks like the guy who shot Lieutenant Leaphorn had shot this guy. I guess he was dragging him up here when we drove up, the lieutenant and me."

"And after he shot the lieutenant he just took off," Gorman said.

"And got clean away," Chee added.

Four flashlights now were illuminating the body. Only the San Juan County deputy was still out in the darkness, doing his fruitless job.

Down in Roosevelt Bistie's yard below, two more vehicles parked. Chee heard doors slam, the voice of Kennedy, the sound of Kennedy and Captain Largo coming up the slope. Chee's flashlight now was focused above the bullet wounds at a place on Bistie's left breast—a reddish mark, narrow, perhaps a half-inch long, where a cut was healing. It would seem, normally, an odd place for such a cut. It made Jim Chee think of Bistie's wallet, and the bone bead he had seen in it, and whether the wallet would have been dragged out of Bistie's hip pocket on his heels-first trip up this rocky slope, and whether the bone bead would still be in it when it was found.

He squatted beside Bistie, taking a closer look, imagining the scene at which this little healing scar had been produced. The hand trembler (or stargazer, or listener, or crystal gazer, or whatever sort of shaman Bistie had chosen to diagnose his sickness) explaining to Bistie that someone had witched him, telling Bistie that a skinwalker had blown the fatal bone fragment into him. And then the ritual cut of the skin, the sucking at the breast, the bone coming out of Bistie, appearing on the shaman's tongue. And Bistie putting the bone in his billfold, and paying his fee, and setting out to save himself by killing the witch and reversing the dreaded corpse sickness.

Chee moved the beam of his light up so that it

reflected again from the glazed, angry eyes of Roosevelt Bistie. How did Bistie know the witch was Endocheeney, the man who all at Badwater agreed was a mild and harmless fellow? The shaman would not have known that. And if the two men even knew each other, Chee had seen no sign of it.

Behind him, the state policeman was shouting to Largo, telling him they'd found a body. The wind kicked up again, blowing a flurry of sand against Chee's face. He closed his eyes against it, and when he reopened them, a fragment of dead tumbleweed had lodged itself against Bistie's ear.

Why was Bistie so certain the witch who was killing him was Endocheeney? He had been certain enough to try to kill the man. How had their paths crossed in this fatal way? And where? And when? Now that Bistie was also dead, who could answer those questions? Any of them?

Largo had joined the circle now, and Kennedy. Chee sensed them standing just behind him, staring down at the body.

"There's what killed him," the state policeman said. "Two gunshots through the chest."

Just on the edge of the circle of illumination, Chee could see the healing cut on Bistie's breast. Those two bullets had completed the death of Roosevelt Bistie. But the little wound high on his breast above them had been where Roosevelt Bistie's death had started.

>15<

THE INDIAN HEALTH SERVICE HOSPITAL at Gallup is one of the prides of this huge federal bureaucracy—modern, attractive, well located and equipped. It had been built in a period of flush budgeting—with just about everything any hospital needs. Now, in a lean budget cycle, it was enduring harder times. But the shortage of nurses, the overspent supplies budget, and the assortment of other fiscal headaches that beset the hospital's bead counters this particular morning did not affect Joe Leaphorn's lunch, which was everything a sensible patient should expect from a hospital kitchen, nor the view from his window, which was superb. The Health Service had located the hospital high on the slope overlooking Gallup from the south. Over the little hump in the sheet produced by his toes, Leaphorn could see the endless stream of semitrailers moving along Interstate 40. Beyond the highway, intercontinental train traffic rolled east and west on the Santa Fe main trunk. Above and beyond the railroad, beyond the clutter of east Gallup, the red cliffs of Mesa de los Lobos rose—their redness diminished a little by the blue haze of distance, and above them was the gray-green shape of the high country of the Navajo borderlands, where the Big Reservation faded into Checkerboard Reservation. For Joe Leaphorn, raised not fifty miles north of this bed in the grass country near Two Gray Hills, it was the landscape of his childhood. But now he looked at the scene without thinking about it.

He had been awake only a minute or two, having been jarred by the arrival of his lunch tray from a hazy, morphine-induced doze into a panicky concern for the welfare of Emma. He remembered very quickly that Agnes was there, had been there for days, living in the spare bedroom and playing the role of concerned younger sister. Agnes made Leaphorn nervous, but she had good sense. She'd take care of Emma, make the right decisions. He needn't worry. No more than he normally did.

Now he had finished the wit-collection process that follows such awakenings. He had established where he was, remembered why, quickly assessed the unfamiliar surroundings, checked the heavy, still cool and damp cast on his right arm, moved his thumb experimentally, then his fingers, then his hand, to measure the pain caused by each motion, and then he thought about Emma again. Her appointment was tomorrow. He would be well enough to take her, no question of that. And another step would be taken toward knowing what he already knew. What he dreaded to admit. The rest of his life would be spent watching her slip away from him, not knowing who he was, then not knowing who she was. In the material the Alzheimer's Association had sent him, someone had described it as "looking into your mind and seeing nothing there but darkness." He remembered that, as he remembered the case report of the husband of a victim. "Every day I would tell her we'd been married thirty years, that we had four children. . . . Every night when I got into bed she would say, 'Who are you?' " He had already seen the first of that. Last week, he had walked into the kitchen and Emma had looked up from the carrots she was scraping. Her expression had been first startled, then fearful, then confused. And she had clutched Agnes's arm and asked who he was. That was something he'd have to learn to live with—like learning to live with a dagger through the heart.

He groped clumsily with his good left hand for the button to summon an attendant, found it, pressed it, glanced at his watch. Outside the glass, the light was blinding. Far to the east, a cloud was building over Tsoodzil, the Turquoise Mountain. Rain? Too early to tell, and too far east to fall on the reservation if it did develop into a thunderstorm. He swung his legs over the edge of the bed and sat, slumped, waiting for the dizziness to subside, feeling an odd, buzzing sense of detachment induced by whatever they'd given him to make him sleep.

"Well," a voice behind him said. "I didn't expect to find you out of bed."

It was Dilly Streib. He was wearing his FBI summer uniform, a dark blue two-piece suit, white shirt, and necktie. On Streib, all of this managed to look slept in.

"I'm not out of bed yet," Leaphorn said. He gestured toward the closet door. "Look around in there and see if you can find my clothes. Then I'll be out of bed."

Streib was holding a manila folder in his left hand. He dropped it at the foot of Leaphorn's bed and disappeared into the closet. "Thought you'd like to take a look at that," he said. "Anybody tell you what happened?"

It occurred to Leaphorn that he had a headache. He took a deep breath. His lunch seemed to consist of a bowl of soup, which was steaming, a small green salad, and something including chicken which normally would have looked appetizing. But now Leaphorn's stomach felt as if it had been tilted on its side. "I know what happened," Leaphorn said. "Somebody shot me in the arm."

"I meant after that," Streib said. He dumped Leaphorn's uniform at the foot of his bed and his boots on the floor.

"After that I'm blank," Leaphorn said.

"Well, to get to the bottom line, the guy got away and he left behind Bistie's body."

"Bistie's body?" Leaphorn reached for the folder, digesting this.

"Shot," Streib said. "Twice. With a pistol, probably. Probably a thirty-eight or so."

Leaphorn extracted the report from the folder. Two sheets. He read. He glanced at the signature. Kennedy. He handed the report back to Streib.

"What do you think?" Streib asked.

Leaphorn shook his head.

"I think it's getting interesting," Streib said. That meant, Leaphorn understood from half a lifetime spent working with the federals, that people with clout and high civil service numbers were beginning to think they had more bodies than could be politely buried. He took off his hospital gown, picked up his undershirt, and considered the problem of how to get it on without moving his right arm around more than was necessary.

"I think we should have kept that Indian locked up a while," Streib said. He chuckled. "I guess that's belaboring the obvious." The chuckle turned into a laugh. "I'm sure his doctor would have recommended it."

"You think we could have got him to change his mind? Tell us what he had against Endocheeney?" Leaphorn asked. He thought a moment. If they had taken Bistie back into custody, Leaphorn had planned to try an old, old trick. The traditional culture allows a lie, if it does no harm, but the lie can be repeated only three times. The fourth time told, it locks the teller into the deceit. He couldn't have worked it on Bistie directly, because Bistie would have simply continued to refuse to say anything about Endocheeney, or bone beads, or witchcraft. But maybe he could have worked around the edges. Maybe. Maybe not.

"I'm not so sure," Leaphorn said. He was even less sure he could have talked Streib into signing his name on the sort of complaint they would have needed. This was a notably untidy piece of work, this business of a man who seemed to think he'd shot a man who'd actually been stabbed. And the FBI hadn't fooled the taxpayers all these years by getting itself involved with the messy ones. Streib was a good man, but he hadn't survived twenty years in the Agency jungle without learning the lessons it taught.

"Maybe not," Streib said. "I defer to you redskins on that. But anyhow . . ." He shrugged, letting it trail off. "This is going to put the heat on. Now we don't just have a bunch of singles. Now we got ourselves a double. And maybe more than a double. You know how that works."

"Yeah," Leaphorn said. Doubling homicides didn't double the interest—it was more like squaring it. And if you had yourself genuine serial killings, nicely mysterious, the interest and the pressure and the potential for publicity went right through the roof. Publicity had never been an issue with Navajo Tribal Police—they simply never got any—but for federals, good press brought the billions pouring in and kept the J. Edgar Hoover Building swarming with fat-cat bureaucrats. But it had damned sure better be good press.

Streib had seated himself. He looked at the report and then at Leaphorn, who was pulling on his pants with left-handed awkwardness. Streib's round, ageless, unlined face made it difficult for him to look worried. Now he managed. "Trouble is, among the many troubles, I can't see how the hell to get a handle on this. Doesn't seem to have a handle."

Leaphorn was learning how difficult it can be to fasten the top button of his uniform trousers with his left-hand fingers after a lifetime of doing it with right-hand fingers. And he was remembering the question Jim Chee had raised. ("I heard gossip at Badwater Trading Post," Chee had said. "They say a bone was found in Endocheeney's corpse.") Had the pathologist found the bone?

"The autopsy on Old Man Endocheeney up at Farmington," Leaphorn said. "I think somebody should talk to the pathologist about that. Find out every little thing they found in that stab wound."

Streib put the report back in the folder, the folder on his lap, pulled out his pipe, and looked at the No Smoking sign beside the door. Beside the sign, Little Orphan Annie stared from a poster that read: "Little Orphan Annie's Parents Smoked." Beside that poster was another, a photograph of rows and rows of tombstones, with a legend reading "Marlboro Country." Streib sniffed at the pipe, put it back in his jacket pocket.

"Why?" he asked.

"One of our people heard rumors that a little fragment of bone was found in the wound," Leaphorn said. He kept his eyes on Streib. Would that be enough explanation? Streib's expression said it wasn't.

"Jim Chee found a little bone bead in his house trailer along with the lead pellets after somebody shot the shotgun through his wall," Leaphorn said. "And Roosevelt Bistie was carrying a little bone bead in his wallet."

Understanding dawned slowly, and unhappily, causing Streib's round face to convert itself from its unaccustomed expression of worry to an equally unaccustomed look of sorrow and dismay.

"Bone," he said. "As in skinwalking. As in witchcraft. As in corpse sickness."

"Bone," Leaphorn said.

"Lordy, lordy, lordy," Streib said. "What the hell next? I hate it."

"But maybe it's a handle."

"Handle, shit," Streib said, with a passion that was rare for him. "You remember way back when that cop got ambushed over on the Laguna-Acoma. You remember that one. The agent on that one said something about witchcraft when he was working it, put it in his report. I think they called him all the way back to Washington so the very top dogs could chew him out in person. That was after doing it by letters and telegrams."

"But it was witchcraft," Leaphorn said. "Or it wasn't, of course, but the Lagunas they tried for it said they killed the cop because he had been witching them, and the judge ruled insanity, and they—"

"They went into a mental hospital, and the agent got transferred from Albuquerque to East Poison Spider, Wyoming," Streib said, voice rich with passion. " 'The judge ruled' don't cut it in Washington. In Washington they don't believe in agents who believe in witches."

"I'd do it myself. Look into it, I mean. But I think you'd have more luck talking to the doctor," Leaphorn said. "Getting taken seriously. I go in there, a Navajo, and start talking to the doc about witch bones and corpse sickness and—"

"I know. I know," Streib said. He looked at Leaphorn quizzically. "A bone bead, you said? Human?"

"Cow."

"Cow? Anything special about cow bones?"

"Damn it," Leaphorn said. "Cow or giraffe, or dinosaur or whatever. What difference does it make? Just so whoever we're dealing with thinks it works."

"Okay," Streib said. "I'll ask. You got any other ideas? I got a sort of a feeling that the one at Window Rock—the Onesalt woman—could be some sort of sex-and-jealousy thing. Or maybe the

Onesalt gal nosed into some sort of ripoff in the tribal paperwork that caused undue resentment. We know she was a sort of full-time world-saver. Usually you just put her type down as a pain in the ass, but maybe she was irritating the wrong fellow. But I sort of see her as one case and those others as another bag. And maybe now we toss that Chee business in with 'em. You have any fresh thinking about it?"

Leaphorn shook his head. "Just the bone angle," he said. "And probably that leads no place." But he was doing some fresh thinking. Nothing he wanted to talk to Streib about. Not yet. He wanted to find out if Onesalt's agency knew anything about the letter that office had mailed to Dugai Endocheeney. If Onesalt had written it, Dilly might be dead wrong about Onesalt not being linked to the other homicides. And now he was thinking that Roosevelt Bistie fell into a new category of victim. Bistie had been part of it, part of whatever it was that was killing people on the Big Reservation. Thus the killing of Bistie was something new. Whatever it was, this lethal being, now it seemed to be feeding on itself.

> 16 <

THE CAT WAS THERE when Chee awakened. It was sitting just inside the door, looking out through the screen. When he stirred, rising onto his side in the awkward process of getting up from the pallet he'd made on the floor, the cat had been instantly alert, watching him tensely. He sat, completed a huge yawn, rubbed the sleep from his eyes, and then stood, stretching. To his mild surprise, the cat was still there when he finished that. Its green eyes were fixed on him nervously, but it hadn't fled. Chee rolled up the sleeping bag he'd been using as a pad, tied it, dumped it on his unused bunk. He inspected the irregular row of holes the shotgun blasts had punched through the trailer wall. One day, when he knew who had done it, when he knew it wouldn't be happening again, he would find himself a tinsmith—or whomever one found to patch shotgun holes in aluminum alloy walls—and get them patched more permanently. He peeled off the duct tape he'd used to cover them and held out his hand, feeling the breeze sucking in. Until the rains came, or winter, he might as well benefit from the improved ventilation.

For breakfast he finished a can of peaches he'd left in the refrigerator and the remains of a loaf of bread. It wasn't exactly breakfast, anyway. He'd got to bed just at dawn—thinking he was too tired, and too wired, to sleep. Even though night was almost gone, he avoided the bunk and used the floor. He had lain there remembering the two black holes in the skin of Roosevelt Bistie's chest, remembering the healing cut higher on Bistie's breast. Those vivid images faded away into a question.

Who had called Janet Pete?

Unless she was lying, it had not been Roosevelt Bistie's daughter. The daughter had driven up just behind the ambulance. She had been following it, in fact—coming home from Shiprock with four boxes of groceries. She had emerged from Bistie's old truck into the pale yellow light of police lanterns, with her face frozen in that expression every cop learns to dread—the face of a woman who is expecting the very worst and has steeled herself to accept it with dignity.

She had looked down at the body as they carried it past her and slid the stretcher into the ambulance. Then she had looked up at Captain Largo. "I knew it would be him," she'd said, in a voice that sounded remarkably matter-of-fact. Chee had watched her, examining her grief for

some sign of pretense and thinking that her pre-
science was hardly remarkablc. For whom else
could the ambulance have been making this
back-road trip? Virtually no one else lived on this
particular slope of this particular mountain—
and no one else at all on this particular spur of
track. The emotion of Bistie's Daughter seemed
totally genuine—more shock than sorrow. No
tears. If they came, they would come later, when
her yard was cleared of all these strangers, and
dignity no longer mattered, and the loneliness
closed in around her. Now she talked calmly
with Captain Largo and with Kennedy—re-
sponding to their questions in a voice too low for
Chee to overhear, as expressionless as if her face
had been carved from wood.

But she had recognized Chee immediately
when all that was done. The ambulance had
driven away, taking with it the flesh and bones
that had held the living wind of Roosevelt Bistie
and leaving behind, somewhere in the night air
around them, his *chindi*.

"Did Captain Largo tell you where he died?"
Chee had asked her. He spoke in Navajo, using
the long, ugly guttural sound which signifies that
moment when the wind of life no longer moves
inside a human personality, and all the dishar-
monies that have bedeviled it escape from the
nostrils to haunt the night.

"Where?" she asked, at first puzzled by the
question. Then she understood it, and looked at
the house. "Was it inside?"

"Outside," Chee said. "Out in the yard. Behind the house."

It might be true. It takes a while for a man to die—even shot twice through the chest. No reason for Bistie's Daughter to believe her house had been contaminated with her father's ghost. Chee had evolved his own theology about ghost sickness and the *chindi* that caused it. It was, like all the evils that threatened the happiness of humankind, a matter of the mind. The psychology courses he'd taken at the University of New Mexico had always seemed to Chee a logical extension of what the Holy People had taught those original four Navajo clans. And now he noticed some slight relaxation in the face of Bistie's Daughter—some relief. It was better not to have to deal with ghosts.

She was looking at Chee, thoughtfully.

"You noticed when you and the *belagana* came to get him that he was angry," she said. "Did you notice that?"

"But I don't know why," Chee said. "Why was he so angry?"

"Because he knew he had to die. He went to the hospital. They told him about his liver." She placed a hand against her stomach.

"What was it? Was it cancer?"

Bistie's Daughter shrugged. "They call it cancer," she said. "We call it corpse sickness. Whatever word you put on it, it was killing him."

"It couldn't be cured? Did they tell him that?"

Bistie's Daughter glanced around her, looked

nervously past Chee into the night. The state policeman's car—on its way back to paved highways—crunched through the weeds at the edge of the yard. Its headlights flashed across her face. She raised her hand against the glare. "You can turn it around," she said. "I always heard you could do that."

"You mean kill the witch and put the bone back in him?" Chee said. "Is that what he was going to do?"

Bistie's Daughter looked at him silently.

"I talked to them already," she said finally. "To the other policemen. To the young *belagana* and the fat Navajo."

Largo would hate hearing that "fat Navajo" description, Chee thought. "Did you tell them that's what your father was doing? When he went to the Endocheeney place?"

"I told them I didn't know what he was doing. I didn't know that man who got killed. All I know is that my father was getting sicker and sicker all the time. He went to see a hand trembler over there between Roof Butte and Lukachukai to find out what kind of cure he would need to have. But the hand trembler had gone off someplace and he wasn't home. He went over on the Checkerboard Reservation, someplace over there by the Nageezi Chapter House, and talked to a listener over there. He told him he had been cooking food over a fire made out of wood struck by lightning and he needed to have a Hail Chant." Bistie's Daughter looked up at Chee with a strained grin. "We burn butane to cook on," she said. "But he charged my father fifty dollars. Then he went to the Badwater Clinic to see if they would give him some medicine. He didn't come back until the next day because they kept him in the hospital. Made X-rays, I think. Things like that. When he came back he was angry. Said they told him he was going to die." Bistie's Daughter stopped talking then, and looked away from Chee. Tears came abruptly but without sound.

"Why angry?" Chee asked, his voice so low she might have thought he meant the question only for himself.

"Because they told him he could not be cured," Bistie's Daughter said in a shaky voice. She cleared her throat, wiped the back of her hand across her eyes. "That man was strong," she continued. "His spirit was strong. He didn't give up on things. He didn't want to die."

"Did he say why he was angry at Endocheeney? Why he blamed Endocheeney? Did he say he thought Endocheeney had witched him?"

"He didn't say hardly anything at all. I asked him. I said, 'My Father, why—'" She stopped.

Never speak the name of the dead, Chee thought. Never summon the *chindi* to you, even if the name of the ghost is Father.

"I asked that man why he was angry. What was wrong. What had they told him at the Badwater Clinic? And finally he told me they said his liver was rotten and they didn't know how to fix it with medicine and he was going to die pretty quick. I told the other policemen all this."

"Did he say anything about being witched?"

Bistie's Daughter shook her head.

"I noticed that he had a cut place on his breast." Chee tapped his uniform shirt, indicating where. "It was healing but still a little sore. Do you know about that?"

"No," she said.

The answer didn't surprise Chee. His people had adopted many ways of the *belagana*, but most of them had retained the Dinee tradition of personal modesty. Roosevelt Bistie would have kept his shirt on in the presence of his daughter.

"Did he ever say anything about Endocheeney?"

"No."

"Was Endocheeney a friend?"

"I don't think so. I never heard of him before."

Chee clicked his tongue. Another door closed.

"I guess the policemen asked you if you know who came here to see your fath— to see him tonight?"

"I didn't know he was home. I was away since yesterday. In Gallup to visit my sister. To buy things. I didn't know he was back from being in jail."

"After we arrested him, did you go and get the lawyer to get him out?"

Bistie's Daughter looked puzzled. "I don't know anything about that," she said.

"You didn't call a lawyer? Did you ask anyone else to call one?"

"I don't know anything about lawyers. I just heard that lawyers will get all your money."

"Do you know a woman named Janet Pete?"

Bistie's Daughter shook her head.

"Do you have any idea who it might have been who came here and shot him? Any idea at all?"

Bistie's Daughter was no longer crying, but she wiped her hand across her eyes again, looked down, and released a long, shuddering sigh.

"I think he was trying to kill a skinwalker," she said. "The skinwalker came and killed him."

And now, as Jim Chee finished the last slice of peach and mopped the residue of juice from the can with the bread crust, he remembered exactly how Bistie's Daughter had looked as she'd said that. He thought she was probably exactly correct. The Mystery of Roosevelt Bistie neatly solved in a sentence. All that remained was another question. Who was the skinwalker who came and shot Bistie? Behind that, how did the witch know Bistie would be home instead of safely jailed in Farmington?

In other words, who called Janet Pete?

He would find out. Right now. The very next step. As soon as he finished breakfast.

He unplugged his coffeepot, filled his coffee cup with water, swirled it gently, and drank it down.

("I never saw anybody do that before," Mary Landon had said.

"What?"

"That with the water you rinsed your cup with." Empty-handed, she had mimicked the swirling and the drinking.

It still had taken him a moment to understand. "Oh," he had said. "If you grow up hauling water, you don't ever learn to pour it out. You don't waste it, even if it tastes a little bit like coffee."

"Odd," Mary Landon said. "What the old prof in Sociology 101 would call a cultural anomaly."

It had seemed odd to Chee that not wasting water had seemed odd to Mary Landon. It still seemed odd.)

He put the pot under the sink. "Look out, Cat," he said. And the cat, instead of diving for the exit flap as it normally did when he came anywhere near this close, moved down the trailer. It sat under his bunk, looking at him nervously.

It took a millisecond for Jim Chee to register the meaning of this.

Something out there.

He sucked in his breath, reached for his belt, extracted his pistol. He could see nothing out the door except his pickup and the empty slope. He checked out of each of the windows. Nothing moved. He went through the door in a crouched run, holding the pistol in front of him. He stopped in the cover of the pickup.

Absolutely nothing moved. Chee felt the tension seep away. But something had driven in the cat. He walked to its den, eyes on the ground. In the softer earth around the juniper there were paw prints. A dog? Chee squatted, studying them. Coyote tracks.

Back in the trailer, the cat was sitting on his bedroll. They looked at each other. Chee noticed something new. The cat was pregnant.

"Coyote's after you, I guess," Chee said. "That right?"

The cat looked at him.

"Dry weather," Chee said. "No rain. Water holes dry up. Prairie dogs, kangaroo rats, all that, they die off. Coyotes come to town and eat cats."

The cat got up from the bedroll, edged toward the doorway. Chee got a better look at it. Not very pregnant yet. That would come later. It looked gaunt and had a new scar beside its mouth.

"Maybe I can fix something up for you," Chee said. But what? Fixing something that would be proof against a hungry coyote would take some thought. Meanwhile he looked through the refrigerator. Orange juice, two cans of Dr. Pepper, limp celery, two jars of jelly, a half-consumed box of Velveeta: nothing palatable for a cat. On the shelf above the stove, he found a can of pork and beans, opened it, and left it on a copy of the Farmington *Times* beside the screen door. When he got back from finding out who called Janet Pete, he'd think of something to do about the coyote. He backed his pickup away from the trailer. In the rearview mirror he noticed that the cat was gulping down the beans. Maybe Janet Pete would have an idea about the cat. Sometimes women were smarter about such things.

But Janet Pete was not at the Shiprock DNA office, a circumstance that seemed to give some satisfaction to the young man in the white shirt and the necktie who answered Jim Chee's inquiry.

"When do you expect her?" Chee asked.

"Who knows?" the young man said.

"This afternoon? Or has she left town or something?"

"Maybe," the man said. He shrugged.

"I'll leave her a message," Chee said. He took out his notebook and his pen and wrote:

"Ms. Pete—I need to know who called you to come and get Roosevelt Bistie out of jail. Important. If I'm not in, please leave message." He signed it and left the tribal police telephone number.

But on the way out, he saw Janet Pete pulling into the parking area. She was driving a white Chevy, newly washed, with the Navajo Nation's seal newly painted on its door. She watched him walk up, her face neutral.

"Ya-tah-hey," Chee said.

Janet Pete nodded.

"If you have just a minute or two, I need to talk to you," Chee said.

"Why?"

"Because Roosevelt Bistie's daughter told me she didn't call a lawyer for her father. I need to know who called you."

And I need to know absolutely everything else you know about Roosevelt Bistie, Chee thought, but first things first.

Janet Pete's expression had shifted from approximately neutral to slightly hostile.

"It doesn't matter who called," she said. "We don't have to have a request for representation from the next of kin. It can be anybody." She opened the car door and swung her legs out. "Or it can be nobody, for that matter. If someone needs to have his legal rights protected, we don't have to be asked."

Janet Pete was wearing a pale blue blouse and a tweed skirt. The legs she swung out of the car were very nice legs. And Miss Pete noticed that Chee had noticed.

"I need to know who it was," Chee said. He was surprised. He hadn't expected any trouble with this. "There's no confidentiality involved. Why be—"

"You have another homicide to work on now," she said. "Why not just leave Mr. Bistie alone. He didn't kill anyone. And he's sick. You should be able to see that. I think he has cancer of the liver. Another homicide. And no arrest made. Why don't you work on that?"

Janet Pete was leaning on the car door while she said this, and smiling slightly. But it wasn't a friendly smile.

"Where did you hear about the homicide?"

She tapped the car. "Radio," she said. "Noon news, KGAK, Gallup, New Mexico."

"They didn't say who was shot?"

" 'Police did not reveal the identity of the victim,' " she said, but the smile faded as she said it. "Who was it?"

"It was Roosevelt Bistie," Chee said.

"Oh, no," she said. She sat down on the front seat again, wrinkled her face, closed her eyes, shook her head against this mortality. "That poor man." She put her hands across her face. "That poor man."

"Somebody came to his house last night. His daughter was gone. They shot him."

Janet Pete lowered her hands to listen to this, staring at Chee. "Why? Do you know why? He was dying, anyway. He said the doctor told him the cancer would kill him."

"We don't know why," Chee said. "I want to talk to you about it. We're trying to find out why."

They left Janet Pete's clean Chevy and got into Chee's unwashed patrol car. At the Turquoise Cafe, Janet Pete ordered iced tea and Chee had coffee.

"You want to know who called me. That's funny, because the man who called lied. I found out later. He said his name was Curtis Atcitty. Spelled with the *A*. Not *E*. I had him spell it for me."

"Did he say who he was?"

"He said he was a friend of Roosevelt Bistie's, and he said Bistie was being held without bond and without any charges being filed against him, and that he was sick and didn't have any lawyer and he needed help." She paused, thinking about it. "And he said that Bistie had asked him to call DNA about a lawyer." She looked at Chee. "That's where he lied. When I told Bistie about it, he said he hadn't asked anybody to call. He said he didn't know anybody named Curtis Atcitty."

Chee clicked his tongue against his teeth, the sound of disappointment. So much for that.

"When you left the jail, I saw you driving back into Farmington. Where did you go? When was the last time you saw him?"

"Down to the bus station. He thought one of his relatives might be there, and they'd give him a ride home. But nobody he knew was there, so I took him back to Shiprock. He saw a truck he recognized at the Economy Washomat and I left him out there."

"Did he ever tell you why he tried to kill Old Man Endocheeney?"

Janet Pete simply looked at him.

"He's dead," Chee said. "No lawyer-client confidentiality left. Now it's try to find out who killed him."

Janet Pete studied her hands, which were small and narrow, with long, slender fingers, and if her fingernails were polished it was with the transparent, colorless stuff. Nice feminine hands, Chee thought. He remembered Mary Landon's hands, strong, smooth fingers intertwined with his own. Mary Landon's fingertips. Mary Landon's small white fist engulfed in his own. Janet Pete's right hand now gripped her left.

"I'm not stalling," she said. "I'm thinking. I'm trying to remember."

Chee wanted to tell her it was important. Very important. But he decided it wasn't necessary to say that to this lawyer. He watched her hands, thinking of Mary Landon, and then her face, thinking of Janet Pete.

"He said very little altogether," she said. "He didn't talk much. He wanted to know if he could go home. We talked about that. I asked him if he knew exactly what he was accused of doing. What law he was supposed to have broken." She glanced at Chee, then turned her eyes away, gazing out the street window through the dusty glass on which THE TURQUOISE CAFE was lettered in reverse. Beyond the glass, the dry wind was chasing a tumbleweed down the street. "He said he had shot a fellow over in the San Juan Canyon. And then he sort of chuckled and said maybe he just scared him. But anyway the man was dead and that was what you had him in jail for." She frowned, concentrating, right hand gripping the left. "I asked him why he had shot at the man and he said something vague." She shook her head.

"Vague?"

"I don't remember. Something like 'I had a reason,' or 'good reason,' or something like that—without saying why."

"Did you press him at all?"

"I said something like 'You must have had a good reason to shoot at a man,' and he laughed, I remember that, but not like he thought it was funny, and I asked him directly what his reason was and he just shut up and wouldn't answer."

"He wouldn't tell us anything, either," Chee said.

Janet Pete had taken a sip from her glass. Now she held it a few inches from her lips. "I told him I was his lawyer—there to help him. What he told me would be kept secret from anyone else. I told him shooting at somebody, even if you missed them, could get him in serious trouble with the white man and if he had a good reason for doing it, he would be smart to let me know about it. To see if we could use it in some way to help keep him out of jail."

She put down the glass and looked directly at Chee. "That's when he told me about being sick. It was easy enough to see anyway, with the way he looked. But anyway, he said the white man couldn't give him any more trouble than he already had, because he had cancer in his liver." She used the Navajo phrase for it—"the sore that never heals."

"That's what his daughter told me," Chee said. "Cancer of the liver."

Janet Pete was studying Chee's face. It was a habit that Chee had learned slowly, and come to tolerate slowly, and that still sometimes made him uneasy. Another of those cultural differences that Mary found odd and exotic.

("That first month or two in class I was always saying: 'Look at me when I talk to you,' and the kids simply wouldn't do it. They would always

look at their hands, or the blackboard, or anywhere except looking me in the face. And finally
one of the other teachers told me it was a cultural
thing. They should warn us about things like
that. Odd things. It makes the children seem evasive, deceptive."

And Chee had said something about it not
seeming odd or evasive to him. It seemed merely
polite. Only the rude peered into one's face during a conversation. And Mary Landon had asked
him how this worked for a policeman. Surely,
she'd said, they must be trained to look for all
those signals facial expressions reveal while the
speaker is lying, or evading, or telling less than
the truth. And he had said . . .)

"You needed to know who called me," Janet
Pete was saying, "because you suspect that who-
ever called is the one who killed Roosevelt Bistie.
Isn't that it?"

Like police academy, Chee thought, law
schools teach interrogators a different conversa-
tional technique than Navajo mothers. The white
way. The way of looking for what the handbook
on interrogation called "nonverbal signals."
Chee found himself trying to keep his face blank,
to send no such signals. "That's possible," he said.
"It may have happened that way."

"In fact," Janet Pete said, slowly and thoughtfully, "you think this man used me. Used me to
get Mr. Bistie out of jail and home . . ." Her voice
trailed off.

Chee had been looking out past the window's

painted lettering. The wind had changed direction just a little—enough to pull loose the leaves and twigs and bits of paper it had pinned against the sheep fence across the highway. Now the gusts were pulling these away, sending them skittering along the pavement. Changing winds meant changing weather. Maybe, finally, it would rain. But the new tone in Janet Pete's voice drew his attention back to her.

"Used me to get him out where he could be killed."

She looked at Chee for confirmation.

"He would have gotten out, anyway," Chee said. "The FBI had him, and the FBI didn't charge him with anything. We couldn't have—"

"But I think that man wanted Mr. Bistie out before he would talk to anyone. Doesn't that make sense?"

It was exactly the thought that had brought him looking for Janet Pete.

"Doubtful," Chee said. "Probably no connection at all."

Janet Pete was reading his nonverbal signals. Rude, Chee thought. No wonder Navajos rated it as bad manners. It invaded the individual's privacy.

"It's not doubtful at all," she said. "You are lying to me now." But she smiled. "That's kind of you. But I can't help but feel responsible." She looked very glum. "I am responsible. Somebody wants to kill my client, so they call me and have me get him out where they can shoot him." She picked up her glass, noticed it was empty, put it down again. "He didn't even particularly want to be my client. The guy who wanted to shut him up just put me on the job."

"It probably wasn't that way," Chee said. "Different people, probably. Some friend called you, not knowing that this madman was coming along."

"I'm getting to be a jinx," Janet Pete said. "Typhoid Mary. A sort of curse."

Chee waited for the explanation. Janet Pete offered none. She sat, her square shoulders slumped a little, and looked sadly at her hands.

"Why jinx?" Chee said.

"This is the second time this happened," Janet Pete said, without looking at Chee. "Last time it was Irma. Irma Onesalt."

"The woman who got killed over by . . . You knew her?"

"Not very well," Janet said. She produced a humorless laugh. "A client."

"I want to hear about it," Chee said. Leaphorn seemed to think there might be some connection between the Onesalt killing and the Sam and Endocheeney cases. The lieutenant had been very interested when Chee had told him about the letter Endocheeney received from Onesalt's office. It didn't seem likely, but maybe there was some sort of link.

"That's how I heard about Officer Jim Chee," Janet Pete said, studying him. "Irma Onesalt said you did her a favor, but she didn't like you."

"I don't understand," Chee said. And he didn't. He felt foolish. The only time he'd met Onesalt, the only time he could remember, had been that business about picking up the patient at the clinic—the wrong Begay business.

"She told me you were supposed to deliver a witness to a chapter meeting and you showed up with the wrong man and screwed everything all up. But she said she owed you something. That you'd done her a favor."

"What?"

"She didn't say. I think it must have been some sort of accident. I remember she said you helped her out and you didn't even know it."

"I sure didn't," Chee said. "And don't." He waved at the man behind the counter, signaling a need for refills. "How was she your client?"

"That's pretty vague too," Janet Pete said. "She called one day and made an appointment. And when she came by, she mostly just asked a lot of questions." She paused while her glass was refilled and then stirred sugar into her tea—two teaspoons.

How did she keep so slim? Chee wondered. Nervous, he guessed. Runs it off. Mary was like that. Always moving.

"I don't think she trusted me. Asked a lot of questions about our relationship at DNA with the tribal bureaucracy and the BIA and all that. When we got that out of the way, she had a lot of questions about what I could find out for her. Financial records, things like that. What was public. What wasn't. How to get documents. I asked her what she was working on, and she said she would tell me later. That maybe it wasn't much of anything and then she wouldn't bother me. Otherwise, she would call me back."

"Did she?"

"Somebody shot her," Janet Pete said. "About ten days later."

"Did you report talking to her?"

"Probably no connection, but finally I did. I checked to find out who was handling the case and then called him and told him—Streib I think it was." She shrugged. "The fed at Gallup."

"Dilly Streib," Chee said. "What did he say?"

She made a wry face. "You know the FBI," she said. "Nothing."

"How about you? Any idea what she was after?"

"Not really." She sipped the tea, slim fingers around the tall glass.

A Navajo complexion, Chee thought. Perfect skin. Smooth, glossy. Janet Pete would never have a freckle. Janet Pete wouldn't have a wrinkle until she was old.

"But she said something that I remembered. It made me curious. Let's see if I can remember just how she put it." She raised a slim hand to her cheek, thinking. "I asked what she would want to look for and she said maybe some answers to some questions, and I said what questions and she said . . . she said how people can look so healthy after they're dead. And then I asked her what that meant. Didn't really ask her exactly, you know. Just looked puzzled, raised my eyebrows or something like that. And she just laughed."

"How people can look healthy after they're dead?"

"That's it," she said. "Maybe not the exact words, but that was the sense of it. Mean anything to you?"

"Absolutely nothing," Chee said, thinking about it so hard that he forgot the refill, and gulped scalding coffee, and spilled it on his uniform shirt—which was not at all what Jim Chee wanted to do in front of Janet Pete.

> 17 <

THE FIRST THING Joe Leaphorn noticed when he rolled Emma's old Chevy sedan to a halt in the yard of the Short Mountain Trading Post was that McGinnis had repainted his Sale sign. The sign had been there the first time Leaphorn had seen the place, coming on some long-forgotten assignment when he was a green new patrolman working in the Tuba City subagency. He sat assessing the pain in his forearm. And remembering. Even then the sign had been weather-beaten. Then, as now, it proclaimed in large block letters:

THIS ESTABLISHMENT
FOR SALE
INQUIRE WITHIN

Around Short Mountain, they said that the store on the rim of Short Mountain Wash had been established sometime before the First World War by a Mormon who, it was said, noticed the lack of competition without noticing the lack of customers. It was also said that he had been convinced that the oil prosperity he saw far to the north around Aneth and Montezuma Creek would spread inexorably and inevitably south and west—that the Just Creator must have blessed this area somehow with something. And since the surface itself offered nothing but scanty grass, scarce wood, and a wilderness of erosion, there surely must be a bountiful treasure of oil below those sterile rocks. But his optimism had finally faltered with the Aneth field, and when his church ruled against multiple wives, he'd opted to join the polygamist faction in its trek to tolerant Mexico. Everyone around Short Mountain Wash seemed to remember the legend. No one remembered the man himself, but those who knew McGinnis marveled at the Mormon's salesmanship.

McGinnis now appeared in his doorway, talking to a departing customer, a tall Navajo woman with a sack of cornmeal draped over her shoulder. While he talked he stared at Emma's Chevy. A strange car out here usually meant a stranger was driving it. Among the scattered people who occupied the emptiness of Short Mountain country, strangers provoked intense curiosity. In Old Man McGinnis, almost anything provoked intense curiosity. Which was one reason Leaphorn wanted to talk to Old Man McGinnis, and had been talking to him for more than twenty years, and had become in some odd way his friend. The other reason was more complicated. It had something to do with the fact that McGinnis, alone, without wife, friend, or family, endured. Leaphorn appreciated those who endured.

But Leaphorn was in no hurry. First he would give his arm a chance to quit throbbing. "Don't move it," the doctor had told him. "If you move it, it's going to hurt." Which made sense, and was why Leaphorn had decided to drive Emma's sedan—which had automatic transmission. Emma had been delighted to see him when he'd come home from the hospital. She had fussed over him and scolded and seemed the genuine Emma. But then her face had frozen into that baffled look Leaphorn had come to dread. She said something meaningless, something that had nothing at all to do with the conversation, and turned her head in that odd way she'd developed—looking down and to her right. When she'd looked back, Leaphorn was sure she no longer recognized him. The next few moments formed another of those all too familiar, agonizing episodes of confusion. He and Agnes had taken her into the bedroom, Emma talking in a muddled attempt to communicate something, and then lying on the coverlet, looking lost and helpless. "I can't remember," she'd said suddenly and clearly, and then she'd fallen instantly asleep. Tomorrow they would keep their appointment with the specialist at the Gallup hospital. Then they would know. "Alzheimer's," the doctor would say, and then the doctor would explain Alzheimer's, all that information Leaphorn had already read and reread in "The Facts About Alzheimer's Disease" sent him by the Alzheimer's Association. Cure unknown. Cause unknown. Possibly a virus. Possibly an imbalance in blood metals. Whatever the cause, the effect was disruption of the cells on the outer surface of the brain, destroying the reasoning process, eroding the memory until only the moment of existence remains, until—in merciful finality—there is no longer a signal to keep the lungs breathing, no longer the impulse to keep the heart beating. Cure unknown. For Emma, he had watched this process of unlearning begin. Where had she left her keys? Walking home from the grocery with the car left parked in the grocery lot. Being brought home by a neighbor after she'd forgotten how to find the house they'd lived in for years. Forgetting how to finish a sentence. Who you are. Who your husband is. The literature had warned him what would be coming next. Fairly early, all speech would go. How to talk. How to walk. How to dress. Who is this man who says he is my husband? Alzheimer's, the doctor would say. And then Leaphorn would put aside pretense and prepare Emma, and himself, for whatever would be left of life.

Leaphorn shook his head. Now he would think of something else. Of business. Of whatever it was that was killing the people he was paid to protect.

He had the cast propped against the steering wheel, letting the pain drain away, sorting what he hoped to learn from this visit to Old Man McGinnis. Witchcraft, he guessed. Much as he hated to admit it, he was probably involved again in the sick and unreal business of the skinwalker superstition. The bits of bone seemed to link Jim Chee, and Roosevelt Bistie, and Dugai Endocheeney. Dilly Streib's call had confirmed that.

"Jim Chee's gossip had it right," Streib had said. "They found a little bead down in one of the knife wounds. Thread, little dirt, and a bead. I've got it. I'll have it checked to see if it matches the first one." And then Streib had asked Leaphorn what it meant, beyond the obvious connection it made between the Endocheeney and Bistie killings and the attempt on Chee. Leaphorn had said he really didn't know.

And he didn't. He knew what it might mean. It might mean that the killer thought Endocheeney was a witch. He might have thought that Endocheeney, the skinwalker, had given him corpse sickness by shooting the prescribed bit of bone into him. Then, instead of relying on an Enemy Way ritual to reverse the witchcraft, he had reversed it himself by putting the lethal bone back into the witch. Or it might mean that the killer in some crazy way thought himself to be a witch and was witching Endocheeney, putting the bone into him at the very moment he killed him with the knife. That

seemed farfetched, but then everything about
Navajo witchcraft seemed farfetched to Leaphorn. Or it might mean that the killer inserted
the notion of witchcraft into this peculiar crime
simply to cause confusion. If that had been the
goal, the project had succeeded. Leaphorn was
thoroughly confused. If only Chee had wormed
it out of Bistie. If only Bistie had told them why
he was carrying the bone bead in his wallet, what
he planned to do with it, why he wanted to kill
Endocheeney.

The pain in his arm had subsided. He climbed
out of the Chevy, and walked across the hard-
packed earth toward the sign that proclaimed the
willingness of McGinnis to leave Short Mountain
Wash for a better world, and stepped through
McGinnis's doorway—out of the glare and heat
and into the cool darkness.

"Well, now," the voice of McGinnis said from
somewhere. "I wondered who it was parked out
there. Who sold you that car?"

McGinnis was sitting on a wooden kitchen
chair, its back tilted against the counter beside
his old black-and-chrome cash register. He was
wearing the only uniform Leaphorn had ever
seen him wear, a pair of blue-and-white-striped
overalls faded by years of washings, and under
them a blue work shirt like those that convicts
wear.

"It's Emma's car," Leaphorn said.

" 'Cause it's got automatic shift and you got
your arm hurt," McGinnis said, looking at Leap-

horn's cast. "Old John Manymules was in here with his boys a little while ago and said a cop had got shot over in the Chuskas, but I didn't know it was you."

"Unfortunately it was," Leaphorn said.

"The way Manymules was telling it, old fella got killed up there at his hogan and when the police came to see about it, one of the policemen got shot right in the middle."

"Just the arm." Leaphorn was no longer surprised by the dazzling speed with which McGinnis accumulated information, but he was still impressed.

"What brings you out here to the wrong side of the reservation?" McGinnis said. "Broke arm and all."

"Just visiting," Leaphorn said.

McGinnis eyed him through his wire-rimmed bifocals, expression skeptical. He rubbed his hand across the gray stubble on his chin. Leaphorn remembered him as a smallish man, short but with a barrel-chested strength. Now he seemed smaller, shrunken into his overalls, the sturdiness missing. The face, too, had lost the remembered roundness, and in the dimness of the trading post, his blue eyes seemed faded.

"Well, now," McGinnis said. "That's nice. I guess I ought to offer you a drink. Be hospitable. That is, if my customers can spare me."

There were no customers. The tall woman was gone and the only vehicle in the yard was Emma's Chevy. McGinnis walked to the door, limping a little and more stooped than Leaphorn remembered. He closed it, slipped the bolt lock. "Got to lock her up, then," he said, half to Leaphorn. "Goddam Navajos they'll steal the panes outta the windows if they need it." He limped toward the doorway into his living quarters, motioning Leaphorn to follow. "But only if they need it. White man, now, he'll steal just for the hell of it. I've known 'em to steal something and then just throw it away. You Navajos, now, if you steal a sack of my meal I know somebody's hungry. Screwdriver's missing, I know somebody lost his screwdriver and has a screw that needs driving. I think it was your granddaddy that first explained that to me, when I was new out here."

"Yeah," Leaphorn said. "I think you told me that."

"Get so I repeat myself," McGinnis said, with no sound of repentance in his voice. "Hosteen Klee, they called him before he died. Your mother's father. I knew him when they was still calling him Horse Kicker." McGinnis had opened the door of a huge old refrigerator. "I ain't offering you a drink because you don't drink whiskey, or at least you never did, and whiskey's all I got," he said into the refrigerator. "Unless you want a drink of water."

"No, thanks," Leaphorn said.

McGinnis emerged, holding a bourbon bottle and a Coca Cola glass. He carried these to a rocking chair, sat, poured bourbon into the glass, examined it, then, with the glass close to his eyes, dripped in more until the level reached the bottom of the trademark. That done, he set the bottle on the floor and motioned Leaphorn to sit. The only place open was a sofa upholstered with some sort of green plastic. Leaphorn sat. The stiff plastic crackled under his weight and a puff of dust arose around him.

"You're here on business," McGinnis declared.

Leaphorn nodded.

McGinnis sipped. "You're here because you think old McGinnis knows something about Wilson Sam. He'll tell you, and you'll put it with what you already know and figure out who killed him."

Leaphorn nodded.

"Outta luck," McGinnis said. "I've known that young fella since he was a buck Indian and I don't know anything about him that's going to help."

"You've been thinking about it," Leaphorn said.

"Sure," McGinnis said. "Fella you've known gets killed, you think about it." He sipped again. "Lost a customer," he said.

"Anything in that?" Leaphorn said. "Unusual, I mean. Like him coming in with money to pay off his pawn. Or buying anything unusual. People coming to ask where to find him."

"Nothing," McGinnis said.

"He make any trips? Go anyplace? Been sick? Any ceremonials for him?"

"Nothing like that," McGinnis said. "He used to come in now and then to do his buying. Sell me his wool. Things like that. Get his mail. I remember he cut his hand bad way back last winter and he went into that clinic that Sioux Indian opened there at Badwater Wash and they sewed it up for him and gave him a tetanus shot. But no sickness. No sings for him. No trips anyplace, except he told me couple of months ago he went into Farmington with his daughter to get himself some clothes." McGinnis took another sip of bourbon. "Too damn fashionable to buy his clothes from me anymore. Everybody's wearing designer jeans."

"How about his mail? Do you write his letters for him? He get anything unusual?"

"He could read and write," McGinnis said. "But he ain't bought no stamps this year. Not from me, anyway. Or mailed any letters. Or got any unusual mail. Only thing unusual, couple of months ago he got a letter in the middle of the month." He didn't explain that, or need to. On the far reaches of the reservation, mail consists primarily of subsistence checks, from the tribal offices in Window Rock or some federal agency. They arrive on the second day of the month, in brown stacks.

"In June was it?" That was when Chee had said Endocheeney received his letter from Irma Onesalt's office. "About the second week?"

"That's what I said," McGinnis said. "Two months ago."

Leaphorn had managed to find a way to be fairly comfortable on the sofa. He had been watching McGinnis, who in turn had kept his watery eyes focused on the bourbon while he talked. And while he talked, he rocked, slowly and steadily, coordinating a motion in his forearm with the motion of his chair. The net result of this was that while the bourbon glass seemed to move, the liquid in it remained level and motionless. Leaphorn had noticed this lesson in hydraulic motion before, but it still intrigued him. But what McGinnis had said about the letter regained his full attention. He leaned forward.

"Don't get excited," McGinnis said. "You gonna expect me to tell you that inside that envelope there was a letter from somebody telling Wilson Sam to hold still because he was coming to kill him. Something like that." McGinnis chuckled. "You got your hopes up too high. It wasn't from anybody. It was from Window Rock."

Leaphorn wasn't surprised McGinnis had noticed this, or that he remembered it. A midmonth letter would have been an oddity.

"What was it about?"

McGinnis's placid expression soured. "I don't read folks' mail."

"All right then, who was it from?"

"One of them bureaus there in Window Rock," McGinnis said. "Like I said."

"You remember which one?"

"Why would I remember something like that?" McGinnis said. "None of my business."

Because everything out here is your business, Leaphorn thought. Because the letter would have lain around somewhere for days while you waited for Wilson Sam to come in, or for some relative to come in who could take it to him, and every day you would look at it and wonder what was in it. And because you remember everything.

"I just thought you might," Leaphorn said, overcoming a temptation to tell McGinnis the letter was from Social Services.

"Social Services," McGinnis said.

Social Services. Exactly. He wished he had found time to check. If the letter wasn't in the file, if no one there remembered writing to Endocheeney, or to Wilson Sam, it would be fair circumstantial evidence that Onesalt had done the writing, and that the letters were in some way unofficial. Why would Social Services be writing to either man?

"Did it have a name on it? I mean on the return address. Or just the office?"

"Come to think of it, yeah." McGinnis sipped again and inspected the bourbon level with watery eyes. "That might be of some interest to you," he said, without taking his eyes off the glass. "Because that woman who had her name on the return address, she was the one that got shot a little later over there in your part of the reservation. Same name, anyway."

"Irma Onesalt," Leaphorn said.

"Yessir," McGinnis said. "Irma Onesalt."

The circle was thus complete. The bone beads linked Wilson Sam and Endocheeney and Jim Chee and Roosevelt Bistie. The letters linked Onesalt into the pattern. Now he had what he needed to solve this puzzle. He had no idea how. But he knew himself. He knew he would solve it.

≫ 18 ≪

Iᴛ ᴡᴀs ᴀ ᴅᴀʏ ᴏғғ ғᴏʀ ᴄʜᴇᴇ, and in a little while it would be time to leave for the long drive to the place of Hildegarde Goldtooth, to meet with Alice Yazzie. Ninety miles or so, some of it on bad roads, and he intended to leave early. He planned to detour past the Badwater Clinic to see if he could learn anything there. And he didn't want to keep Alice Yazzie waiting. He wanted to do her Blessing Way. Now Chee was passing the time in what Captain Largo called his "laboratory." Largo had laughed about it. "Laboratory, or maybe it's your studio," Largo had said when he found Chee working there. In fact, it was nothing but a flat, hard-packed earthen surface up the slope from Chee's trailer. Chee had chosen it because a gnarled old cottonwood shaded the place. He had prepared it carefully, digging it up, leveling it, raking out bits of gravel and weed roots, making it an approximation of the size and shape of a hogan floor. He used it to practice dry painting the images used in the ceremonials he was learning.

At the moment, Chee was squatting at the edge of this floor. He was finishing the picture of Sun's Creation, an episode from the origin story used in the second night of the Blessing Way. Chee was humming, mouthing the words of the poetry that recounted this episode, letting a controlled trickle of blue sand sift between his fingers to form the tip of the feather that was hung from Sun's left horn.

Sun will be created—they say it is planned
  to happen.
Sun will be created—they say he has
  planned it all.
Its face will be blue—they say he has
  planned it all.
Its eyes will be yellow—they say he
  planned it all.
Its forehead will be white—they say he
  planned it all.

Feather finished, Chee rocked back on his heels, poured the surplus blue sand from his palm into the coffee can that held it, wiped his hand on the leg of his jeans, and surveyed his work. It was good. He had left off one of the three plumes that should have extended eastward from the headdress of Pollen Boy, standing against Sun's face—thus not completing the power of the holy image at this inappropriate time and place. Otherwise, the dry painting looked perfect. The lines of sand—black, blue, yellow, red, and white—were neatly defined. The symbols were correct. The red sand was a bit too coarse, but he would fix that by running a can of it through the coffee grinder again. He was ready. He knew this version of the Blessing Way precisely and exactly—every word of every song, every symbol of the dry paintings. It would cure for him. He squatted, memorizing again the complicated formula of symbols he had created on the earth before him, feeling its beauty. Soon he would be performing this old and holy act as it had been intended, to return one of his people to beauty and harmony. Chee felt the joy of that rising in him, and turned away the thought. All things in moderation.

The cat was watching him from the hillside above its juniper. It had been in sight much of the morning, vanishing down the bank of the San Juan for a while but returning after less than an hour to lie in the juniper's shade. Chee had put the shipping case under the tree the previous evening—fitting it beneath the limbs as near to the cat's sleeping place as he could force it. In it he'd put an old denim jacket, which the cat sometimes sat on when it came into the trailer. He had added, as lure, a hamburger patty from his refrigerator. He'd been saving the patty for some future lunch, but the edges had curled and turned dark. This morning he noticed the meat was missing and he presumed the cat had gone into the case to retrieve it. But he could see no

sign that the cat had slept there. No problem.
Chee was patient.

The case was really a cage with a carrying
handle and had cost Chee almost forty dollars
with taxes. It had been Janet Pete's idea. He had
brought up the problem of cat and coyote as they
left the Turquoise Cafe, trying to extend the
conversation—to think of something to say that
would prevent Miss Pete from getting into her
clean white official Chevy sedan and leaving him
standing there on the sidewalk.

"I don't guess you'd know anything about
cats?" Chee had said, and she'd said, "Not much,
but what's the problem?" And he'd told her about
the cat and the coyote. Then he'd waited a
moment while she thought about it. While he
waited (Janet Pete leaning, gracefully, against
her Chevy, frowning, lower lip caught between
her teeth, taking the problem seriously), he
thought about what Mary Landon would have
said. Mary would have asked who owned the cat.
Mary would have said, Well, silly, just bring the
cat in, and keep it in your trailer until the coyote
goes away and hunts something else. Perfectly
good solutions for a *belagana* cat in a *belagana*
world, but they overlooked the nature of Jim
Chee, a Navajo, and the role of animals in Dine'
Bike'yah, where Corn Beetle and Bluebird and
Badger received equal billing when the Holy
People emerged into this Earth Surface World.

"I don't guess you'd want a cat," Janet Pete
said, looking at Chee.

Chee grinned.

"Can you fix up something out there? So the coyote can't get to it?"

"You know coyotes," Chee said.

Janet Pete smiled, looked wry, brightened. "I know," she said. "Get one of those airline shipping cages." She described one, cat-sized, with her hands. "They're tough. A coyote couldn't get her in that."

"I don't know," Chee said, doubting the cat would get into such a thing. Doubting it would foil a coyote. "I don't think I've ever seen one. Where can you get 'em? Airport?"

"Pet store," Janet Pete said. And she'd driven him to the one in Farmington. The shipping cage Chee eventually bought had been designed for a small dog. It was made of stiff steel wire that looked coyote-proof. And it was large enough, in Chee's opinion, to seem hospitable to the cat. Janet Pete had remembered an appointment and hurried him back to his car at the courthouse.

Even as he was driving to Shiprock with the cage on the seat beside him it was seeming less and less of a good idea. He'd have to narrow the doorway to make it just big enough for the cat and too small for the coyote's head. That looked simple enough In fact, it had been merely a matter of using some hay baling wire. But there was still the question of whether the cat would accept it as a bedroom, and whether she would be smart enough to recognize the safety it offered when the coyote was stalking her.

Chee thought about that as he swept up the sand, using the feathered wand from his *jish* bundle for the task. After she had created the first of the Navajo clans, Changing Woman had taught them how to perform their curing ceremonials. She'd made the first dry paintings out of the clouds, blowing each away with her breath as its purpose was completed. And she'd taught the first of the Navajos to scatter their painting sand to the winds, just as Chee did now—collecting it on a dustpan and then throwing it into the air to drift away. He brushed the last traces of the picture away and collected the coffee cans in which he kept his supply of unused sands. No use thinking about the cat now. Time would tell. Perhaps the cat would use the cage. If it didn't, there would be the time to seek another solution. And there were other, tougher problems. How would she fare when she grew big with pregnancy? How would the litter survive? Worse, she was hunting less now—or seemed to be. Relying more on the food he provided her. That was exactly what he couldn't allow to happen. If the cat was to make the transition—from someone's property to self-sufficient predator—it couldn't rely on him, or on any person. To do so was to fail. Chee had been surprised when he first realized that he cared how this struggle ended. Now he accepted it. He wanted the cat to tear itself free. He wanted *belagana* cat to become natural cat. He wanted the cat to endure.

Chee stacked the cans of sand back into the outside storage compartment in the wall of his trailer, where he kept all his ceremonial regalia. He would take with him, he decided, his *jish* just in case the circumstances at his meeting with Alice Yazzie required some sort of blessing. Besides, the *jish* case itself and the ceremonial items in it were impressive. In this, Chee was a perfectionist. His prayer sticks were painted exactly right, waxed, polished, with exactly the right feathers attached as they should be attached. The bag that held his pollen was soft doeskin; labeled plastic prescription bottles held the fragments of mica, abalone shell, and the other "hard jewels" his profession required. And his Four Mountain bundle—four tiny bags contained in a doeskin sack—included exactly the proper herbs and minerals, which Chee had collected from the four sacred mountains exactly as the *yei* had instructed. Chee would take his *jish*. He would hope that the opportunity would arise to get it out and open it.

Inside the trailer, he exchanged his dusty jeans for a pair he'd just bought in Farmington. He put on the red-and-white shirt he saved for special occasions, his polished "go-to-town" boots, and his black felt hat. Then he checked himself in the mirror over his washbasin. All right, he thought. Better if he looked a lot older. The Dinee liked their *yataalii* to be old and wise—men like Frank Sam Nakai, his mother's brother. "Don't worry about it," Frank Sam Nakai had told him. "All the famous singers started when they were young. Hosteen Klah started when he was young. Frank Mitchell started when he was young. I started when I was young. Just pay attention and try to learn."

Now, finally, he would be beginning to use what Frank Sam Nakai had been teaching him for so many years. As he drove up the slope away from the river, he noticed that the cloud formation that built every afternoon over the slopes behind Shiprock was bigger today, dark at the bottom, forming its anvil top of ice crystals earlier than usual in this dry summer. Howard Morgan, the weatherman on Channel 7, had said there was a 30 percent chance of rain in the Four Corners today. That was the best odds of the summer so far. Morgan said the summer monsoon might finally be coming. Rain. That would be the perfect omen. And Morgan was often right.

When he turned west on 504, it looked as if Morgan was right again. Thunderheads had merged over the Carrizo range, forming a blue-black wall that extended westward far into Arizona. The afternoon sun lit their tops, already towering high enough to be blowing ice crystals into the jet stream winds. By the time he turned south beyond Dennehotso across Greasewood Flats, he was driving in cloud shadow. Proximity winds were kicking up occasional dust devils. But Chee had been raised with the desert dweller's conditioning to avoid disappointment.

He allowed himself to think a while about rain, sweeping its cool, wet blessing across the desert, but not to expect it. And now he needed to think of something else. The Badwater Clinic was over the next ridge.

The quirky wind generated by the thunderstorms' great updrafts bounced a tumbleweed across the unpaved clinic parking lot just as he pulled his truck to a stop. He turned off the engine and waited for the gust to subside. The place had been built only five or so years ago—a long one-story, flat-roofed rectangle set in a cluster of attendant buildings. A cube of concrete housing the clinic's water well was just behind the building, surmounted by a once-white storage tank. Beyond that stood a cluster of those ugly frame-and-brown-plaster housing units that the Bureau of Indian Affairs had scattered by the thousands across Indian reservations from Point Barrow to the Pagago Reservation. New as the clinic compound was, the reservation had already touched it, as it seemed to touch all such unnatural shapes imposed upon it, with an instant look of disrepair. The white paint of the clinic building was no longer white, and blowing sand had stripped patches of it from the concrete-block walls. None of this registered on the consciousness of Chee, who, Navajo fashion, had looked at the setting and not the structures. It was a good place. Beautiful. A long view down the valley toward the cliffs that rose above Chilchinbito Canyon and Long Flat Wash, toward the massive shape of Black Mesa—its dark green turned a cool blue by cloud shadow and distance. The view lifted Chee's spirits. He felt exultant—a mood he hadn't enjoyed since reading Mary Landon's letter. He walked toward the clinic entrance, feeling a gust of sand blown against his ankles and guessing that today it would finally rain and he would be lucky.

He was. The person sitting behind the counter-desk in the entrance foyer was the Woman from the Yoo'l Dinee, the Bead People. Chee's excellent Navajo-trained memory also produced her name—Eleanor Billie. She had been the receptionist on duty that cold late-spring day when he had come with the Onesalt woman to collect the wrong Begay. Her memory seemed to be as good as Chee's.

"Mister Policeman," she said, smiling very slightly. "Who can we get for you today? Do you need another Begay?"

"I just need you to help me understand something," Chee said. "About the time we got the wrong one."

Mrs. Billie had nothing to say to that. That smile, Chee realized, had not been a warm one. Maybe he wasn't so lucky.

"What I need to know is whether the woman who was with me—that woman from Window Rock—if she ever contacted anybody about that. Wrote a letter. Telephoned. Anything like that. Did she have any questions? Who would I ask about that?"

Mrs. Billie looked surprised. She produced an ironic chuckle. "She raised hell," she said. "She came in here the next day and acted real nasty. Wanted to see Dr. Yellowhorse. I don't know how she acted with him. She acted nasty with me."

"She came back?" Chee laughed. "I guess I shouldn't act surprised. She was mad enough to kill somebody." He laughed again. Mrs. Billie smiled, and now, he noticed, it seemed genuine. In fact, it was spreading into a broad grin.

"I always wondered what happened. To get that bitch in such a rage," Mrs. Billie said.

"Well, we took Begay to the chapter house over at Lukachukai. They were having a meeting— trying to settle whether a family from the Weaver Clan or an outfit from the Many Hogans Dinee had a right to live on some land over there. Anyway, Irma Onesalt had found out that this old Begay man had lived over there for about a thousand years and he was supposed to tell the council that the Many Hogans family had lived there first, and had the grazing and the water and all that. I didn't see all of it, but what I heard was that when they called on that Begay you gave us to talk about it, he gave them this long speech about how he never had lived there at all. He was born to the Coyote Pass People, and born for the Monster People, and him and his outfit lived way over east on the Checkerboard Reservation."

Chee was grinning as he finished, remembering Irma Onesalt's incoherent rage as she stomped out of the chapter house and back to his patrol car. "You should have heard what she said to me," he said. What Irma Onesalt had said would translate precisely from Navajo to English. It was the equivalent of: "You stupid son-of-a-bitch, you got the wrong Begay."

Mrs. Billie's grin showed an array of very white teeth in a very round face.

"I'd like to have seen that," Mrs. Billie said, with Chee now firmly established as a fellow victim. "You should have heard what she said to me. I just reminded her she'd called and said she was picking up Frank Begay to take him to the hearing, and we gave her the only Begay we had. Franklin Begay. Pretty damn close."

"Pretty close," Chee agreed.

"And the only Begay we had," Mrs. Billie said. "Still is, for that matter."

"Wonder what caused her to get the wrong name—or whatever happened."

"Oh, Frank Begay used to be here. He was diabetic, with all sorts of complications. But he died way back in the winter. Earlier than that. It was in October. He was the one from Lukachukai."

"I wonder if that's what caused the confusion," Chee said. "She didn't seem like a woman who'd get confused much."

Mrs. Billie nodded, agreeing. She looked thoughtful. "What she said was that we had our records all screwed up. Said we had him on our list as a patient. I looked, and told her we didn't. And she said, Damn it, yes we did. Maybe not today, she said, but a couple of weeks ago." Mrs. Billie was showing her white teeth in another joyful grin, remembering. "That's why I know just when Frank Begay died. October three. I went back into the files and found it."

Chee allowed himself to imagine for a moment how much pleasure Mrs. Billie had attained by giving that news to Irma Onesalt. He remembered his own discomfort at the chapter house, with the woman leaning on the door of his patrol car, staring at him contemptuously, bombarding him with questions about why he had delivered Franklin Begay when she had told him to deliver Frank Begay. An unusually arrogant woman, Irma Onesalt. He wondered, half seriously, if Dilly Streib, or whoever was working her homicide for the FBI, had considered that as a motive for her murder. Someone might simply have got tired of suffering Irma Onesalt's bad conduct.

"What else did Onesalt say?" Chee asked.

"Wanted to see the doctor to argue about it."

"Dr. Yellowhorse?"

"Yeah. So I sent her on in."

Yellowhorse and Onesalt, Chee thought. Two tough coyotes. For different reasons, he didn't like either of them—but Yellowhorse he respected. His differences with the doctor were purely philosophical—the believer and the agnostic exploiting the belief. Onesalt was, or had been, simply an obnoxious jerk. "I wish I could have seen those two," Chee said. "What happened?"

Mrs. Billie shrugged. "She went in. Maybe five minutes she came out."

The telephone at Mrs. Billie's plump elbow buzzed. "Badwater Clinic," she said. "What? Okay. I'll tell him." She hung up. "Came out steaming," she continued, grinning again. "Pure rage now. The doctor, he can be rough, you get him stirred up."

Chee was remembering what Janet Pete had told him—of Irma Onesalt's remark about the wrong Begay business tipping her off to something. This conversation hadn't opened any doors to what that might be. Or had it?

"She say anything else? Any remarks or anything?"

"No," Mrs. Billie said. "Well, not much. She got almost to the door and then she turned around and came back and asked me what that date was when Frank Begay died."

"You told her October third?"

"No. I hadn't looked it up yet. I told her last fall, I guess. And then she asked me if she could see a list of the patients we had in here." Mrs. Billie's face expressed disapproval of this remembered outrage. "Imagine that kind of brass!" she said. "And I said she'd have to ask the doctor about that and she said to hell with it then, she'd get it another way." Mrs. Billie looked even more disapproving. "Actually she said a little worse than that. Rough-talking woman."

A middle-aged black woman in a nurse's uniform came down the hall with a young Navajo who was pushing a wheelchair. The wheelchair contained a woman with her leg in a cast. "Now tell her again that it will itch, but she's not supposed to scratch it. Just let it itch. Think about something else." The Navajo said, "Don't scratch," in Navajo, and Woman in Cast said, in English, "Don't scratch. You told me that before."

"She speaks English," Mrs. Billie told the nurse. "Better than I do."

"That was it? Nothing else?" Chee asked, getting Mrs. Billie's attention again.

"Just walked out after that," Mrs. Billie said.

"She said she could get the list of patients another way?"

"Yeah," Mrs. Billie said. "I guess she could, too. They'd all be on some sort of medical-cost reimbursement list. Medicare, or Medicaid, or some insurance claim if they had insurance. Most of them wouldn't."

"Just have to go through the red tape?"

"Probably no big deal. She worked in Window Rock with all the other bureaucrats. Probably just get somebody in the right accounting office to get her a Xerox, or let her take a peek."

Chee had been remembering Leaphorn in his trailer, putting the list on his countertop. Leaphorn watching his face as he looked at the list. Leaphorn asking if he knew any of them. Looking disappointed when he didn't. Asking if the names suggested anything to him. They had suggested nothing. But now they did. Now they seemed terribly important.

"I haven't got any friends among the bureaucrats at Window Rock. Any way I could find out who was here that day?"

"You could ask Dr. Yellowhorse."

"Good," Chee said. "Can I get in to see him?"

"He's not here," Mrs. Billie said.

Chee looked as disappointed as possible. He shrugged, made a wry face.

"You're a policeman. I guess you could say it was police business."

"It's police business," Chee said.

"It will take a while," Mrs. Billie said, getting up. "Call me if the telephone rings."

It took about ten minutes and the telephone didn't ring. "I just copied them off for that date," Mrs. Billie said. "I hope you can read my writing."

Mrs. Billie's writing was a beautiful, clear, symmetrical script—a script that would win penmanship competitions, if there were still penmanship competitions. Chee noticed that before he looked at the names.

> *Ethelmary Largewhiskers*
> *Addison Etcitty*
> *Wilson Sam*

This was the list Leaphorn had told him about. The names for which Irma Onesalt was seeking death certificate dates. Wilson Sam's name was third. And second from the bottom Chee saw Dugai Endocheeney.

"Thanks," he said. He folded the paper absently and put it into his billfold, thinking: Sam and Endocheeney were alive when Onesalt was hunting their death certificates. Endocheeney had been into the clinic for that broken leg Iron Woman had told him about, and Sam for God knows what. But they were still alive. What was Onesalt . . . ?

His mind answered the question even before he completed it. He knew why Irma Onesalt had died, and almost all the rest of it. All that remained of the puzzle was why someone had tried to kill him. He glanced at his watch. He'd spent more time here than he'd intended.

"Need to use your telephone," he told Mrs. Billie.

He would call Leaphorn and tell him what he'd learned. Then he had to hurry. He'd been hearing thunder and it seemed to be getting closer. He'd have to leave a little time in case it got muddy. After he made a deal with Alice Yazzie to conduct a Blessing Way, he'd see if he could figure out why Jim Chee's ghost was supposed to join the *chindis* of Onesalt, Sam, and Endocheeney. Now was not the time to be thinking such unpleasant thoughts.

≫ 19 ≪

THE TELEPHONE WAS BUZZING when Leaphorn came through his office door. "You just missed a call," the operator told him. "I took the message for you."

"Okay," Leaphorn said. He was tired. He wanted to clean off his desk in a hurry, go home, take a shower, try to relax for a few minutes, and then drive back to Gallup. Emma had to stay overnight for the tests they were making, for the things they do when something is wrong inside the head. Why? Leaphorn didn't understand that. Uncharacteristically for him, he hadn't insisted on an explanation. Everything about Emma's illness left him feeling helplessly out of control. Things were happening to them that would change their lives—devastate his life—and there was nothing he could do that would affect it. He felt surrounded by inevitability—something new for Joe Leaphorn. It made him feel as he'd heard people felt when caught in earthquakes, with the solid earth no longer solid.

He worked quickly through the "Immediate Action" memos, and found none that required immediate action. The most urgent two concerned the rodeo. First, a bootlegger, a woman in a blue Ford 250 pickup, seemed to be selling more or less openly, according to the complaints, but hadn't been arrested. Second, a problem with traffic management had developed at points where the rodeo grounds access routes tangled with mainstream flow on Navajo Route 3. Leaphorn wrote the necessary order to deal with the traffic first. The bootlegger required thought. Who would the woman be? He sorted through a career-long accumulation of bootlegger knowledge, studied his map briefly. Usually five or six bootleggers would work an event as popular as the rodeo, two or three of them female. One of these women was sick, Leaphorn knew, maybe even in the hospital. Of the other two, the one who lived down at Wide Ruins drove a big pickup. Leaphorn conjured up her family connections. She was born to the Towering House Clan, born for the Rock Gap People? He compared this mentally with the clans of the policemen he had working the rodeo—following the simple and true theory that no one is going to arrest his own clan sister if he can avoid it. He found what he expected to find. The sergeant in charge of internal order was a Towering House man.

Leaphorn tore up the order he'd written to deal with the access problem and wrote another, switching the Towering House sergeant to traffic control and replacing him with the corporal who had been handling traffic. Then he looked at his telephone messages.

The call he had just missed was from Jim Chee.

Lieutenant Leaphorn: Irma Onesalt came back to Badwater Clinic the day after I picked up Franklin Begay there. She was angry. She found out that Frank Begay had died last October. She asked for a list of patients in the clinic, went to see Dr. Yellowhorse about it, got a turndown, said she could get the names elsewhere. I got a list of the names on list on the date Onesalt was there. The list included both Endocheeney and Wilson Sam. I remember hearing that Endocheeney had been in the clinic about then with a broken leg.

The remainder of the message was a listing of all those who had been patients in the Badwater Clinic that April day. They included the names Dr. Jenks had remembered, the quaint names.

Leaphorn read the note again. Then he let it drop from his fingers and picked up the telephone.

"Call Shiprock and get me Chee," he said.

"Doubt if we can," the dispatcher said. "He was calling from the Badwater Clinic. Said he was just leaving. Going over toward Dinebito Wash and he'd be out of touch for a while."

"Dinebito Wash?" Leaphorn said. What the hell would he be doing there? Even on the reservation, where isolation was the norm, Dinebito country was an empty corner. There the desert rose toward the northern limits of the Black Mesa highlands. Leaphorn told the switchboard to get Captain Largo at Shiprock.

He waited, standing by the window. The entire sky, south and west, was black with storm now. Like all people who live a lot out of doors and whose culture depends upon the weather, Leaphorn was a student of the sky. This one was easy enough to read. This storm wouldn't fade away, as storms had been doing all this summer. This one had water in it, and force. It would be raining hard by now across the Hopi mesas, at Ganado and on the grazing country of his cousins around Klagetoh and Cross Canyons and Burntwater. By tomorrow they'd be hearing of the flash floods down Wide Ruins Wash, and the Lone Tule, and Scattered Willow Draw, and those dusty desert-country drains that converted themselves into roaring torrents when the male rains came. Tomorrow would be a busy day for the 120 men and women of the Navajo Tribal Police.

Leaphorn watched the lightning, and the first cold drops splattering themselves across the glass, and did not think of Emma sleeping in her hospital room. Instead he let the links offered in

Chee's message click into place. Onesalt's motivation? Malice, of course. Leaphorn thought about it. It was unproductive thought, but it was better than thinking of Emma. Better than thinking about what he would learn tomorrow when the tests were finished.

The telephone rang.

"I've got Captain Largo," the operator said, with Largo's voice behind him saying something about quitting time.

"This is Leaphorn," Leaphorn said. "Do you know where Jim Chee was going today?"

"Chee?" Largo laughed. "I do. Son-of-a-bitch finally got himself a sing. He was going out to see about it. All excited."

"I need to talk to him," Leaphorn said. "Is he working tomorrow? Could you call in and check for me?"

"I am in," Largo said. "I don't have any better luck getting away from the office than you do. Just a minute."

Leaphorn waited, hearing Largo's breathing and the sounds of papers shuffling. "It raining down there yet?" Largo asked. "Looks like we might finally get some up here."

"Just starting," Leaphorn said. He drummed his fingertips against the desktop. Through the rain-streaked window he saw a triple-flash lightning.

"Tomorrow," Largo said. "No, Chee's off."

"Well, hell," Leaphorn said.

"But let's see now. He was supposed to keep in

touch. Because of somebody trying to shoot him. I told him, and sometimes Chee does what he's told. Let's see if there's a note on that."

More rustling of papers. Leaphorn waited.

"Be damned. He did it for once." Largo's tone changed from man talking to man reading. " 'Will go today to the place of Hildegarde Goldtooth out near Dinebito Wash to meet with her and Alice Yazzie about doing a sing for a patient.' " Largo's voice switched back to normal. "He got invited to do that sing last week. Real proud of it. Going around showing everybody the letter."

"Nothing about when he'll be back?"

"With Chee, that'd be asking too much," Largo said.

"I haven't been out there since I worked out of Tuba City," Leaphorn said. "Wouldn't he have to go past Piñon?"

"Unless he's walking," Largo said. "That's the only road."

"Well, thanks," Leaphorn said. "I'll call our man there and get him to catch him going in or out."

The policeman assigned to work out of the Piñon Chapter House was a Sleep Rock Dinee named Leonard Skeet. Leaphorn had worked with him in his younger days at Tuba City and remembered him as reliable if you weren't in a hurry. The voice that said "Hello" was feminine—Mrs. Skeet. Leaphorn identified himself.

"He's gone over to Rough Rock," the woman said.

"When you expect him?"

"I don't know." She laughed, but the storm, or the distance, or the way the telephone line was tied to miles of fence posts to reach this outpost, made it difficult to tell whether the sound was amused or ironic. "He's a policeman, you know."

"I'd like to leave a message for him," Leaphorn said. "Would you tell him Officer Jim Chee will be driving through there. I need your husband to stop Chee and tell him to call me." He supplied his home telephone number. It would be better to wait there until it was time to go back to Gallup.

"About when you think he'll come by? Lenny's going to ask me that."

"It's just a guess," Leaphorn said. "He's gone out somewhere around Dinebito Wash. Out to see Hildegarde Goldtooth. I don't know how far that is."

There was something as close to silence as the crackling of the poorly insulated line allowed.

"You there?" Leaphorn asked.

"That was my father's sister," Mrs. Skeet said. "She's dead. Died last month."

And now it was Leaphorn's turn to produce the long silence. "Who lives out there now?"

"Nobody," Mrs. Skeet said. "The water was bad, anyway. Alkaline. And when she died, there was nobody left but her daughter and her son-in-law. They just moved away."

"The place is empty, then."

"That's right. If anybody moved in, I'd know it."

"Can you tell me exactly how to get there from Piñon?"

Mrs. Skeet could. As Leaphorn sketched out her instructions on his notepad, his mind was checking off other Navajo Police subagency offices that might be able to get someone to Piñon quicker than he could get there himself from Window Rock. Many Farms would be closer. Kayenta would be closer. But who would be working at this hour? And he could think of nothing he could tell them—nothing specific— that would instill in them the terrible sense of urgency that he felt himself.

He could be there in two hours, he thought. Perhaps a little less. And find Chee, and be back here in time to get to Gallup by midnight or so. Emma would be asleep, anyway. He had no choice.

"You taking off for home?" the desk officer asked him when he came down the stairs.

"Going to Piñon," Leaphorn said.

≫ 20 ≪

IN ALBUQUERQUE, in the studio of KOAT-TV,
Howard Morgan was explaining it. The newscast
was picked up and relayed by drone repeater sta-
tions to blanket the Checkerboard Reservation
and reach into the Four Corners country and
into the eastern fringes of the Navajo Big Reservation. Had Jim Chee been at home in his trailer
with his battery-powered TV turned on, he would
have been seeing Morgan standing in front of a
projection of a satellite photograph, explaining
how the jet stream had finally shifted south, pulling cool, wet air with it, and this mass was meeting more moisture. The moisture coming up
from the south was serious stuff, being pushed
across Baja California and the deserts of northwest Mexico by Hurricane Evelyn. "Rains at
last," said Morgan. "Good news if you're growing
rhubarb. Bad news if you're planning picnics.
And remember, the flash flood warnings are out
for all of the southern and western parts of the

Colorado plateau tonight, and for tomorrow all across northern New Mexico."

But Chee was not at home watching the weathercast. He was more or less racing the storm front—driving through the cloud-induced early twilight with his lights on. Just past Piñon he had run into a quick and heavy flurry of rain—drops the size of peach stones kicking up spurts of dust as they struck the dirt road ahead of him. Then came a bombardment of popcorn snow which moved like a curtain across the road, reflecting his headlights like a rhinestone curtain. That lasted no more than a hundred yards. Then he was in dry air again. But rain loomed over him. It hung over the northeast slopes of Black Mesa like a wall—illuminated to light gray now and then by sheet lightning. The smell of it came through the pickup vents, mixed with the smell of dust. In Chee's desert-trained nostrils it was heady perfume—the smell of good grazing, easy water, heavy crops of piñon nuts. The smell of good times, the smell of Sky Father blessing Mother Earth.

Chee drove with the map Alice Yazzie had drawn on the back of her letter spread on his lap. The volcanic outcrop rising like four giant clenched fingers just ahead must be the place she'd marked to watch for a left turn. It was. Just beyond it, two ruts branched from the dirt road he'd been following.

Chee was early. He stopped and got out to stretch his muscles and kill a little time, partly

to check if the track was still in use and partly
for the sheer joy of standing under this huge, violent sky. Once, the track had been used fairly
heavily, but not recently. Now the scanty weeds
and grass of a dry summer had grown on the
hump between the ruts. But someone had driven
here today. In fact, very recently. The tires were
worn, but what little tread marks they left were
fresh. Jagged lightning streaked through the
cloud and repeated itself—producing a thunder-
clap loud as a cannon blast. A damp breeze
moved past, pressing the denim of his trousers
against his legs and carrying the smell of ozone
and wet sage and piñon needles. Then he heard
the muted roar of the falling water. It moved toward him like a gray wall. Chee climbed back
into the cab, as an icy drop splashed against the
back of his wrist.

He drove the final 2.3 miles that Alice Yazzie
had indicated on her map with his windshield
wipers lashing and the rain pounding on the
roof. The track wandered up a wide valley, rising
toward the Black Mesa highlands, becoming in-
creasingly rocky. Chee had been worried a little,
despite the mud chains he always carried. The
rockiness eliminated that worry. He wouldn't get
stuck on this. Abruptly, the sky lightened. The
rain eased—one of those brief respites common
to high-altitude storms. The tracks climbed a
ridge lined with eroded granite boulders, followed it briefly, and then turned sharply downward. Below him Chee saw the Goldtooth place.

A round stone hogan with a domed dirt roof, a peak-roofed frame house, a pole corral, a storage shed, and a lean-to of poles, planks, and tar-paper, built against the wall of a low cliff. Smoke was coming from the hogan, hanging in the wet air and creating a blue smudge across the narrow cul-de-sac where the Goldtooth outfit had built its place. An old truck was parked beside the plank house. From behind the house, the back end of an ancient Ford sedan was visible. Chee could see a dim light, probably a kerosene lamp, illuminating one of the side windows of the house. Except for that, and the smoke, the place had an abandoned look.

He parked a polite distance from the house and sat for a moment with his headlights on it, waiting. The front door opened and the light outlined a shape, wearing the voluminous long skirt and long-sleeved blouse of the traditional Navajo woman. She stared out into Chee's headlights, then made the traditional welcoming motion and disappeared into the house.

Chee switched off the lights, opened the door, and stepped out into the resuming rain. He walked toward the house, past the parked truck. He could see now that the Ford had no rear wheels. The damp air carried the thousand smells aroused by rain. But something was missing. The acrid smell that fills the air when rain wets the still-fresh manure of corrals and sheep pens. Where was that? Chee's intelligence had its various strengths and its weaknesses—a superb memory, a tendency to exclude new input while it focused too narrowly on a single thought, a tendency to be distracted by beauty, and so forth. One of the strengths was an ability to process new information and collate it with old unusually fast. In a millisecond, Chee identified the missing odor, extracted its meaning, and homogenized it with what he had already noticed about the place of the Goldtooth outfit. No animals. The place was little used. Why use it now? Chee's brain identified an assortment of possible explanations. But all this changed him, midstride, from a man happily walking through the rain toward a long-anticipated meeting, to a slightly uneasy man with a memory of being shot at.

It was just then that Chee noticed the oil.

What he saw was a reflection in the twilight, a slick blue-green sheen where rainwater had washed under the truck and picked up an oil emulsion. It stopped him. He looked at the oily spot, then back at the house. The door was open a few inches. He felt all those odd, intense sensations caused when intense fear triggers the adrenaline glands. Maybe nothing, one corner of his brain said. A coincidence. Leaky oil pans are usual enough among the old trucks so common on the reservation. But he had been foolish. Careless. And he turned back toward his pickup, walking at first, then breaking into a trot. His pistol was locked in the glove compartment.

He was not conscious of any separation between the boom of the shotgun and the impact that staggered him. He stumbled against the hogan, catching the edge of the door lintel for support. Then the second shot hit him, higher this time, the feel of claws tearing against his upper back and neck muscles and the back of his head. It knocked him off balance and he found himself on his knees, his hands in the cold mud. Three shots, he remembered. An automatic shotgun legally choked holds three shells. Three holes torn through the aluminum skin of his trailer. Another shot would be coming. He slammed against the hogan door, pushed his way through it, just as he heard the shotgun again.

He pushed the door shut, sat against it, trying to control the shock and the panic. The hogan was empty, stripped bare and lit by flickering coals of a fire built on the earthen floor under the smoke hole. His ears were ringing with the sound of the shots, but through that he could hear the splashing sound of someone running through the rain. His right side felt numb. With his left hand he reached behind him and slid the wooden latch.

Something pushed, tentatively, against the door.

He pressed his shoulder against it. "If you open the door, I'll shoot you," Chee said.

Silence.

"I am a police officer," Chee said. "Why did you shoot me?"

Silence. The ringing in his ears diminished. He could distinguish a pinging noise—the sound of the rain hitting the metal shield placed over the smoke hole to keep the hogan dry. The sound of feet moving on muddy ground. Metallic sounds. Chee strained to hear them. The shotgun was being reloaded. He thought about that. Whoever had shot him hadn't bothered to reload before running after him. He had seen Chee had been hit, knocked down. Apparently it was presumed the shots had killed him. That Chee was no danger.

The pain was fierce now—especially the back of his head. He touched it gingerly with his fingers and found the scalp slick with blood. He could also feel blood running down his right side, warm against the skin over his ribs. Chee looked at his palm, tilted it so that the weak glow from the coals would reach it. In that light the fresh blood looked almost black. He was going to die. Not right away, probably, but soon. He wanted to know why. This time he shouted.

"Why did you shoot me?"

Silence. Chee tried to think of another way to get an answer. Any response. He tried his right arm, found he could move it. The worst pain was the back of his head. A teeth-gritting ache in what seemed to be twenty places where shotgun pellets had struck the skull bone. Overlying that was the feeling that his scalp was being scalded. The pain made it hard to think. But he had to think. Or die.

Then the voice: "Skinwalker! Why are you killing my baby?"

It was a woman's voice.

"I am not," Chee said, slowly and very plainly.

No reply. Chee tried to concentrate. In not very long, he would bleed to death. Or, before that happened, he would faint, and then this crazy woman would push open the hogan door and kill him with her shotgun.

"You think I'm a witch," he said. "Why do you think that?"

"Because you are an *adan'ti,*" she said. "You shot a bone into me before my baby was born, or you shot a bead into my baby, and now it is dying."

That told him just a little. In the Navajo world, where witchcraft is important, where daily behavior is patterned to avoid it, prevent it, and cure it, there are as many words for its various forms as there are words for various kinds of snow among the Eskimos. If the woman thought he was *adan'ti*, she thought he had the power of sorcery—to convert himself into animal form, to fly, perhaps to become invisible. Very specific ideas. Where had she gotten them?

"You think that if I confess that I witched your baby, then the baby will get well and pretty soon I will die," Chee said. "Is that right? Or if you kill me, then the witching will go away."

"You should confess," the woman said. "You should say you did it. Otherwise, I will kill you."

He had to keep her here. Had to keep her talking until he could make his mind work. Until he could learn from her what he had to learn to save his life. Maybe that was impossible. Maybe he was already dying. Maybe his life wind was already blowing out of him—out into the rain. Maybe there was nothing he could learn that would help him. But Chee's conditioning was to endure. He thought, frowning with concentration, willing away the pain and the dreadful consciousness of the blood running down his flanks and puddling under his buttocks. Meanwhile he had to keep her talking.

"It won't help your baby if I confess, because I am not the witch. Can you tell me who told you I was the witch?"

Silence.

"If I were a witch . . . if I had the power of sorcery, did someone teach you what I could do?"

"Yes, I was taught." The voice was hesitant.

"Then you know that if I was a witch, I could turn myself into something else. Into a burrowing owl. I could fly out the smoke hole and go away into the night."

Silence.

"But I am not a witch. I am just a man. I am a singer. A *yataalii*. I have learned the ways to cure. Some of them. I know the songs to protect you against a witching. But I am not a witch."

"They say you are," the woman said.

"Who are they? They who say this?" But he already knew the answer.

Silence.

The back of Chee's head was on fire, and beneath the fire the shattering pain in the skull was beginning to localize itself into a dozen spots of pain—the places where shotgun pellets had lodged in the bone. But he had to think. This woman had been given him as her witch just as Roosevelt Bistie must have been given Endocheeney as his scapegoat. Bistie had been dying of a liver disease. And this woman was watching her infant die. A conclusion took its shape in Chee's mind.

"Where was your baby born?" Chee asked. "And when it got sick, did you take it to the Badwater Clinic?"

He had decided she wouldn't answer before the answer came. "Yes."

"And Dr. Yellowhorse told you he was a crystal gazer, and that he could tell you what caused your baby to be sick, is that right? And Dr. Yellowhorse told you I had witched your child."

It was no longer a question. Chee knew it was true. And he thought he might know how to stay alive. How he might talk this woman into putting down her shotgun, and coming in to help stop his bleeding and to take him to Piñon or someplace where there would be help. He would use what little life he had left telling this woman who the witch really was. Chee believed in witchcraft in an abstract way. Perhaps they did have the power, as the legends claimed and the rumors insisted, to become were-animals, to fly, to run faster than any car. On that score, Chee was a skeptic willing to accept any proof. But he knew witchcraft in its basic form stalked the Dinee. He saw it in people who had turned deliberately and with malice from the beauty of the Navajo Way and embraced the evil that was its opposite. He saw it every day he worked as a policeman—in those who sold whiskey to children, in those who bought videocassette recorders while their relatives were hungry, in the knife fights in a Gallup alley, in beaten wives and abandoned children.

"I am going to tell you who the witch is," Chee said. "First I am going to throw out the keys to my truck. You take 'em and unlock the glove box in the truck, and you will find my pistol there. I said I had it in here with me because I was afraid. Now I am not afraid any more. Go and check, and see that I don't have my pistol with me. Then I want you to come in here where it is warm, and out of the rain, and where you can look at my face while I tell you. That way you can tell whether I speak the truth. And then I will tell you again that I am not a witch who harmed your child. And I will tell you who the witch is that put this curse on you."

Silence. The sound of gusting rain. And then a metallic clack. The woman doing something with the shotgun.

Chee's right arm was numb again. With his left hand he extracted his truck keys, slid back the latch, and eased the door toward him. As he tossed the keys through the opening, he waited for the shotgun. The shotgun didn't fire. He heard the sound of the woman walking in the mud.

Chee exhaled a gust of breath. Now he had to hold off the pain and the faintness long enough to organize his thoughts. He had to know exactly what to say.

≫ **21** ≪

THE PATROL CAR OF Officer Leonard Skeet, born
to the Ears Sticking Up Clan, the man in charge
of law and order in the rugged vacant places surrounding Piñon, was parked in the rain outside
the subagency police station. The station, a
double-width mobile home, stood on the bank of
Wepo Wash. It also served as home for Leonard
Skeet and Aileen Beno, his wife. Leaphorn pulled
off the asphalt of Navajo Route 4 and into the
mud of Skeet's yard, tapped on Skeet's door, and
collected him.

Skeet had seen no sign of Chee's pickup. His
house was located with a view of both Navajo 4
and the road that wandered northwestward toward the Forest Lake Chapter House and, eventually, to the Goldtooth place. "He was probably
already past here long before I got home," Skeet
said. "But he hasn't come back through. I would
have seen his truck."

At Emma's car, Skeet hesitated. "This isn't

good for mud, and maybe I oughta drive," he said, looking at Leaphorn's cast. "You probably oughta give that arm some rest."

Under the cast, the arm arched from wrist to elbow. Leaphorn stood in the rain, common sense wrestling with his conditioned instinct to be in control. Common sense won. Skeet knew the road. They switched to Skeet's patrol car, left the tiny scattering of buildings that was Piñon behind, left asphalt for gravel, and soon, gravel for graded dirt. It was slick now and Skeet drove with the polished skill of an athletic man who drives the bad back roads every working day. Leaphorn found himself thinking of Emma and turned away from that. Skeet had asked no questions and Leaphorn's policy for years had been to tell people no more than they needed to know. Skeet needed to know a little.

"We may be wasting our time," Leaphorn said. He didn't have to tell Skeet anything about the attempt on Chee's life—everyone in NTP knew everything about that and everyone, Leaphorn guessed, had a theory about it. He told Skeet about Chee being invited to the Goldtooth place to talk about doing a sing.

"Uh huh," Skeet said. "Interesting. Maybe there's some explanation for it." He concentrated on correcting a rear-end skid on the muddy surface. "He didn't know nobody lives there," Skeet said. "No way he could have, I guess. Still, if somebody was shooting at me . . ." He let the statement trail off.

Leaphorn was riding in the back, where he could lean against the driver-side door and keep the cast propped along the top of the backrest. Despite the cushioning, the jolts and jarring of the bumpy road communicated themselves to the bone. He didn't feel like talking, or like defending Chee. "No IQ test required for the job," he said. "But maybe I'm just overnervous. Maybe there's an explanation for having the meeting there."

"Maybe so," Skeet said. His tone was skeptical.

Skeet slowed at an oddly shaped outcrop of volcanic basalt. "If I remember right, the turnoff's here," he said.

Leaphorn retrieved his arm from the backrest. "Let's take a look," he said.

On a clear evening, this lonely landscape would still have been lit by a red afterglow. In steady rain, the dark was almost complete. They used their flashlights.

"Some traffic," Skeet said. "One out pretty recently."

The rain had blurred the track of the tires without erasing them. And the depth of the rut in the softer earth at the juncture showed the vehicle had passed after the moisture had soaked in. And these fresher tracks had partly overlapped earlier, shallower tracks which the rain had almost smoothed away.

"So maybe he's come and gone," Skeet said. But as he said it he doubted it. At least two vehicles had gone in. One had come out since the rain became heavy.

Their headlights reflected first from the rain-slick roof of a truck, then they picked up the windows of the Goldtooth house. No lights visible anywhere. Skeet parked fifty yards away. "Leave 'em on?" he said. "What do you think?"

"Turn 'em off for now," Leaphorn said. "Until we make sure that's Chee's truck. And find out who's here."

They found a wealth of half-erased, rain-washed tracks but no sign of anyone outside. "Check the truck," Leaphorn said. "I'll take the house."

Leaphorn pointed his light at the building, holding it gingerly in his left hand, as far from his body as was practical. "Kicked once, double careful," his mother would have told him. And in this case, they might be dealing with a shotgun. Leaphorn thought, wryly, that he should have a telescoping arm, like Inspector Gadget in the television cartoon.

The house door was open. The beam of Leaphorn's light shined through it into emptiness. In front of the door, on the wet, packed earth, it lit a small red cylinder. Leaphorn picked it up, an empty shotgun shell. He switched off the light, sniffed the open end of the cartridge, inhaled the acrid smell of freshly burned powder. "Shit," Leaphorn said. He felt bleak, defeated, conscious of the cold rainwater against his ribs.

Skeet splashed up behind him.

"Truck unlocked," Skeet said. "Glove box open. This was on the seat." He showed Leaphorn a .38 caliber revolver. "That his?"

"Probably," Leaphorn said. He checked the cylinder, sniffed the barrel. It hadn't been fired. He shook his head, showed Skeet the empty shotgun shell. They would find Jim Chee's body and they would call it a homicide. Maybe they should call it suicide. Or death by stupidity.

The house was empty. Absolutely empty. Of people, of furniture, of anything except a scattered residue of trash. They found small footprints around the door, damp but not muddy. Whoever had been here had come before the rain turned heavy. Had left. Hadn't returned.

From the front door, Leaphorn shined his flash on the hogan. Its door was half open.

"I'll check it," Skeet said.

"We will," Leaphorn said.

They found Jim Chee just inside the door, slumped against the wall just south of the entrance—the correct place for a proper Navajo to be if he had entered the hogan properly "sunwise"—which was from east to south to west to north. In the light of the two flashes, the back of his head and his side seemed clotted with grease. In the reflected light, Skeet's long face was pinched and stricken.

Grief? Or was he conscious that he was standing in a ghost hogan, being infected with the virulent ghost of Officer Jim Chee? Leaphorn, who had long since come to terms with ghosts, stared at Skeet's face, trying to separate out the sorrow and find the fear.

"I think he may be alive," Skeet said.

> 22 <

As IT USUALLY DOES on the Colorado Plateau, night defeated the storm. It drifted northeastward, robbed of the solar power that had fed it, and exhausted its energy in the thin, cold air over the Utah canyons and the mountains of northern New Mexico. By midnight there was no more thunder; the cloud formation had sagged into itself, flattening to a vast general rain—the sort Navajos call female rain—which gently drenched an area from the Painted Desert northward to Sleeping Ute Mountain.

From the fifth-floor windows of the Indian Health Service hospital in Gallup, Joe Leaphorn saw the deep blue of the newly washed morning sky—cloudless except for scraps of fog over the Zuni Mountains to the southeast, and the red cliffs stretching eastward toward Borego Pass. By afternoon, if moisture was still moving in from the Pacific, the towering thunderheads would be building again, bombarding earth with lightning, wind, and rain. But now the world out-side the glass where Leaphorn stood was bril-liant with sun—clean and calm.

He was hardly aware of it. His mind was full of what the neurologist had told him. Emma did not have Alzheimer's disease. Emma's illness was caused by a tumor pressing against the right front lobe of her brain. The doctor, a young woman named Vigil, had told Leaphorn a great deal more, but what was important was simple enough. If the tumor was cancerous, Emma would probably die, and die rather soon. If the tumor was benign, Emma would be cured by its removal through surgery. "What are the odds?" Dr. Vigil didn't want to guess. This afternoon she would call a doctor she knew in Baltimore. A doctor she had studied with. Cases like this were his field. He would know.

"I want to discuss it with him before I do any guessing." Dr. Vigil was in her early thirties, Leaphorn guessed. One of those who went to medical school with a government grant and worked it off in the Indian Health Service. She stood, hands on desk, waiting for Leaphorn to leave. "Leave word where I can get in touch with you," she said.

"Call now," Leaphorn said. "I want to know."

"He does his surgery in the mornings," she said. "He won't be in."

"Try it," Leaphorn said. "Just try."

Dr. Vigil said, "Well, now, I don't think . . ."

Then her eyes met Leaphorn's. "No harm trying," she said.

He'd waited in the hall, just outside the doctor's door, staring out at the morning, digesting this new data. The news was good. But it left him off balance, trying to live again with hope. It was a luxury he had given up weeks before. The exact moment, he thought, was when he sat at his desk reading the literature the Alzheimer's organization had sent him and seeing Emma's awful confusion described in print. It had been a terrible morning—the worst pain he'd ever endured. Now all his instincts cried out against enduring it again—against reentering that door which hope held open for him. But there was the ultimate fact: Emma might be well again. He wanted to celebrate. He wanted to shout for joy. But he was afraid.

So he waited. To avoid the trap of hope, he thought of Jim Chee. Specifically he thought of what Jim Chee had told them when the ambulance unloaded him at the Badwater Clinic. Just a few words, but a lot of information in them if only Leaphorn knew how to read it.

"Woman," Chee had said, in a voice so weak that Leaphorn had heard it only because he was leaning with his face just inches from Chee's lips.

"Who shot you?" Leaphorn had asked while attendants shifted the stretcher onto the hospital cart. Chee had moved his head. "Do you know?" Chee had moved his head again, a negative motion. And then he had said: "Woman."

"Young?" Leaphorn had asked, and got no response.

"We'll find her," Leaphorn had said, and that had provoked the rest of the information Chee had provided.

"Baby dying," Chee said. He said it clearly, in English. And then he repeated it in mumbled Navajo, his voice fading away.

So it would seem that the person who had shot Chee at the Goldtooth place was a woman with a fatally ill infant. Probably the same person had fired the three shotgun blasts through Chee's trailer wall. When Chee came out of surgery it would be easy enough to find her. He would be able to identify the vehicle she was driving, probably even give them the license number if he had been halfway alert before the shooting. And if he knew she had a sick child, he had to have talked to her face to face. They would also have a physical description. But even if Chee didn't survive to describe her, they could find her. A young woman with a critically ill child who knew about the Goldtooth place, about it being abandoned. That would give them all the narrowing they needed.

They would find the woman. She would tell them why she wanted Jim Chee dead. Then all this insane killing would make sense.

Below Leaphorn, a flock of crows moved toward the center of Gallup, their cawing muted by the glass. Far beyond, an endless line of tank

cars moved eastward down the Santa Fe main-
line.

Or, Leaphorn thought, they wouldn't find the
woman. Or they would find her dead. Or she, like
Bistie, would tell them absolutely nothing. And
he would be exactly where he was now. And
where was that?

The crows disappeared out of his line of vision.
The freight crawled inexorably eastward. Leaphorn considered why he was nagged with the
feeling that these homicides made perfect sense,
that Chee had somehow, in those three words,
put the key in the lock and turned it.

"Woman," Chee had said. A woman Chee
didn't know. How did that help? Of the victims,
only Irma Onesalt was female. She had been
killed with a rifle shot, not a shotgun. No apparent connection there. "Baby dying," Chee had
said. Presumably the baby of the woman who
had shot him. Presumably she had told Chee
about it. Why?

"Mr. Leaphorn?" a woman's voice said at Leaphorn's elbow. "She asked me to get you. Dr.
Vigil."

Dr. Vigil had come to the door to meet him. "I
can give you the statistics now," she said, smiling
slightly. "Recovery from the actual surgery, close
to ninety-nine percent. Nature of tumor: malig-
nant twenty-three-plus percent, benign seventy-
six-plus percent."

And so Joe Leaphorn allowed himself again
the heavy risk of hope. He went to Emma's room

to tell her, found her sleeping, and left her a note. It told her what Dr. Vigil had told him, and that he loved her, and that he would be back as soon as he could be.

Then he left on the long drive to the Badwater Clinic. He wanted to be there when Chee recovered from the anesthesia. And he wanted to talk to Yellowhorse about Irma Onesalt's list, and learn what Onesalt had said to Yellowhorse about it; specifically if she had told him why she wanted the dates of death of people who had not yet died. The Cambodian doctor who had been in charge when they'd brought Chee in had said Yellowhorse was in Flagstaff—that he would be driving back today, that he should be back by early afternoon.

Leaphorn stopped for gas at Ganado and called the clinic while his tank was being filled. Yes, Chee had survived the surgery. He was still in the recovery room. No, Yellowhorse was not back from Flagstaff yet. But he'd called and they expected him sometime after lunch.

Leaphorn was finding it difficult to think about homicides. He was preoccupied, indeed fascinated, by his own emotions. He had never felt quite like this before—this immeasurable joy. This relief. Emma, who had been lost forever, was found again. She would live. She would be herself again. He thought of Dr. Vigil, watching him receive her hopeful news. Doctors must see a lot of such violent emotional reaction—even more than policemen do. Understanding the intensity love can produce would be a by-product of that profession. Dr. Vigil would understand how a dying infant could motivate a murder. If not yet, she would when she was older. Leaphorn was thinking this as he passed the turnoff to Blue Gap. He moved from that into analyzing his own emotions. Watching what was happening to Emma had caused everything else to recede into triviality. Other values ceased to exist for him. Had there been anything he could do to help her, anything, he would have done it. Beyond the turnoff to Whippoorwill School, his thoughts moved back to a question that had intrigued him earlier. Why had the woman told Chee her baby was dying? He seemed to know the answer. She had told Chee to explain why she was killing him. She was killing him to reverse the witchcraft that was killing her baby. Logical. Why did something keep tugging him back to this?

Just then, Leaphorn saw how it all had worked. All the pins on his map came together into a single cluster at the Badwater Clinic. Four and a half homicides became a single crime with a single motive. His car fishtailed on the muddy road as he jammed down the accelerator. If he didn't reach the clinic before Dr. Yellowhorse, the four and a half homicides would become five.

➤ 23 ◄

IT WAS ALL VERY VAGUE to Chee. The nurse who moved him down the hall from the recovery room had shown him a paper cup containing a spoonful of shot. "What Dr. Wu dug out of your back and your neck and your head," she explained. "Dr. Wu thought you'd want to keep it."

Chee, woozy, could think of nothing to say to that. He raised his eyebrows.

"Sort of a souvenir," she explained. "To help you remember." And then she had added something about Dr. Wu being Chinese, but actually a Cambodian Chinese, as if this would clarify why he thought Chee would want a souvenir.

"Um," Chee said, and the nurse had looked at him quizzically and said, "Only if you want to."

The nurse had talked a lot more, but Chee remembered little of it. He recalled wanting to ask her where he was, and what had happened, but he didn't have the energy. Now the back of his head was helping him remember. Whatever

painkiller they had used to numb it was wearing
off and Chee could isolate and identify about
seven places where the surgeon had dug a piece
of shot out of the thick bone at the back of his
skull. It reminded Chee of a long time ago when
a yearling horse they were branding had kicked
him squarely on the shinbone. Bruised bone
seemed to issue a peculiarly painful protest to the
nervous system.

But he kept the pain at bay by celebrating
being alive. It surprised him. He could only
dimly remember the woman coming hesitantly
into the hogan, the shotgun pointing at him. He
remembered the seconds when he had thought
she would simply shoot him again and that
would be the end of it. Perhaps that was what
she'd intended to do. But she had let him talk,
and he had forced himself into a kind of coher-
ence. Now it was all hazy, much of it simply
blank. The medics called it temporary post-
trauma amnesia, and Chee had seen it in enough
victims of knife fights and traffic accidents to recognize it in himself. He didn't try to force his
memory. What was important, obviously, was
that the woman had believed him. She seemed
to have brought him here, although Chee
couldn't remember that happening, or imagine
how she had gotten him from the hogan to her
truck. The last he remembered was describing
for her what must have happened, relying on his
recollection of the time he himself had been
taken to a crystal gazer as a child, remembering

the old man's eye, immensely magnified and distorted, looking into his own eye, remembering his own fear.

"I think I know what happened," Chee had told her. "Yellowhorse pretends to be a crystal gazer. I think you took your sick baby to the Badwater Clinic and Yellowhorse looked at it, and then Yellowhorse got out his crystal, and pretended to be a shaman, and he told you that the baby had been witched. And then he did the sucking ceremony, and he pretended to suck a bone out of your baby's breast." Chee remembered that at this point he began to run out of strength. His eyes were no longer focusing and it was difficult to generate the breath to form the guttural Navajo words. But he had gone on. "Then he told you that I was the skinwalker who had witched your baby and that the only way to cure it was to kill me. And he gave you the bone and told you to shoot it into me."

The woman, hazy and distant, had simply sat there, holding the shotgun. He couldn't see well enough to know if she was listening.

"I think he wants to kill me because I have told people that he is not really a shaman. I told people he had no real powers. But maybe there is some other reason. That doesn't matter. What matters is that I am not the skinwalker. Yellowhorse is the skinwalker. Yellowhorse witched you. Yellowhorse turned you into someone who kills." He had said a lot more, or he thought he had, but maybe that was part of the dream that he had drifted into as he fell asleep. He couldn't separate it.

The nurse was back in the room. She put a tray on the table beside his bed—a white towel, a syringe, other paraphernalia. "You need some of this by now," she said, glancing at her watch.

"First I need to do some things, know some things," Chee said. "Are there any policemen here?"

"I don't think so," the nurse said. "Quiet morning."

"Then I need to make a call," Chee said.

She didn't bother to look at him. "Fat chance," she said.

"Then I need somebody to make a call for me. Call the tribal police headquarters at Window Rock and get a message to a Lieutenant Leaphorn."

"He's one of them who brought you in. With the ambulance," she said. "If you want to tell him who shot you, I'll bet that can wait until you're feeling a little better."

"Is Yellowhorse here? Dr. Yellowhorse?"

"He's in Flag," the nurse said. "Some sort of meeting at the Flagstaff hospital."

Chee felt dizzy, and a little nauseated, and vastly relieved. He didn't understand why Yellowhorse wanted to kill him—not exactly, anyway. But he knew he didn't want to be sleeping in his hospital when Yellowhorse was here.

"Look," he said. Trying to sound like a policeman when your head and your arm and shoulder and side were encased in bandages and you were flat on your back wasn't easy. "This is important. I have to tell Leaphorn some things or a murderer might get away. Might kill somebody again."

"You're serious?" the nurse asked, still doubting it.

"Dead serious."

"What's the number?"

Chee gave her the number at Window Rock. "And if he's not in, call the substation at Piñon. Tell 'em I said we need a policeman out here right away." Chee tried to think of who was stationed at Piñon now, and drew a blank. He was conscious only that his eyes were buzzing and that his head hurt in at least seven places.

"You know that number?"

Chee shook his head.

The nurse went out the door, leaving the tray. "Here he comes now," she said.

Leaphorn, Chee thought. Great!

Dr. Yellowhorse came through the door, moving fast.

Chee opened his mouth, began a yell, and found Yellowhorse's hand clamped across his jaws, cutting off all sound.

"Keep quiet," Yellowhorse said. With his other hand he was pressing something hard against Chee's throat. It was another source of pain—but no competition for the back of his head.

"Struggle and I cut your throat," Yellowhorse said.

Chee tried to relax. Impossible.

Yellowhorse's hand came off his mouth. Chee heard it fumbling in the tray.

"I don't want to kill you," Yellowhorse said. "I'm going to give you this shot so you'll get some sleep. And remember, you can't yell with your windpipe cut."

Chee tried to think. Whatever was pressing against his throat was pressing too hard to make yelling practical. Almost instantly he added the feel of the needle going into his shoulder to the battery of other pains. And then Yellowhorse's hand was over his mouth again.

"I hate to do this," Yellowhorse said, and his expression said he meant it. "It was that damned Onesalt woman. But in the long run, it more than balances out."

Chee's expression, as much as Yellowhorse could see of it around his smothering hand, must have seemed skeptical.

"It balances way out in favor of saving the clinic," Yellowhorse said, voice insistent. "Four lives. Three of them were men past their prime and one of them was dying fast anyway. And on the balance against that, I know for sure we've saved dozens of lives already, and we'll save dozens more. And better than that, we're stopping birth defects, and catching diabetes cases early." Yellowhorse paused, looking into Chee's eyes.

"And glaucoma," he said. "I know we've caught a dozen cases of that early enough to save good vision. That Onesalt bitch was going to put an end to all that."

Chee, who was in no position to talk, didn't.

"You feeling sleepy?" Yellowhorse said. "You should be by now."

Chee was feeling—despite an intense effort of will—very sleepy. There was no question at all that Yellowhorse was going to kill him. If there were any other possibility, Yellowhorse would not be telling him all this, making this apology. Chee tried to gather his strength, tense his muscles for a lunge against the knife. All he had to muster was a terrible weakness. Yellowhorse felt even that and tightened his grip.

"Don't try it," he said. "It won't work."

It wouldn't. Chee admitted it to himself. Time was his only hope, if he had a hope. Stay awake. He made a questioning sound against Yellowhorse's palm. He would ask him why Onesalt and the rest had to be killed. It was to cover up something at the clinic, clearly, but what?

Yellowhorse eased the grip on Chee's mouth. "What?" he said. "Keep it low."

"What did Onesalt know?" he asked.

The hand gripped again. Yellowhorse looked surprised. "I thought you had guessed," he said. "That day when you came and got the wrong Begay. Onesalt guessed. I figured you would. Or she would tell you."

Chee mumbled against the palm. "You gave us the wrong Begay. I wondered what had happened to the right one. But I didn't guess you were keeping him on your records."

"Well, I thought you were guessing," Yellowhorse said. "I always knew you would guess sooner or later. And once you did, it would take time but it would be inevitable. You would find out."

"Overcharging?" Chee asked. "For patients who weren't here?"

"Getting the government to pay its share," Yellowhorse said. "Have you ever read the treaty? The one we signed at Fort Sumner. Promises. One schoolteacher for every thirty children, everything else. The government never kept any promises."

"Charging for people after they were dead?" Chee mumbled. He simply could not keep his eyes open any longer. When they closed, Yellowhorse would kill him. Not immediately, but soon enough. When his eyes closed they would never open again. Yellowhorse would keep him asleep until he could find a way to make it look normal and natural. Chee knew that. He must keep his eyes open.

"Getting sleepy?" Yellowhorse asked, his voice benign.

Chee's eyes closed. He went to sleep, a troubled sleep, dreaming that something was hurting the back of his head.

≫ 24 ≪

Leaphorn parked right at the door, violating the blue handicapped-only zone, and trotted into the clinic. He'd made his habitual instant eyeball inventory of the vehicles present. A dozen were there, including an Oldsmobile sedan with the medical symbol on its license plate, which might be Yellowhorse's car, and three well-worn pickup trucks, which might include the one driven by the woman determined to kill Chee. Leaphorn hurried through the front door. The receptionist was standing behind her half-round desk screaming something. A tall woman in a nurse's uniform was standing across the desk, hands in her hair, apparently terrified. Both were looking down the hallway that led to Leaphorn's right, down a corridor of patients' rooms.

Leaphorn's trot turned into a run.

"She has a gun," the receptionist shouted. "A gun."

The woman stood in the doorway four rooms

down, and she did, indeed, have a gun. Leaphorn could see only her back, a traditional dark blue blouse of velvet, the flowing light blue skirt which came to the top of her squaw boots, her dark hair tied in a careful bun at the back of her head, and the butt of the shotgun protruding from under her arm.

"Hold it," Leaphorn shouted, digging with his left hand for his pistol.

Aimed as the shotgun was into the room and away from him, the sound it made was muted. A boom, a yell, the sound of someone falling, glass breaking. With the sound, the woman disappeared into the room. Leaphorn was at the door two seconds later, his pistol drawn.

"The skinwalker is dead," the woman said. She stood over Yellowhorse, the shotgun dangling from her right hand. "This time I killed him."

"Put down the gun," Leaphorn said. The woman ignored him. She was looking down at the doctor, who sprawled face-up beside Jim Chee's bed. Chee seemed to be sleeping. Leaphorn shifted his pistol to the fingers that protruded from his cast and lifted the shotgun from the woman's hand. She made no effort to keep it. Yellowhorse was still breathing, unevenly and raggedly. A man in a pale blue hospital smock appeared at the door—the same Chinese-looking doctor who had been on duty when they delivered Chee. He muttered something that sounded like an expletive in some language strange to Leaphorn.

"Why did you shoot him?" he asked Leaphorn.

"I didn't," Leaphorn said. "See if you can save him."

The doctor knelt beside Yellowhorse, feeling for a pulse, examining the place where the shotgun blast had struck Yellowhorse's neck at point-blank range. He shook his head.

"Dead?" the woman asked. "Is the skinwalker dead? Then I want to bring in my baby. I have him in my truck. Maybe now he is alive again."

But he wasn't, of course.

It took Jim Chee almost four hours to awaken and he did so reluctantly—his subconscious dreading what he would awaken to. But when he came awake he found himself alone in the room. Sunset lit the foot of his bed. His head still hurt and his shoulder and side ached, but he felt warm again. He removed his left hand from under the covers, flexed the fingers. A good strong hand. He moved his toes, his feet, bent his knees. Everything worked. The right arm was another matter. It was heavily bandaged elbow to shoulder and immobilized with tape.

Where was Yellowhorse? Chee considered that. Obviously he had guessed wrong about the doctor. The man hadn't killed him, as common sense said he should have. Apparently Yellowhorse had run for it, or turned himself in, or went to talk to a lawyer, or something. It seemed totally unlikely that Yellowhorse would come back now to finish off Chee. But just in case, he decided he would get up, put on his clothes, and go somewhere else. Call Leaphorn first. Tell him about all this.

Just about then it also occurred to Chee how he would solve the problem of the cat. He would put the cat in the forty-dollar case, and take it to the Farmington airport and send it off to Mary Landon. But first he would write her and explain it all—explain how this *belagana* cat simply wasn't going to make it as a Navajo cat. It would starve, or be eaten by the coyote, or something like that. Mary was a very smart person. Mary would understand that perfectly. Probably better than Chee.

Carefully, slowly, he turned himself onto his good side, swung his feet off the bed, pushed himself upright. Almost upright. Before he completed the move, weakness and faintness overcame him. He was on his side again, the back of his head throbbing, and a metal tray he'd tumbled from the bedside stand still clattering on the floor.

"I see you're awake," a female voice said. "Tell the lieutenant that Officer Chee is awake."

Lieutenant Leaphorn's expression, when he came through the door behind the nurse, could best be described as blank. He sat on the chair beside Chee's bed, resting his cast gingerly on the cover.

"Do you know her name? The woman who shot you?"

"No idea," Chee said. "Where is she? Where's Yellowhorse? Do you know—"

"She shot Yellowhorse," Leaphorn said. "Right here. Did a better job on him than she did on you. We have her in custody, but she won't tell us her name. Anything else, for that matter. Just wants to talk about her baby."

"What's wrong with it?"

"It's dead," Leaphorn said. "The doctors say it's been dead for a couple of days." Leaphorn shifted his cast, which was generally grimy and had a streak of dried blue-black mud on its bottom side.

"She thought it was witched," Chee said. "That's why she wanted to kill me. She thought I was the witch and she could turn the witching around."

Leaphorn looked disapproving. "It had something they call Werdnig-Hoffmann disease," Leaphorn said. "Born with it. The brain never develops properly. Muscles never develop. They live a little while and then they die."

"Well," Chee said. "She didn't understand that."

"No cure for it," Leaphorn said. "Not even by killing skinwalkers like you."

"Do you know why Yellowhorse was doing all this?" Chee asked. "He told me he was trying to get the government to pay its share, or something like that, and Onesalt found out about it, or was finding out, and he figured sooner or later I would understand it too, because of what I knew." Chee paused, slightly abashed by the admission he would be making. "I guess he figured

I'm smarter than I am. I guess I was supposed to figure out that he was turning in hospitalization claims on patients after they were dead. I guess that's why Onesalt was looking for those death dates."

"About right," Leaphorn said. "After they died, or long after they'd checked out and gone home. Dilly Streib is in the business office now. They're going through the billing records."

"I began to see how he was doing it," Chee said. "I couldn't see why. Wasn't he using a lot of his own money to run this place?"

"Yeah," Leaphorn said. "Mostly his own money. Through his foundation. And he had other private foundation money. And some tribe support. Medicare. Medicaid. Guess it wasn't enough. Not even with hiring immigrant doctors."

"I understand how he killed Endocheeney and Wilson Sam. How about why?"

"Streib thinks he's going to find they were out of here for months before Yellowhorse stopped billing for them," Leaphorn said. "I guess there were a lot of them like that. But they were the only two on Onesalt's list. After he shot Onesalt, it took the pressure off. No rush anymore. But I guess he figured that since you were with Onesalt, you'd know about the list and sooner or later you'd just naturally find out about it. Or if you didn't, somebody else would. So he decided to get rid of Sam and Endocheeney, and you too."

"He told me it balanced out," Chee said. "Onesalt was going to put an end to the clinic and it was saving more lives than those he had to kill."

Leaphorn had nothing to say to that. He raised his cast off the bed, grimaced, put it down again. *"Anti'll,"* he said sourly, using the Navajo word for witchcraft.

Jim Chee just nodded.

"Pretty smart, really," Leaphorn added. "No hurry, so he could pick his people carefully. From desperate people. Like Bistie, who was dying. Or the woman he sent after you. People won't talk about witches, so there wasn't much risk of tracking anything back here."

"I guess he sent two after Endocheeney. Maybe Bistie was too slow and he thought he wasn't going to do it."

"Apparently," Leaphorn said. "And then he found out we'd arrested Bistie, so he had to kill him—just in case we did trick him into talking."

"I guess we could find them now," Chee said. "The one who killed Endocheeney. The one who killed Wilson Sam. Just work down through the records of the caseload here, looking at them the way Yellowhorse would have looked."

"I guess we could," Leaphorn said.

Chee considered that answer awhile. It was, after all, a federal problem.

"You think Streib will think of it?"

"I doubt it," Leaphorn said. He laughed a humorless laugh. "People say I hate witchcraft. Dilly, he hates to even think about witches."

"Doesn't matter, anyway," Chee said. "It's finished."

Here's chapter one from Tony Hillerman's
The Fly on the Wall,
available from HarperPaperbacks!

JOHN COTTON HAD BEEN in the pressroom almost an hour when Merrill McDaniels came in. He had written a five-hundred-word overnighter wrapping up the abortion-bill hearings in the House Public Affairs Committee. He had teletyped that—and a shorter item on a gubernatorial appointment—to the state desk of the *Tribune.* Then Cotton had stood at the window— a tall, wiry man with a longish, freckled, somber face. He had thought first about what he would write for his political column, about how badly he wanted a smoke, and then had drifted into other thoughts. He had considered the dust on the old-fashioned window panes, and the lights— the phosphorescent glow of the city surrounding the semidarkness of the state capitol grounds. In the clear, dry air of Santa Fe there wouldn't be this glow. Each light would be an individual glitter without this defraction of cold, misty humidity. Twenty blocks away, by the river below Statehouse Hill, the glow was faintly pink with the neon of the downtown business district. It outlined vaguely the blunt, irregular skyline: the square tower of Federal Citybank, the black glass monolith of the Hefron Building, the dingy granite of the Commodity Exchange— the seats of money and power rising out of a moderately dirty middle-aged midwestern city, clustered beside a polluted midwestern river. Not very large and not very small. About 480,000 people, the Chamber of Commerce said. Exactly 412,318 by the last federal census, not counting the satellite towns and not counting those who farmed the infinity of cornfields and the hilltops of wheat that surrounded it all.

Farm-belt landscape. Rich. Nine-hundred-dollar-an-acre country. Beautiful if you liked it and Cotton had thought again that he didn't like it. The humid, low-level sky oppressed him. He missed the immense skyscapes of the mountains and the deserts. And he thought, as he had thought many times before, that one day he would write Ernie Danilov a letter and tell the managing editor he was quitting. He would enjoy writing that letter.

And then, just a few minutes before McDaniels walked in, he sat down again at his desk. He typed "At the Capitol" and his byline on a sheet of copy paper and wrote rapidly.

Governor Paul Roark remains coy about the U.S. Senate race upcoming next year. But if you make political bets, consider these facts:

1. The tax-reform package the governor and his supporters are now trying to ram through the legislature would make an excellent plank for a campaign in the Democratic senatorial primary.

2. Friends of incumbent U.S. Senator Eugene Clark say privately that they're dead certain Roark will fight Clark for the nomination. They see Roark's campaign as a last-gasp effort of the once-dominant liberal-labor-populist-small-farmer coalition to retain its slipping control over the Democratic party machinery.

3. Roger Boyden, Senator Clark's press secretary and hatchet man, has moved back from Washington. Boyden isn't talking, but those he has been contacting say he's mobilizing Clark's supporters for a primary battle against Roark.

4. An "Effective Senate Committee" has been registered with the secretary of state as a repository for senatorial campaign funds. The listed directors include an aide of Congressman William Jennings Gavin and two long-time allies of National Committeeman Joseph Korolenko. The veteran congressman and Korolenko—himself a former governor and ex-congressman—are close friends of Roark's and supported his race for governor four years ago.

It was exactly at this point that McDaniels came through the pressroom doorway. Cotton was leaning back in his chair, looking at his notepad. Halfway up the empty room, the Associated Press teletype said, *ding, ding, ding,* and typed out a message in a brief flurry of clicking sounds. And there was McDaniels wobbling into the room, fat, rumpled and obviously drunk.

"Johnny," McDaniels said, "you're working late." McDaniels's smile was a joyous, drunken smile.

"Yeah," Cotton said. His voice was curt. Cotton didn't like drunkenness. It made him nervous. When he drank seriously himself, he drank in the safety of solitude. He didn't know exactly why he didn't like drunks, any more than he knew why he didn't like people putting their hands on him, why he always shrugged the hand off his shoulder even when it was a friendly hand. He recognized it as a weakness and he had tried once or twice—without success—to understand this quirk.

McDaniels tossed a stenographer's notebook onto his desk, sending an avalanche of papers cascading to the floor. He sat down heavily and fumbled with the copy paper. Cotton felt himself relaxing, relieved that McDaniels was not in the mood for alcoholic soul baring. The Western Union clock above the pressroom door showed 9:29, which meant Cotton had thirty-one minutes to write four or five more brief items to complete his column, punch it into perforated tape, and teletype it three hundred miles across the state to the *Tribune* newsroom before the overnight desk shut down. Plenty of time. Cotton wasted a few moments of it wondering where the *Capitol-Press* reporter had been doing his drinking. Probably down the hall in the suite of the speaker of the house. Bruce Ulrich always had a bottle open.

Across the room, the UPI telephone rang. It rang four times, loud in the stillness. Two page boys, working late for some committee, walked past the open door, arguing about something. Their voices diminished down the corridor, trailing angry echoes. McDaniels started typing, an erratic clacking. Cotton inspected him, regretting his curtness. It hadn't been necessary. Mac's drunkenness was past the stage at which it would threaten the arm-around-the-shoulder, the maudlin, all-guards-down indecent exposure of the private spirit. And since the snub hadn't been necessary it had been simply rude. Cotton looked at the humped figure of McDaniels and felt penitent.

McDaniels mumbled something.

"What?"

"Said can't find my notebook."

"You threw it on the desk," Cotton said.

Mac groped among the papers, found a notebook, peered at it, put it down. "That's an old one," he said. "Full. Need to find the one I'm using now."

"Maybe it fell off," Cotton said. He got up and looked over McDaniel's shoulder. In the lead sentence, Mac had misspelled the name of the committee chairman and left out the verb.

"You know what you ought to do, Mac? You need to go home and sleep it off. I'll call your desk and tell 'em you got sick and had to go home."

"Maybe so," McDaniels said.

"If you send in a story like you're going to write with all that booze in you, you're in real trouble. I'll tell 'em you got food poisoning."

McDaniels thought, his forehead wrinkled with concentration.

"Yes," he said. "Good idea," He got up carefully.

"I can tell them you said to use AP on the committee hearing," Cotton said. He said it hurriedly. Mac was peering at him, his eyes watery.

"Y'know what I'm celebrating?" McDaniels asked. He spoke slowly, forming each word gingerly, beaming at Cotton now. "I've got me a hell of a story. A real, screaming, eight-column ninety-six-point, earth-shaking bastard." He put his glasses on, slightly askew, and then took them off again and put them carefully back in the case. "Going to make the heads roll, and thrones topple, and rock this old statehouse right down. I got it solid now and in a day or two I'll have all the loose ends, and when I break it, Johnny, you know what I'm going to do?" He waited for an answer, peering at Cotton.

"What?" Cotton said reluctantly.

"You son-of-a-bitch, I'm going to give you part of it."

"That's fine," Cotton said. "But how're you going to do that? You print in the morning and the *Tribune* is an afternoon paper."

"Got more than I can use," McDaniels said, careful with the shape of each word. "I'll give you the background the night before I bust it and you can get it out in advance for your column the next day. Make it look like you were right on top of it."

"What the hell is it?" Cotton asked. "Something about somebody big?"

"Something about stealing the taxpayers' money. Something about a big screwing for the good old taxpayer."

"That's not news," Cotton said. "Who's doing the screwing this time?"

But McDaniels wasn't listening to the question. McDaniels was looking at him, his eyes watery. And then McDaniels was saying: "Johnny, you're a good son-of-a-bitch. You know that? You know, all my life I never broke a really big one like this. Never did. Mostly worked on little *pissant* stuff. All my life I wanted to win the Pulitzer Prize. Wanted one of the big prizes." He put his hand on Cotton's arm. Cotton flinched, his biceps rigid. "Wanted somebody to pay attention to me. Always wanted . . ."

Cotton pulled away from the hand. "Go home," he said. "Take a cab."

"Yes," McDaniels said. "O.K." He paused at the door. "You're a good son-of-a-bitch, Cotton."

From McDaniels's retreating figure Cotton glanced upward at the white face of the clock. It was an act of professional habit, and now of nervous release. It was twenty-two minutes before ten, still plenty of time. He dialed the *Capitol-Press* city-desk number on McDaniels's phone, gave Mac's excuse to a harassed-sounding copy editor, and went back to his own typewriter. He spent perhaps a minute wondering about Mac's story—about whom he had caught stealing. Then he put the question aside and typed rapidly.

A primary-election showdown between the young governor and Gene Clark would split the state's Democratic party machinery approximately down the middle. If Roark runs and loses, the losing effort would almost certainly cost the Korolenko-Gavin bloc its balance of power in party decision making.

Backers of Senator Clark have made obvious inroads into that balance in the past three years. The election last year of George Bryce as District Attorney of the Third Judicial District illustrated how Clark's forces have extended their grip.

Bryce is a former partner in Clark's law firm. He won the Democratic nomination despite the bitter animosity of the Gavin-

Korolenko people. The election put a Clark man in control of law enforcement in the state's most politically sensitive area—the district which includes the state capital.

Whether or not . . .

Cotton stopped typing, aware of movement to his left.

A tall, dark-haired man in a blue topcoat was poking through the litter of papers on McDaniels's desk.

"Looking for something?"

The man didn't look up. "McDaniels forgot his notebook," he said. "He asked me to get it for him."

"I think he threw it on top of all that stuff," Cotton said. He went back to his typing, finishing a summary paragraph and adding four much briefer items. A lot of it wasn't new but it made a fairly good column, Cotton thought. It would be read by maybe 40 percent of the *Tribune*'s 380,000 subscribers, of whom—if the *Tribune*'s latest readership survey was accurate—less than half would plow their way to the final sentence.

Cotton noticed the man in the topcoat was gone. The pressroom was empty. He thought again about McDaniels's story. Mac had been excited, which was surprising. No one in the pressroom was ever excited. He glanced at the clock. Nine forty-four. Sixteen minutes left. He pulled the copy paper from the typewriter, pushed the lever on the teletype to SEND, tapped on the BELL key, and then punched out:

HV COLUM REDY. YOU THERE? JC944P

The machine was silent. Cotton pushed the key to TAPE and began retyping the column into tape, his fingers moving fast on the electric keyboard.

The teletype thumped twice, then typed out:

OK, JOHNNY. GO HED. TL

It was then Cotton heard the sound. He jerked his head toward the pressroom door and listened. The sound lasted maybe three seconds, or four. It started abruptly, loud, and then diminished. Then there was only silence. Above the pressroom door the clock clicked, inhaled electricity, and purred briefly. It became officially 9:45 P.M.

Cotton punched MIN PLEASE on the keyboard and stood up—still looking toward the door. By day, this echoing fourth-floor Senate wing of the capitol was a buzzing, rattling medley of sounds. Laughter, angry conversation, shouts, tapping high heels, slamming doors, and the whine of elevator motors were bounced by the grimy marble of the corridors and mixed in a discordant symphony always present just outside the pressroom door. But at night the immense old building was virtually empty and its silence imposed a hush on the few who still occupied it.

Thus the sudden sound violated custom and protocol. But it wasn't that which took Cotton through the pressroom door into the semi-darkness of the corridor. There was something animal in the sound, something ugly and primeval which prickled the skin and demanded investigation.

The sound had come from the left, from the direction of the central rotunda. Cotton walked slowly from the corridor into the broad foyer directly under the capitol dome. The lights here were off but there was a dim illumination from below—lights from the lobby three floors below reflecting upward.

Cotton stood, listening. Footsteps. A figure emerged from a corridor in the House wing and then stopped at the edge of the foyer.

"Was that you?"

"I heard it, but it wasn't me," Cotton said.

The man walked toward him, skirting the marble railing which circled the open center of the rotunda. Cotton recognized him, a clerk in the office of the House sergeant at arms. But he couldn't remember his name.

"What the hell was it?" the man asked. He looked around the foyer carefully, at the four broad corridors which led into it from the House and Senate wings and then upward at the fourth-floor mezzanine railing above. "Nobody here," he said, looking at Cotton again.

"It damned sure wasn't me," Cotton snapped. "I heard it down in the pressroom."

From a floor somewhere below came a stutter of voices—an excited sound. Cotton suddenly understood the noise, what had made it. He and the clerk walked to the railing, looking down.

"Good God," the clerk said. "God."

At the edge of the Great Seal of the Commonwealth embossed in the marble tile of the lobby floor a body was sprawled. It looked from this height, Cotton thought, like a broken doll. By the body, a man in the khaki of a capitol custodian was kneeling. Another man stood beside him, only the top of his hat and his shoulders visible.

"That's what we heard," the clerk said. "He fell from here."

"Here or over the third-floor railing," Cotton said. "Let's hope it was that. That would give him some chance of being alive."

There was no use calling the *Tribune* on it now. The next edition wasn't until 11 A.M. tomorrow. He thought about it. The later the A.M. reporters knew about it the better. They would get the story soon but every minute that passed before they did would mean more missed editions and more details that would be fresh for the afternoon cycle. Still, he had sent McDaniels home. He should protect him at the *Capitol-Press*.

Cotton leaned over the balustrade and cupped his hands. "Is he dead?"

The man in the hat looked upward, his face a small white oval. Cotton didn't hear his answer.

"What?" he shouted.

"He's dead," the man yelled.

Cotton trotted back to the pressroom and switched the teletype key from tape to manual.

BE MIN WITH THE COLUM. JUST HAD
FATAL. UNIDENTIFIED DROPPED
DOWN CENTRAL ROTUNDA. WILL
ADVISE. JC

And then he called the *Capitol-Press* desk and asked for the city editor. The switch button clicked. In the receiver Cotton heard the background sound of teletypes. A voice near the phone was saying, "All right, then, damn it, get it written." And then it was talking into Cotton's ear.

"Yeah?"

"This is John Cotton. McDaniels went home sick and I'm backstopping for him. Your mail edition out?"

"Running now," the voice said. "What ya got?"

"Just had a fatal out here. Somebody did a dry dive in the rotunda. Just a minute ago. I'll go down and get an identification and call you back."

"We're locking up the two star at ten-fifteen," the voice said. "We can save a hole for it."

"It may not amount to much," Cotton said. "But if it's a biggie, I work for the *Tribune*, and if anybody asks you, it's McDaniels covering for you."

"O.K.," the voice said. "If it's a good one— somebody big—call me back quick, before you wrap it up. I'm playing a second-cycle story on the President's press conference, and if your fatal is some hotshot, I could move the President inside and lead with your jumper."

On the way down in the elevator Cotton thought that it might be somebody fairly big. At least it would most likely be somebody in state government. A tourist wouldn't be in the capitol at night and there must be more convenient places for an intended suicide to do his jumping. It would be somebody in government, probably not a run-of-the-mill clerk. Probably somebody with enough responsibilities to keep him working in his office at night. Or maybe some legislator. Suicide of anyone on the public payroll raised interesting possibilities. Might be worth a two-column head, or one column above the fold.

Cotton pulled the door of the antique elevator open on the first floor and trotted toward the lobby floor of the rotunda. The feeling was familiar, a knotting in his stomach, a tightness in his chest. When he had been a police reporter, he had felt it often—this approach to violent death—without getting used to it. They always looked surprised. No matter the circumstances. The suicide gassed in his garage, the motel night clerk with a robber's bullet through his neck, the middle-aged woman pinned beneath her car. The details were different but the eyes were the same. The intellect believed in death but the animal in man thought it was immortal. The eyes were always glossy with outraged surprise.

Four men stood by the body now, talking quietly. Cotton recognized the clerk from the fifth floor, and the custodian, and the man in the hat. The fourth man was fat, a Game and Fish Department employee, but Cotton didn't know his name.

And then he looked downward. He saw it would not be a big one for the night city editor of the *Capitol-Press*. Not a play story. Probably a one-column head below the fold at best. Maybe no better than page two. The surprised eyes staring sightlessly up at the capitol dome six floors above were those of Merrill McDaniels.

≡ HarperPaperbacks *By Mail*

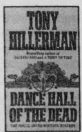